# KISSED BY A COWBOY

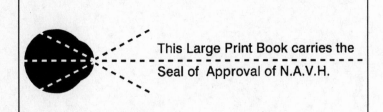

This Large Print Book carries the
Seal of Approval of N.A.V.H.

A FOUR OF HEARTS RANCH ROMANCE,
BOOK 3

# KISSED BY A COWBOY

# DEBRA CLOPTON

**THORNDIKE PRESS**

*A part of Gale, Cengage Learning*

GALE
CENGAGE Learning·

Farmington Hills, Mich • San Francisco • New York • Waterville, Maine
Meriden, Conn • Mason, Ohio • Chicago

## GALE
### CENGAGE Learning·

Copyright © 2016 by Debra Clopton.
Thorndike Press, a part of Gale, Cengage Learning.

Thorndike Press® Large Print Christian Romance.
The text of this Large Print edition is unabridged.
Other aspects of the book may vary from the original edition.
Set in 16 pt. Plantin.

LIBRARY OF CONGRESS CATALOGING-IN-PUBLICATION DATA

Names: Clopton, Debra, author.
Title: Kissed by a cowboy : a four of hearts ranch romance / Debra Clopton.
Description: Large print edition. | Waterville, Maine : Thorndike Press Large Print, 2016. | © 2016 | Series: A four of hearts ranch romance ; 3 | Series: Thorndike Press large print Christian romance
Identifiers: LCCN 2015047152 | ISBN 9781410487445 (hardback) | ISBN 141048744X (hardcover)
Subjects: LCSH: Large type books. | BISAC: FICTION / Christian / Romance. | GSAFD: Love stories. | Christian fiction.
Classification: LCC PS3603.L67 K57 2016b | DDC 813/.6©dc23
LC record available at http://lccn.loc.gov/2015047152

Published in 2016 by arrangement with Thomas Nelson, Inc., a division of HarperCollins Publishing, Inc.

Printed in Mexico.
1 2 3 4 5 6 7 20 19 18 17 16

*As always this book is dedicated
to my family with all my love . . .
now and forever.*

# 1

Strawberry Hill. Cassidy Starr's headlights shined on the faded words of the wooden sign, which looked nearly ready to collapse. She knew exactly how it felt.

Taking a deep breath, she pushed her kinky mass of red hair behind her ears, then took hold of the steering wheel of her truck and drove up the dark, tree-lined lane. Up the hill, the two-story, yellow Victorian appeared in her headlight beams, and a wave of nostalgia and relief washed over Cassidy. She was home.

Humiliated, but home.

Tears dampened her eyelashes and she blinked them away. "I will not get emotional. I will not get emotional," she chanted to the silence around her.

She was done with tears.

Seriously done.

So over them.

These days the only thing tears did was

make her mad when they dared to threaten.

Coming back here must have been pulling these feelings from her, because it had been months since the divorce, since she'd walked away. Coming back to Aunt Roxie's was just . . . well, it was emotional.

She hadn't planned on getting here this late, but on the way her truck's battery died in some tiny town in the middle of nowhere. She'd been lucky when an older man had finally come along and given her battery a jump-start.

Pulling to the rear of the house, she parked, then nearly rocketed out of her skin when the truck backfired. The engine sputtered and died.

"Terrific. Par for the course."

She was suddenly shrouded in darkness as her truck lights died. She groaned — it was blacker than Texas oil out here. Other than the ones coming from the ranch house half a mile away, there wasn't a light or even a moonbeam anywhere to be seen.

Cassidy swallowed hard and tried to crank her engine. It made a sad attempt, but then the battery completely flew the coop as just a clicking noise sounded when she turned the key.

"Well, how do ya like them beans?" she muttered while fumbling around for her cell phone. When she finally found it and turned it on, she groaned again — the battery life meter registered in the red. Two percent life was all she had — this wasn't looking good.

Clicking on the phone's flashlight app, she reached for the truck door. She had to act fast before the little light she had ran out. The heated air of the early June night hit her as she climbed out of the truck, then slammed the door extra hard, trying to make noise, just in case any unwanted visitors were roaming around. Hopefully the noise would scare them off. She remembered that once when she'd been here as a girl, she'd met a skunk face-to-face. Not a good situation at all.

"Yah! Get on outta here!" she yelled loudly into the night. She remembered Pops saying that when he wanted to move cattle along. Pops owned the ranch next door, and she'd been able to tag along with him and his grandsons a few times on roundups. She didn't want to round up anything now, but yelling should run off things too.

At this moment, all she wanted was to get inside Aunt Roxie's house — her house now. It had been six years since her aunt passed away and left the house to her, as if she'd known Cassidy would need it someday. And she'd been right. The thought settled depressingly on her shoulders and she shoved it away.

A bed and sleep were all Cassidy needed for now. It had been an exhausting day of travel from Plano, which had started with catching all the morning commuters in Dallas and then gone downhill from there. If it could go wrong, it had, and all this was more of the same.

Heart thundering, Cassidy moved toward the back porch. Memories greeted her as she approached the house, but now was not the time to be waylaid by them. So she shoved them away, too, and trudged forward.

She stomped up the steps and stooped down to feel beneath the flowerpot that had sat next to that back door since she was a kid. No key.

She should have made certain the Burke brothers, who kept watch on the place, still kept it in the same spot. She just hadn't thought to ask about that when she'd made arrangements to have the electricity turned on.

The eerie sound of a hoot owl sounded from the direction of the barn's hayloft, and Cassidy shivered despite the warmth of the summer night. She shined the phone's light that direction just in time to see the bird fly off into the darkness.

She swallowed hard, then turned back to the door and gave the handle a twist, hoping that maybe . . . Nope, nothing. She eyed the doggie door with skeptical eyes. No, no way. Striding over to a window on the porch, she tried opening it. No budge.

She was worried about her phone battery too.

"Why couldn't there have been a full moon tonight?" she grumbled, then promptly tripped over the step as she hurried off the porch. Managing not to fall, she found the rock that sat in the flower bed beside the porch and lifted it, hoping maybe . . . A couple of bugs scurried away, but there was still no key.

Clomping around the house, she tried each window and the front door.

"Come on!" Weariness was starting to get to her.

She should have felt some excitement at being here, but instead she felt weighed down by the trepidation swirling in the pit of her stomach. She was here, but it was not looking good.

*Stop that.* She might not be inside her new home yet, but she would find a way. She would —

*"Umph,"* she grunted as she fell facedown

on the ground, her phone flying out of her hand. She knew instantly that she'd hit the water spigot that had always protruded from the earth in the middle of the yard. She'd forgotten it was there despite having tripped over it several times growing up. Either it had rained at some point or the water hose had been leaking, because dampness instantly began seeping through her clothes. Then her phone light died, the battery evidently giving out.

"Great. Just great."

She jerked up to her hands and knees and felt around on the ground. Finally she gave up, knowing she'd find it in the morning. Her knees were soaked now, and her determination was wavering.

Sleeping in the hot truck might be her only option. Her head was starting to thump, a lingering ailment from the accident that had pushed her to move to Strawberry Hill. Being hit by a car and spending two days in a coma made a person take a serious look at her life. Rubbing her temple, Cassidy scrambled up and eased around to the back of the house, still wary of what critters she might run into.

She seriously needed to be in the house and get some light. Her stomach was churning, her head was thumping harder, and now her knee throbbed where she'd hit that metal water spigot. She grimaced with each uncertain step.

Aunt Roxie would have plowed through this inky black and dared something to jump out at her. Her aunt had lived her entire adult life single, independent, and self-sufficient. She'd been able to do anything. Cassidy remembered the roof once sprang a leak during a rainstorm and there went Roxie, stomping out to the barn, grabbing her ladder. The next thing Cassidy knew, the woman was up on that roof with a blue tarp and tacks, covering it up until the rain stopped.

"It's just going from point A to point B," she'd tell Cassidy. "You can do anything you want in life if you think about it like that — and read lots of books." To prove that belief she had shelves and shelves of books on every subject imaginable.

The bottom line was her aunt Roxie wasn't afraid of anything. She'd lived fully and on her terms until she'd dropped dead in her garden. She was probably up there in heaven right now with her big, floppy, brimmed red gardening hat and her oversized chambray shirt and her gardening gloves, telling the Lord where she wanted the strawberries, tomatoes, and marigolds to go.

And he was probably saying, "Have at it, Roxie. Things have never looked so good before."

Cassidy smiled in the darkness, consoling herself with the knowledge that her aunt had died doing what she loved. Working in her garden, living her simple, uncomplicated, single life.

And that was exactly what Cassidy had come home to do.

She made it to the back porch by feel and memory, then knelt down and felt for the doggie door. When she'd been younger she'd fit through this opening. Loopy, Aunt Roxie's cocker spaniel, hadn't been big, but she hadn't been tiny either. If Loopy could fit, maybe Cassidy could. She pushed on the heavy flap and felt it give. She weighed the idea of sleeping in her truck, no light, and no shower against sleeping in a bed, light, hot water, and all the comforts of Aunt Roxie's things around her.

It was a no-brainer. She needed sleep tonight. She had a lot to do. Starting tomorrow she was making plans for her organic strawberry farm and beginning the process of making her new home into a bed-and-breakfast.

*You won't make it on your own. You need me.*

Jack the Jerk's chiding words echoed through her mind, words he'd smugly tossed at her the day they'd signed the papers that had cut their legal ties.

But like Roxie, she could make it on her own.

She *would* make it on her own.

Because from here on out that was the way it would be.

A fist of fear knotted in her chest, but she ignored it as best she could and stuck her head through the doggie door.

She was going in.

Jarrod Monahan clicked off the computer, scrubbed his eyes, and pushed his chair back from the desk as the clock on the mantel struck midnight and chimed. He'd been going over the cattle records in his office for hours now and he was tired. It had been a long day.

The clock on the mantel seemed to tick louder than usual in the silence. The house, as always, was quiet. When a man lived by himself, watched a little TV, and basically did nothing but work in his office or sleep when he was home, quiet was all it would be. He told himself he should get another

15

dog. His Blue Heeler had died two years ago, but Jarrod just hadn't taken the time to replace it.

Needing something more than a computer to stare at and the sound of a ticking clock, he went outside to sit on the back porch. As soon as he stepped out the door, he breathed in the scent of the rose bushes beside the porch, a leftover reminder of his mom when they'd all lived here as a family. The heat met him too. The first week of June had hit with a vengeance and he and other ranchers in the area needed rain already. Walking to the edge of the porch, he let the haunting sounds of the coyotes and the crickets settle around him, much preferring them to the silence inside his home that seemed to permeate his soul tonight.

He might think about that dog more seriously.

Tonight he was restless. In more ways than one. Lonesome feelings had been grabbing hold of him lately and dragging behind him like dead weight. The feelings set him off center and they were distracting. But he wanted to focus on the only issue that mattered right now — the fact that the ranch had cattle missing.

The numbers didn't lie.

Jarrod passed up the chairs on the porch

and sat on the steps instead as he gazed into the darkness. He heard the sound of an owl in the distance as his thoughts churned. He wasn't going to jump the gun, but he was pretty certain these cattle were being stolen, which meant only one thing — he had rustlers.

He turned the numbers over in his mind again. It was possible the theft could be the work of one person. Then again, he hadn't checked all the sections of the ranch, which was expansive with a lot of cattle. He didn't know the exact number of missing cattle he was dealing with, but he would know soon. At the moment it was just a rough estimate.

He did know one thing, though. Whoever was taking their cattle was in for trouble when he caught them. And he would catch them. He and his brothers, Tru and Bo, had been working too hard for too long to let this go. He'd catch them and then he'd —

His gaze suddenly locked on a small pin of light across the pasture.

He stood up and watched the light creep along for a moment. The only thing out here on the far side of the ranch was his house, with no neighbors for miles — except for the Starr place. But that had been empty for over six years. Roxie Starr had passed away suddenly and left her property to her great-niece. Cassidy had been here only long enough to pay her respects to her great-aunt at the funeral, sign papers, and make a few arrangements for caretakers. Then she'd gone back to life in the city. And her husband.

Jarrod strode into the house and grabbed his shotgun from the gun safe. He either had rustlers sneaking onto his property through his neighbor's place or there were vandals next door.

Either way, with the mood he was in, if they were lookin' for trouble, they'd come to the right place.

# 2

Cassidy had almost made it through the doggie door when the belt loop of her jeans caught on something on the outside of the door. "No," she grunted. She tried to back out so she could unhook herself, but she couldn't. She yanked her body hard. Nothing happened. "This is ridiculous." She was stuck, and no amount of yanking or jerking was doing her a bit of good.

It was icing on the awful day.

In the darkness the musty scent of dust and disuse assaulted her senses. She sneezed, then dropped her forehead to her arm. Could it get any worse than this? She sneezed again as coyotes howled in the distance. What if they showed up and there she was hanging halfway out the doggie door for them to nibble on her bones? A shiver ran through her at the thought.

She jerked harder but it was useless.

"This is just so not right," she muttered

as a deeper weariness and feelings of ineptitude filled her. What was she going to do?

"Okay. Back out *real* slow and easy," a deep, gravelly voice warned.

Cassidy froze and screamed silently, *Who?* And where had the man come from? She hadn't heard a vehicle drive up.

"Come on, do as I say."

Her weary eyes narrowed and fear shot straight to mad. "I don't know who you are," she growled, saying the first thing that popped into her exhausted brain, "but I warn you, I'm armed, so you better back off." *What? Are you crazy, Cassidy?*

"Well, that makes two of us," the man drawled. "Now, come on out here."

Her heart leapt in her chest — he was armed. What if he was here to rob the place?

"My patience is wearing thin and my trigger finger is itchin', so hurry it up."

"This is ridiculous. Look here, bucko," she warned, not liking yet another man trying to push her around. "I guess we will have to have our shoot-out at the O.K. Corral in a little while, because the truth is I'm stuck here. So there isn't much that can be done until I get loose. Either help me or get off my property."

Laughter from the other side of the door was her only answer. A husky, wonderful laugh that she would know anywhere. "Jarrod Monahan, is that you out there?"

"Cassidy Starr, I have seen you in some predicaments, but this one wins hands down. What in the name of thunder are you doing?"

"What does it look like I'm doing, knitting a sweater?"

"Well, you could be, but since your hands aren't exactly the part of your anatomy I have a visual on, I don't know what you're doing over there on that side of the door."

Drop her in a hole and push dirt over her! She was pretty certain she was glowing with mortification in the pitch-dark house as she growled, "Get me loose, please. And stop gawking."

"You've got me on that one. I cannot tell a lie," he drawled and chuckled at the same time.

Memories from the past rushed by her in living color. "You're incorrigible." She yanked her hips hard.

"Hey, I'm not the one stuck halfway through a doggie door."

"Would you please help me get unhooked from this thing so I can move?" She wondered what he looked like after all these years. She'd glimpsed him a couple of times at Aunt Roxie's funeral, but he'd stayed well away from her at the back of the packed church. And outside he'd had his cowboy hat on, which cast his face in shadow.

She suddenly felt his hand on her hip and she tensed.

"I'm sorry to have to do this. Hold still."

He tugged on her waistband, then she heard an odd sound and felt the tightening of the hooked area. She realized she was feeling the blade of a pocket knife sliding through material.

"You're cutting my jeans!"

And then she was free. Cassidy wasted no time after that. She pulled herself through the door and into the dark house. She stood up and felt along the wall beside the back door for the light switch. Thankfully she'd made sure to have the utilities turned on. She'd even asked for them to be turned on a few days before she told them she would be here, just in case. Sure enough, she'd been ready to come back home earlier than she thought she'd be, and today she'd made her escape.

Light flooded the kitchen, and floral overload hit her as burgundy and pink rose-patterned wallpaper jumped out at her in a busy Pepto-Bismol swirl.

It was awful, making her head bang harder. And she sneezed again.

Aunt Roxie had inherited this decor from the original owner of the home, and she'd despised it. But she had never taken the time to do anything about it. She'd been too busy working outside to change anything inside. Now it brought back so many memories of early-morning breakfast at the old table in the corner and canning and cooking with Roxie over the large stove.

Cassidy glanced around and felt Roxie's absence intensely. Then she flipped on the porch light and unlocked the door. She was completely unprepared when she found herself face-to-face with Jarrod Monahan.

He was pure, undiluted, male charisma personified, standing in the bright beam of the porch light. He had dark good looks that were intensified by the blackness of his hair, the sideburns enhancing the dark shadow on his jaw. He'd always looked like the man you'd want in your corner if the going got rough. And once upon a time he'd been in her corner.

"Jarrod, so nice of you to drop by," she drawled, trying for a little humor to ease her sudden, acute discomfort.

He chuckled. "Yeah, I was just in the neighborhood and thought I'd swing over. You wouldn't have a cup of sugar I could borrow, would you?"

Cassidy studied him with a smile tugging reluctantly to her lips. Despite their history, it appeared he could still make her smile. He had always been able to make her smile. And rile her up at the same time. Her smile faltered.

"It's been a long time, Cass."

The way he said her name, the name he and he alone had ever called her, was like a caress, and it brought an unwanted longing along with the memory of the last time she'd seen him. She stiffened. "Yes, it has been. Where's your truck?" she asked, needing something to distract from the awkwardness swamping her. And curious as to how he'd gotten here so silently.

"Down the lane. I cut the lights and the engine in case you were a vandal. I wanted to surprise you."

Oh, he'd done that all right. "I see."

"So I gather you've just arrived?"

"Yup, drove in thirty minutes ago." Awkward silence descended around them and stretched between them as they studied each other.

He rubbed his jaw. "You know you could have left your truck lights on and shined them this way."

Did he think she had no sense? "Yes, I

certainly could have if my battery hadn't died."

"That explains the light I saw from my porch."

"So you don't normally just come snooping around the place at all hours of the night."

His brow crinkled and the corner of his lips —

Cassidy's pulse jumped, startling her. *Stay calm, stay calm.*

"I do keep a watch out for things going on over here. An abandoned house is prime target material to vandals and thieves, you know, and since we are the only two houses out here for miles —"

"Yes, I realize that, but I have the Burke twins watching out for the place." She crossed her arms and tried not to let her gaze linger on him. She didn't need him watching over things.

"And Doobie and Doonie asked me to help them out since it is right next door to me."

She bristled and clamped her lips together, biting back so many things she could say to him. But those things were better left unsaid. "Well, I'm here now. I'll keep watch on it. And it's been a long day. I need to settle in and get some sleep."

"Sure. Anything I can help you with before I leave?"

"No. I'm fine. Um, thanks for . . . rescuing me." Boy, it hurt to admit that to him. If she could pick up her property and plop it down miles away from Jarrod's house, she would.

He tapped the edge of his hat, then took a step back. "Anytime. You know where to find me. My cell number should still be on Roxie's bulletin board beside her desk."

"Good night." She didn't acknowledge his offer. If there was one thing certain other than death and taxes, it was that she would not in any way, shape, or form be calling Jarrod Monahan for help.

Head pounding like a thousand drums, she closed the door and just stood there.

When she made the decision to come home, she'd known Jarrod would be her neighbor. She'd known it.

And she thought she could handle it.

But now the reality was here and, well, there might be a bit of a hitch in that plan.

And that knowledge was about as welcome as crawling through that doggie door had been.

Cassidy Starr was back. Jarrod mulled that news over in his mind all the way back to

26

his place. The distance between his house and hers was about half a mile. He could see her barn and back porch from his back porch.

Jarrod had a few regrets in his life and Cassidy was one of them. What was she doing here? How long was she staying? For all he knew she was cleaning up the place and then moving on.

He'd put her out of his mind and heart for eight years now. She'd been a married woman, after all, and there'd been no reason to dwell on the past too long because of that fact.

There was no reason to dwell on it now either.

He slammed his truck door and tromped back into his house, his boots thudding in the dark silence that suddenly seemed almost unbearable. Crossing to his kitchen window, he was drawn to the lights glowing inside her house. Memories swirled like a hurricane inside of him. He stared across the distance, unable to move for the longest time.

Finally, he walked through his quiet, still house to his bedroom. Twenty minutes later, after a long, hot shower that should have eased the knots of tension from his shoulders and neck but didn't, he was still thinking about Cassidy. When he finally climbed into bed, it was only to toss and turn as the fiery, green-eyed redhead remained firmly on his mind.

He told himself he'd messed up royally where she was concerned, but it was a long time ago. Now he had commitments to the ranch and trouble brewing with rustlers. He had Pops to help and this property to get into shape. Truth was, a lot had changed since that night when he'd stepped across a line and then made the mistake of his life.

But now she was back — *and* single.

But for how long?

And what was he going to do about it?

The morning sun streamed through the windows and woke Cassidy. She popped one eye open, then the other. She was home. Back in her old room on the second floor overlooking the barn.

She felt sluggish, jet lagged without the jet. Her mouth was dry and she knew water would do her good, but instead of getting up she rolled over and stared out the window. She needed a few more minutes of laziness before she got up and started working. The big double doors of the large barn were closed, but she knew the inside was packed.

Her gaze lingered on the smaller door of the hayloft. Her place. She'd been a lonely little girl when she climbed up to that loft and spent many hours, doors open, feet dangling out as she chewed on a stalk of hay and studied the house across the pasture. A lonely young girl watching the three boys who lived in the house next door. They liked to rope anything that was standing still and sometimes moving.

And Jarrod had been the best at roping.

And there he was in her thoughts again.

He didn't come say hello or anything at Roxie's funeral, but that had been for the best. It didn't matter any longer anyway, not after all these years.

What mattered now, today and for her future, was building a life for herself where her happiness was no longer dependent on a man.

She climbed out of bed on that thought, knowing that dwelling on such things would only depress her.

The bedroom, like the barn and rest of the house, was packed full of flea market and rummage sale finds. Hordes of knick-knacks and other assortments of mismatched dust catchers sat on every available surface. An old washbasin was on an even older table in the corner. The bed

29

frame was wrought iron. Roxie figured it had been carted to Texas in a covered wagon. Come to think of it, the lumpy mattress felt like it might have made the same trip.

It was actually worse downstairs. Cassidy groaned as she looked about. She had loved her aunt, but this was bad, much worse than she remembered. At least, she thought, there was probably enough usable furniture in the house for the B and B.

After a hot shower, she dug into the one suitcase she'd brought in last night and dressed in clothes ratty enough for barn cleaning. Then she walked downstairs.

In addition to the house being full of old paintings, framed photos of her growing up, and knickknacks, it had all the books Roxie had collected. Cassidy loved those high bookshelves in the sitting room where many of them were stored. Each time her parents dropped her off at Roxie's, she'd discover that her aunt had bought a few new books just for her. She'd even placed them on the shelves at eye level where Cassidy loved to read, sitting on the floor.

Her aunt Roxie had taken care to do special things for her. Cassidy had needed that.

She smiled, feeling her aunt's warmth

envelop her. This place was cluttered, but there had been love here. And for a kid thirsty for love, that was priceless. Even now, her parents were so caught up in their own lives that they seldom called, and Cassidy had given up trying to reconnect. Maybe one day. For now, she didn't have the energy to think about it. Dealing with one failure was enough. Thinking about it wore her down.

And she needed her energy to start new, to make this home into a lovely bed-and-breakfast. It would ooze charm. Aunt Roxie had taught her how to refurbish furniture. She had in fact gotten the flea market bug herself, though not as much as Aunt Roxie. And unlike Roxie, Cassidy knew how to say no to some things. But refurbishing the old furniture she did bring home thrilled her.

It had always bugged Jack, though. He thought everything had to be new. Things that old meant trash to him.

She wondered about that in all areas of her ex-husband's life. She'd been his wife, the old love, so he'd gotten a new love. Out with the old, in with the new — well, technically, before his latest replacement, he'd had a *lot* of new loves. She resisted the urge to roll her eyes or have any feeling at all where Jack was concerned. She'd gone numb to any and all things that had to do with him. She cringed thinking about how fooled she'd been by him. It still dug at her pride that she hadn't recognized he had problems from the very beginning. But she hadn't, and there were a lot of people in his life who still had no idea with whom they were dealing. Oh, she could recognize his type from a mile away now, so there was that at least. Thankfully, she could hold up her head because she had finally decided to do the "out with the old" herself when she'd walked out.

There just wasn't going to be an "in with the new" for her. Nope, she wasn't bringing in anyone new ever again.

Knowing she had been the one to finally end the disastrous marriage, a marriage that never should have happened in the first place, helped. She should have kicked Jack to the curb in the very beginning when she'd first caught him cheating. But no, she'd been a fool.

Okay, she hadn't been a fool, she'd been forgiving — or tried to be. Then she'd felt dirty and angry and sometimes mean. And one of the things she hated about the person she'd turned into during the divorce. She felt ugly through and through.

She would change that, though.

She was getting her life back. She felt like this musty old house she was about to rejuvenate. With some house cleaning and thinning out, this farmhouse would be the most charming little inn within a hundred mile radius. Shoot, in all of Texas.

She felt warm inside, as if she were that little girl once more being enfolded in Aunt Roxie's exuberant hugs. Or God's, as her aunt always reminded her. No matter what she was going through she was to put her trust in the Lord because he loved her the most.

Cassidy blinked at sudden tears. She just wasn't at that place right now. She knew Aunt Roxie would be upset about that, but Cassidy couldn't help it. She was being honest.

After the nightmare of the last few years — especially since Roxie died — she'd begun to wonder what use believing was. Where *was* God, anyway? She was tired of being the only one in a relationship putting out any effort, and in the end she hadn't cared about anything except that she'd wasted years of her life on Jack.

On that heavy note she headed outside to unpack the rest of her belongings and some supplies from her truck, affirming her new outlook as she went. "Today I will start my new life! But coffee first." She pulled open the door and gasped — Jarrod Monahan stood on her porch again.

"Huggley-muggley," she muttered. The man's deep blue eyes stalled her breath and sent her pulse into the stratosphere. The porch light hadn't done him justice last night, but the morning sunlight showed off just exactly how good the years had been to Jarrod. He'd always been ridiculously good-looking, but age, the maturing of those rugged features . . . It was all superficial, she well understood, but nonetheless still a heart-soaring sight. Her head had stopped pounding, but with blood pressure like this it was only a matter of moments before the knocking started again.

"Mornin'," he drawled.

There was a hint of pure tease in that drawl that scrapped her nerves raw. She frowned. "What are you doing here?" Okay, that was mean. She was supposed to be leaving mean behind.

"I'm here to jump-start your battery."

She did not need her battery jump-started, thank you very much. "My battery?" she croaked, hoping he couldn't read her mind.

He nodded and pointed to his truck. It was parked hood to hood with hers.

Had she been so lost in thought that she

hadn't heard his truck? The shower — he must have driven up while she'd been showering.

"Oh, right. Thanks." She breathed a sigh of relief and moved past him, needing to clear her head, which meant getting away from the spicy, rich scent of the man. *He's not a cinnamon roll!*

She needed that coffee and bad. She had awakened in an odd frame of mind. Maybe it was the dust and the mustiness of the house.

"I was going to call Charlie to come take a look at it. I know you have things to do."

"Not a problem. I figured I'd drop by on my way to Pops's house. We're taking him riding today."

"How is Pops? He was always so nice to me." She was glad to have a new focus. And she was truly interested in Pops.

Jarrod's eyes dimmed. "He's healthy as a horse, but his mind is . . . He's got Alzheimer's."

Shock rocked through her. "No! He was always so stinkin' witty and quick," she said, then worried she was being insensitive. "I mean, I'm sorry. What a shame. He's such a good man."

Jarrod was studying her. "Yeah, he was — and is. We try to do what we can to keep life normal for him, and for the most part he's happy as can be. Give him a TV and *Walker, Texas Ranger* and he's okay." He chuckled dryly, but there was pain in the sound. "I think the disease is harder on us now than him."

She could hardly believe it even as she took in the news. How much harder it had to be on all of his boys, as he called Jarrod and his brothers. "I'll have to go see him. Does he still remember people?"

"Sometimes. He has good days and bad days. He'd like to see you, I'm sure. And I'll make sure to invite you over on a good day." He turned his attention to her truck and lifted the hood. Her gaze followed the movement, noting his broad shoulders and trim waist.

"Hop in and start her up."

Cassidy jumped. "Yeah, sure." Glad to have something to do, she hurried inside the truck and cranked the key. It gave a *grrrr*, then just when she thought it wasn't going to turn over, it grabbed charge and rattled to life.

"Thank you!" she hollered out the window. He gave her a thumbs-up, then started unhooking the cables.

"Don't turn it off for a while. Give it time to charge, and you might want to see about getting yourself a new battery. Charlie will have them down at his garage in town. It'll just take a few minutes to install. Or I can pick you up one and do it for you —"

"No, I've got it. But thank you. I'd planned on going there this morning. I'll take care of it."

He shut his hood. "Okay, if you're sure."

"I'm perfectly capable of picking up my own battery. But I appreciate the jump. And the rescue last night. You don't have to keep getting me out of situations."

He grinned. "I've been doing that since the day I met you when we were kids."

"I'm not a kid any longer." Heat crept up her neck. "Well, I need to get to work and I wouldn't want to keep you from your ride." She moved toward the house feeling stiff and awkward with the way things were between them. He seemed to have no memory of how their friendship had ended.

That both baffled her and maddened her.

"Hey," he called, drawing her to turn back.

He had a serious expression on his face but he didn't speak. She didn't say anything, giving him a moment. Instead, he crossed to her.

"I want to say I'm sorry. I heard you went through a pretty rough divorce. That had to be hard on you."

He sounded gentle, sincere. She was expecting anything but this. Maybe it was his sincerity, or maybe the surprise that he'd offered sympathy, but Cassidy instantly felt the humiliation of her failed marriage. Her brow crimped and her vision blurred. She'd fought so hard not to go down the same path her parents had, and Jarrod was one of the few people who understood how affected she'd been by the choices her parents had made. He would know how hard admitting she'd failed would be.

"It was very hard. But it happens." She put up a façade tougher than she felt. Jarrod had once been her friend . . . once. Now she fought not to squirm under his scrutiny. "I don't really want to discuss this." She started backing toward the house. This was too close. Too personal.

"Okay." He looked as baffled by her reaction as she felt by his words. "So are you just here to fix the place up and sell?"

She swallowed the lump that knotted in her throat. "I'm . . . staying. In fact, I'm, uh, turning the place into a bed-and-breakfast and starting the Strawberry Hill business up again." Trepidation filled her. But his eyes widened a touch and a slow smile spread across his face. That smile could send men to the moon, it was so explosive.

"Good. Roxie would be glad."

*What about you?*

The instant the question crossed her mind she frowned. "Um, I better get busy. Thanks again for charging the battery for me." She gave an awkward wave, then hurried up the steps and into the house.

"See you," he called. "Let me know if you need anything."

*Not on your life.* "I'm fine. Gotta go."

She closed the door, resisting the strong urge to look over her shoulder at him. This was not going to do.

Not going to do at all.

# 3

Jarrod's saddle creaked as he shifted to the left to get a better count of the herd. His brothers flanked Pops, who had ridden out with them to check the herd and fences.

"That one there looks like she's going to drop her calf any minute. What do you think, Pops?" Jarrod shot his grandfather a questioning look and studied his expression for signs that he was connecting. When he smiled, the lights were on behind his eyes and Jarrod's heart hitched.

The consummate rider, Pops sat straight in the saddle and grinned at Jarrod, his blue eyes twinkling. "One more for the herd."

"Always room for one more," Tru said in agreement, meeting Jarrod's gaze with knowing eyes.

"Hey, Pops, you ready to pull that calf if we need to?" Bo hiked a teasing eyebrow.

Pops nodded. "Done a many." He spoke in short sentences these days and repeated things often. He'd never been a big talker. Jarrod took after him in that respect.

"Taught me how to do it too." Bo clapped him on the shoulder, his horse stepping to the side a little at the movement. "Maybe you can teach Levi all about the cattle sometime."

Pops beamed at the mention of Bo's toddler. His nearly two-year-old was a real joy in Pops's life. But they all knew the likelihood of Pops teaching him anything was long past. Didn't mean it wasn't wished for.

"He'll be a good 'un," Pops said, grinning.

Next to his family, this ranch was Pops's pride and joy. He'd built it with the three of them in mind. It had always been important to him to leave a legacy behind. And though they'd had challenges over the last couple of years that almost caused them to lose the ranch, Pops's legacy was basically safe again. Those challenges knotted Jarrod's insides with boiled-down anger each and every time he thought of how his own dad had nearly gambled it all away. He still couldn't believe it. He'd thought he knew his dad, but he hadn't known him at all. Disappointment cut like sheet metal every time he thought of his dad. Once he'd planned to name his son Joe — when he had one. But not now. His dad had left a legacy of shame as far as Jarrod was concerned, and he never mentioned his name these days.

Almost from the moment Pops learned what his son had done he'd started fading on them. The stress of believing everything he'd worked for was about to be lost and the heartbreak of knowing what his last living son had done took its toll.

They hadn't learned about the massive debt until Jarrod's dad and mother were killed when their private plane crashed. Pops had to grieve so much at one time, and after he had already experienced so much sorrow in his life too. He not only had already lost his wife but also his other three sons — all from different causes.

But it was Joe, Jarrod's dad, who'd not only caused Pop's grief at his death, but broken his heart at the same time when Pops had learned after the crash what Joe had done: borrowed mind-blowing amounts of money using the ranch as collateral. So much money, from banks and not-so-reputable loan sharks too. The amount had been staggering, and if Joe hadn't died in that crash, they'd have lost the ranch before they'd even known it was in trouble.

Jarrod should have seen it coming and stopped it. He'd missed all the signs, though looking back now he saw some of them.

As the oldest grandson, he had felt an immense responsibility to save Pops's legacy for him and Jarrod's brothers. To get the ranch out of debt, though, they'd all had to buckle down and work hard. Tru with his riding, Bo with his handmade Four of Hearts Ranch stirrups, and Jarrod with the cattle business and running the ranch. They were all busy, but they worked hard to make time for Pops. And they'd agreed to take it one day at a time.

But he'd have plenty of time to dwell on all that when he was alone. Today was a good day. Tru was in from the cutting horse competition circuit for a couple of weeks, so they'd decided it was an ideal time for an outing. It was a beautiful, mild June day, and Pops knew all of them by name, which wasn't always the case.

"We're adopting a baby." Tru's words came out of nowhere, drawing Jarrod's and Bo's attention.

Jarrod busted out a big smile. "Well, it's about time. I'm glad for you." Satisfaction pushed hard at the confines of his heart.

"That's fantastic," Bo added. The youngest of the three, Bo was the first to have a baby; Levi had just come to be with them about nine months ago when Bo found him on the front porch of his house, left there by a friend of Levi's mother who had recently died. Bo hadn't even known he had a child until that moment. The sweet kid had changed all their lives for the better and had fulfilled Pops's desire to see a great-grandchild playing on the ranch.

"Pops, you're going to have another great-grandchild," Tru said, then chuckled when Pops nodded happily.

"Maggie's got to be excited." Jarrod was pleased to see his brother looking so happy.

"She is. We thought we were going to wait until toward the end of the year when I'll start slowing down from competing so much, but one of the girls at Over the Rainbow asked Maggie to take her baby and be its mother. And, well, we've been considering it. Did some praying and decided now was the time."

Over the Rainbow was a home on the outskirts of town for unwed pregnant girls. Maggie had become heavily involved in helping the girls there, as had several of the other women in town. Maggie had a way with the young women since she had once been in a tough situation as a teen herself and she understood where many of them were coming from. It had been almost a year since his brother had found out he couldn't father children.

"I think that's great." Jarrod's heart tightened at the idea of family, and he immediately thought of Cassidy. He'd been thinking about her ever since their crazy meeting last night.

He'd had his shotgun in tow, and the last thing he'd expected to find was a female hanging halfway out of the dog's door. But more shocking was that it was Cassidy. It was obvious she wanted as little to do with him as possible, but he couldn't get her off his mind.

"So, when do you think you're going to slow down enough to have a date every once in a while?" Tru was studying him, and for a moment Jarrod was so caught up thinking about seeing Cassidy that he didn't answer.

Bo patted his horse's neck and shot Jarrod a glance. "We've bit the bullet and gotten married. When are you going to join up with us?"

"Don't y'all start," he warned. "I am not looking for a wife."

"Come on, big brother," Tru said. Seriousness etched his expression. "It would do you good to settle down, to have someone to share your life with."

Jarrod scowled at his brothers in disgust. "I'm happy that y'all are happy, but I do not have the time or the inclination to jump on that wagon with y'all." That wasn't entirely true, since lately he'd been feeling lonelier and lonelier over there in that big house. The nights were getting quieter and longer, and that restlessness wouldn't let go.

Tru looked skeptical. "And I *did* have time? We both know that isn't the truth. I should remind you that I spend more than two-thirds of my life on the road between exhibitions, competitions, and sponsor obligations. If I was able to find time to find my soul mate, then I know for a fact everyone, including you, has time to look for love."

"I'm on the road too, hauling cattle here, there, and yonder." Jarrod knew he sounded defensive, but he did not like justifying his workday. "Not so much as you, by any means, but I'm usually working daylight to dark somewhere here on the ranch, and that leaves little time for anything else. What woman wants to start a relationship with a cowboy who isn't around?"

Bo shook his head. "Hey, I get it, Jarrod. I was so there with ya, buddy — until Abby nearly ran me over, and then Levi showed up. You need someone, man."

Cassidy jumped back to the forefront of

his thoughts. She was here after all these years and he'd seen pain in her eyes. She was hurting right now, and she'd come to Roxie's just like when she was a little girl. Only this time it was her own divorce that brought her here, not one of her parents' dramas.

As he watched two calves romping around together, his mind was full with the past. With Cassidy. But now was not the time to think about that. He glanced at his brothers and reiterated his focus. "This ranch is still not where it needs to be —"

"There's no reason for you to work as hard as you do," Tru jumped in sternly. "We have plenty of hired help, and if we don't, then hire them. You *need* and can have a life, Jarrod. I know you feel responsible, being the oldest and all. But that's hogwash. We're all in this together, and while Bo and I have held up our end of the bargain by bringing in the extra money, you've done amazing things keeping this ranch making money even with the noose tied around its neck."

"We owe you, man," Bo added.

Jarrod's wrists were crossed over the saddle horn as he'd been leaning in and studying the cattle in the distance. Now he raised his hand and tugged on the brim of his hat as he tried to be patient with his younger brothers. They only wanted what they thought was best for him. And right now he only wanted what was best for the ranch. He wasn't ready to deal with anything else. And Cassidy had just shown up, after all. She might be gone in a month.

No matter what they said, he had obligations and pressures of his own driving him, and Tru and Bo wouldn't understand. His personal life was his own business and he'd go at it with his own ideas.

"I'm fine. Stop worrying about me."

Bo's dimples showed up with his grin, reminding Jarrod of the mischievous little brother he'd been growing up, tagging along and looking up to Jarrod. Much like Cassidy had been when she'd first shown up.

"Come on, man," Bo said. "We just want you to have someone."

"Look." Exasperation tightened inside him. "The ranch day is long and the week is longer. If the good Lord wants me to have someone then he'll have to bring her to my doorstep, or she'll have to run me over with her car or something, because I'm not lookin' for her right now."

Bo and Tru looked from him to each other and then grinned. He wasn't finding their amusement real funny.

"You're just being stubborn now." Tru grunted his opinion as if he hadn't heard a word Jarrod had just said. "Let's get real here. Truth is, Bo and I are worried about you. Since all this started after Dad died, you've gotten way too serious and quiet. You don't do anything unless it has to do with the ranch. You smile less than any man I know, and I'm a pretty serious fella myself."

"Yeah," Bo agreed. "Levi's got you smiling more, and then Maggie and Abby when you're around them. That's why we think a family of your own is what you need."

Jarrod's mood darkened, feeling like the whole lot of them had been conspiring about poor, poor Jarrod.

"Don't go lookin' like that." Bo kept going. "We're trying to do a successful intervention here and you, big brother, are not cooperating."

"You deserve some time for yourself." Tru's expression was firm while Bo's look was more a challenge.

"Stop." Jarrod growled the word. "I thought the ladies at the Cut Up and Roll Salon were the ones I'd have to ward off on the matchmakin'. Believe me, boys, it doesn't look good on you."

"And being a grump doesn't look good

on you." Bo's usually teasing eyes were full of concern.

Jarrod felt like he'd stepped into some weird alternate world. Where were his brothers? "What has gotten into y'all? Now, can we get back to ranching?" With that he nudged his horse and loped to meet the calves being herded toward him. His brothers had just tromped into territory they weren't welcome.

He'd date when he was ready and not before. Besides, all he had going this time of year meant he had more responsibility on his plate than he needed without adding anything else. If he was going to date anyone right now, God would have to put her right in front of him, and even then he might miss her in passing.

*How about next door?*

He slowed his horse and studied the heifer eating grass beside him. His thoughts were back on Cassidy. When he'd walked away from her all those years ago, he'd made that mistake on an impulse and he was not going to make that same mistake again. Everything he did these days was thought out, planned, and well executed. And that was the way it would remain.

Pebble Howard pushed her grocery cart

through the store, pausing to survey the vegetables without any real inclination toward what she was doing. She'd been feeling listless and melancholy ever since she woke today. She was feeling at loose ends. Something had to give and soon. Her life needed a change — maybe that was it.

Maybe it was time to sell the motel.

She loved the Sweet Dreams Motel. She and Cecil had opened it when they were young and it had been good to them. But ever since her husband's death over ten years ago, she'd been running it on her own. And recently she'd realized her life had become completely dictated by life around the motel. She'd settled into a safe, predictable existence, and she needed to shake things up.

The idea to sell the motel had come out of the blue and startled her. But it was a very good idea. Cecil would back her 100 percent if he were here to give her advice. He'd want her to move on, and lately she'd come to realize that she hadn't —

"Pebble."

Her pulse skittered like a schoolgirl's as she looked across the apple bin to see her old friend Rand Ratliff. He looked wonderful today. His checkered fedora sat at a slight tilt and his thick, gray hair looked freshly cut against his tanned skin. He smiled that slightly crooked smile and her heart tilted on its axis. She tried to slow the emotion running through her, but she'd learned a long time ago that there was no controlling the feelings she felt inside for Rand. She could, however, control her outward reaction.

"Hello, Rand," she said softly, feeling just as soft inside at being in his presence. No, she could not allow him to see exactly how she was feeling. So much had happened over the last few months that had put a strain between them — even threatened their friendship. Their past went all the way back to high school when she'd been the prim and proper girl in school and he'd been the rebel, pushing limits and hanging out with the so-called rougher crowd. An unlikely pair, he'd been her first love, but that had fallen apart in the end when he left Wishing Springs to find a life filled with more adventure. Young love. Lost love.

Her life had been wonderful in between then and now. She'd married the love of her life and lost him a decade ago. But she'd always had a soft spot in her heart for Rand.

Now he strode her way, his blue eyes clear, no sign that he'd been drinking. No sign that he'd fallen off the wagon since getting out of rehab a few months ago. Pebble wanted to believe he would be strong enough to remain sober, but her fear for him was great.

"It's nice to see you, and you look lovely today," he said gently. Always the gentleman, he tipped his hat.

She picked up an apple and placed it inside a plastic bag, needing something to do with her hands, something to concentrate on other than the ache in her heart that was synonymous with Rand. "Thank you. How is everything at the paper this week?" she said, knowing his newspaper was a safe topic.

"Everything is good. Not a lot of excitement happening in Wishing Springs this week, however, so the news section will be lacking. Though I believe Cassidy Starr has just arrived in town. I haven't seen her yet, but she called Doobie and Doonie earlier this week down at the real estate office and had them turn on the electricity and water."

"That's wonderful. Roxie would be so happy to know that sweet girl is finally home. Roxie always did have a deep worry for the life Cassidy was living." Roxie had been Pebble's friend and had always worried about her young niece. She'd worried about her up until the day she died.

"Her parents put that poor girl through unreasonable trauma." Rand's brow creased.

"True. I'm sure she's relieved to be here." She wondered if he was thinking about the trauma he'd put those who loved him through. "Well, I'd better finish up. I need to get back to the motel."

He nodded, always polite, always just distant enough that they both kept the small wall between them. They were walking on eggshells these days, and her nerves and her heart were showing it.

It took everything she had to push her buggy forward and walk away.

When she arrived at her small apartment attached to the motel office, she went to her bedroom, set her purse on the chair in the corner, and caught sight of herself in the mirror. She smoothed her graying hair and saw the uncertainty in her blue eyes.

A framed photo of Cecil sat on the dresser and she picked it up, ran her hand along the smooth glass. "What do you think?" she asked softly. His handsome, kind face stared back at her, steadied her. She set down the photo.

She could not go on this way. Something had to change.

# 4

It was mid-morning before Cassidy tugged on the first heavy wooden door of the barn and pulled it around until it was wide open and snug against the barn. Then she opened the other side. The door creaked and the stale scent of the interior engulfed her. She slammed her hands on her hips and stared into the shadowy barn. She'd decided clearing it out was the priority so she could make room for her organic gardening supplies. She also needed to take inventory to see what she had on hand, what was useable, and what had to go.

She'd peeked in here after the funeral, so she'd known she would have her work cut out for her because of Aunt Roxie's love of collecting things. The building was packed.

The house cleaning could happen at night, but this was her day life for the immediate future. After Jarrod left last night, she'd really been thankful she'd been too exhausted to stay awake and dwell on the past. And she'd been too intent on her to-do list today to let him take over her thoughts. But then he'd shown up again and thrown her all off balance.

Rebuilding the strawberry farm Aunt Roxie had loved was going to be good for her. More and more organic produce was in demand, and the whole idea went well with the B and B plan. Roxie had never considered having strangers in her home. The idea would have cramped her independent nature, and she had some old royalties on a weak-producing oil well she had a stake in that helped her manage when times got tough. Those royalties had dwindled down to almost nothing now, and Cassidy didn't think about them much. But they'd helped sustain Aunt Roxie.

It was time to see what was inside the barn, and she took determined steps that direction.

She didn't feel the same way Roxie would have about the bed-and-breakfast. She liked the idea of meeting people from all over. Well, maybe she was weird, but the thought of having folks — even strangers — in her home might help make the decision to remain alone from here on out a little easier. While she was taking care of them, it would be almost like she had family.

It was pathetic reasoning, actually, but it was all she had at the moment. Eventually she would be comfortable and satisfied, just like Aunt Roxie had been.

Grabbing hold of two old patio chairs, she backed toward the entrance of the barn and got them outside. She heard a hum in the distance and glanced up to see a low-flying plane. As she looked up, the plane turned in a wide arc, its wings tilted toward her, and she clearly saw they were bright yellow. *Yellow.* It was a crop duster.

*Crop duster!*

Cassidy gasped. "No! No, no, *no!*"

Everything else forgotten, she ran for the truck, slammed the tailgate shut, and hurried to slide behind the wheel and crank the engine. A crop duster could ruin everything! She was going to grow organic strawberries. Crop dusting and organic did not go well together. Cassidy stomped the gas pedal of her old truck and shot forward.

She had to stop that plane.

Jarrod drove up the drive to his ranch house, relieved to have left his brothers back at the stables on the other side of the ranch where Pops's home and the main ranch setup was. He had wasted no time saying good-bye to Pops, then he'd headed home to work.

He paused on the porch at the sound of the plane. He'd hired a crop duster to get the ranch's weed situation back under control. Seeing the plane in the sky gave Jarrod a sense of accomplishment after four years of moving, shaking, scraping, scrimping to make the ranch profitable while debt suffocating in its magnitude had weighed down on him and his brothers.

But though he'd managed to keep the ranch bringing in income, he hadn't been able to keep the ranch in shape. All manner of aggressive weeds, mesquite trees, yaupon bushes, and prairie roses had begun taking over many areas because he hadn't had the funds to keep them under control.

The plane in the sky represented the fact that for the first time since his father put the ranch in jeopardy with his betrayal, Jarrod had been able to hire a crop duster to begin the process of eliminating the insidious weeds.

Over the next few weeks he would get the Four of Hearts Ranch back on the road to being the prettiest land in Texas.

He glanced up to see Cassidy's truck traveling up his gravel drive. By the sound of the old Ford, it was in dire need of a tune-up or a complete engine overall . . . or the junkyard. He moved to the edge of the porch, wondering what the hurry was. Just then the truck hit a rut and fishtailed. Cassidy kept control and swerved to an unsteady halt, momentarily disappearing in a plume of dust as the trail following her caught up with the truck.

The door flew open and Cassidy, long-legged and wild-haired, barreled from the truck and stormed his way. Her hair was tousled around her face in complete mayhem, but the wildness of it didn't hold a candle to the wildfire in her eyes as she rushed him.

"What's wrong?" His heart raced as he stepped off the porch to meet her. "Are you all right?"

Breathing hard, she pointed skyward. "Stop that plane."

"The crop duster?"

She looked like she was ready to take him down if she didn't do what she wanted.

"You have to stop the plane."

Eyes so vivid green they looked backlit by flame glowed at him.

She continued, "I can't have chemicals floating all over my property. I need you to radio the pilot or something. But stop him now."

His pulse calmed knowing she wasn't hurt or no disaster had happened. "Okay, hold on, Cassidy. The plane is way over there." He pointed to the plane in the distance.

Her eyes narrowed. "*Hold on?* Jarrod, I don't have time to hold on. That plane is about to drop its load, and this wind is going to catch it and it's going to *contaminate* my land."

This was a little over the top. "There is almost no wind."

"If he dumps those chemicals any closer, you know they could drift to my land with barely any breeze. Not to mention if he gets careless and drops before he flies over your property line."

"I seriously doubt it. He's an excellent pilot." Jarrod squinted back toward the sky, then back at her. Her cheeks were going to ignite if they got any redder. He swept his hat from his head. His memory kicked into rewind and he was suddenly back to that first day she'd shown up here. A wild-haired, ten-year-old girl with skinned knees and unshed tears glistening in her eyes.

"I'll call him off anyway." He pulled his cell from the holster at his hip and called Jasper, the ag pilot who owned the company. Within moments he'd explained what he needed and Jasper had radioed his man to

60

move over to an area of land on the other side of the ranch. For now. It was going to have to get done sooner or later, though.

"He should be flying off any moment."

"Thank you." Everything about her seemed to soften in an instant as she went from warrior mode to regular person. Well, maybe not exactly regular. Nothing about Cassidy Starr was regular. She'd been an unusual kid. He was six years older than she was, and the first time he met her she'd come crawling across that fence and into this very yard, which at the time had been where he and his parents and brothers called home. She'd been a kid and he'd been a cocky teen.

To this day he didn't remember much else about that moment except that she'd looked about as wild-eyed and fierce then as she had moments ago.

"Now, why are you so frantic about my crop duster? I believe he was far enough away from your place that there wouldn't have been a problem. I'm not the kind of man who would knowingly put something on someone else's land. He'll have to finish —"

"But he can't. You can't predict wind flow. It's totally understandable that you'd be crop dusting your land. Weed control and all of that." Her hand went to her temple now where she rubbed small circles with long fingers. A small gasp escaped. "Aw, bonkers! Look, I'm sorry. This isn't your problem. I just realized that I haven't thought out my organic gardening completely."

"Are you okay?"

"I'm fine," she sighed. "My head just hurts some. It's left over from an accident I had before I moved here. But it seems I have made a really bad error in judgment."

"Nah, it couldn't be that bad." Jarrod wasn't one to enjoy watching a woman look worried and depressed.

"It's bad, all right. I just realized I've based my future on organic gardening and the property I'm planning to do that organic gardening on is probably contaminated beyond repair by years of crop dusting from all of the acreage surrounding it. Your grandfather has had his land dusted for years. What was I thinking?"

He grimaced. It was true. The ranch needed to be sprayed. It was the best way they'd found to corral the weeds and keep the cattle pasture healthy. "Look, can't you have the ground tested? I haven't crop dusted in over four years."

Her eyes brightened. "*Four* years? Really?"

Even after all this time he liked the way she looked when her eyes lit up. "Yeah, today is the first time in around four years anything has been sprayed on the pastures. Believe me, if we loaded up and went out there to the interior of the ranch where he was about to spray, you'd definitely see that's true by the weed and scrub growth and the prairie roses, which sounds nice but is awful if let run unchecked like it's been."

"Four years! You are my hero. *Thank you,*" she gushed. And then grinning like he'd just pulled her from the edge of a cliff, she completely knocked him off one when she threw her arms around him in an exuberant hug.

Cassidy couldn't contain her relief. She had her arms around Jarrod before her good sense could kick in and put a halt to her mistake. She was wrapped around him like shrink-wrap when it hit her that she was molded to his hard chest and mauling the man she most needed not to be touching!

Dropping her arms, she stumbled back and away from him. His hooded gaze hid his reaction from her, but she wouldn't have seen it anyway because she was too en-grossed in saving face.

"Four years," she croaked. "That saves

me. That's over the actual three-year quali-fying time it takes for ground that might have been contaminated by chemicals to be eligible for becoming organic certified."

He rubbed his neck and squinted in the sunlight at her. "That so?"

Her stomach dipped as he suddenly re-minded her of the serious teen she'd idol-ized. "Yes, and since the house has been vacant, which means no one else has been spraying chemicals, and you haven't been crop dusting, there shouldn't be any prob-lem getting my certification process started . . . I mean, the truth is, I don't have to be certified yet. The farm is too small to have to worry about that, but I want to be as compliant as possible for my peace of mind. And ground that's continually drenched in pesticides is bad for everyone."

He frowned. "It's not like we use poison. I raise healthy cattle using minimal chemi-cals."

"I'm sure you do. Look, you just rescued me from a long and lengthy process before I could officially say my fruit is organic. I had completely forgotten about your family crop dusting as a means of land control. I never factored that into my plan until this very moment. I easily could have raised my crops just like Roxie did and claimed that I was organic and had peace of mind about it. After all, pest control done her way meant using a fly swatter or a rock. But knowing I'm compliant with organic standards that help people who need to have minimal chemical exposure is what I'm trying to do. You know, give them peace of mind when they come here to pick my fruit. Does that make sense?"

His very serious, navy eyes crinkled at the edges. "Yes, it makes sense. But we have a problem. I'm going to have to spray the area soon. The outfit I use is excellent, but something tells me that doesn't matter where organic certification is concerned."

"You're right. Can you use something organic instead of the chemicals you normally use?"

Her pulse raced as she watched him contemplate their situation. Surely he wouldn't insist on spraying chemicals after this, would he? Her stomach felt sick waiting for his response. Or was it from attraction? She felt her eyebrows bunch together at the unwelcomed possibility. She'd been through too much with Jack. So much that she was completely shocked that she'd react to any man. Even Jarrod. Especially Jarrod.

He'd broken her young heart.

And then she, like a fool, had run back to

Plano and soon after jumped into marriage with Jack. It had been a rebound relationship, she understood now. Doomed from the start because she'd not known him nearly well enough, as his later actions proved.

She had overlooked the signs of certain tendencies when they were dating, like the fact that when they were out together he had no problem watching other women. She should have realized if he was that bold when he was with her then he was probably even more so when he was alone.

Her head began to thump. She hated how upset she got when thinking of the man. A skirt chaser, Aunt Roxie would have called him had she met him. But she hadn't because Roxie hadn't been back to visit in all that time. Guilt swallowed her up as it always did when she thought about that. She closed her fingers into fists and clenched them, trying to force down the building anger, resentment, and disappointment in her own actions.

"Hey, no need to look so upset," Jarrod said. Concern rumbled in his tone, drawing her from her thoughts.

She blinked hard, tried to relax, and started to speak, "I . . ." His gaze softened, grabbing something deep inside her, and she lost her words.

"I'll talk to the owner about it. We'll see what can be done. I'll let you know what I find out. Are you sure you're fine? You're rubbing your temple again."

She hadn't even realized she was rubbing her temple. She had always worn her emotions on her face too. At least that was what Roxie used to say. Well, now was not the time to be showing anything. "I'm fine." She backed up. "I need to get back to work. I'm going to be cleaning the house in the evenings right now and working in the barn during the day, trying to make room for any supplies I'll need for my gardening." *Too much information, Cassidy.* She clamped her lips shut. He did not need to know the details of her plan.

"I'm here if you need me. I'm gone some, but mostly around," he drawled in a gravelly voice as he squinted again in the sunlight.

Dear goodness, he looked good. And he'd been almost too helpful.

"I'm fine," she croaked, backing up some more. She wouldn't be calling him if she needed anything. She had all kinds of books on everything from planting her organic strawberries to house repair. And what she didn't have in paperback she had on her e-reader, and what she didn't have there she could always search for on the Internet. How hard could it be?

She started back to her truck. The dust she'd stirred up had settled, and yet her throat felt as if she'd been caught in a dust storm. With her mouth open.

Jarrod Monahan had been her hero from the moment she'd arrived at her aunt's house as a ten-year-old kid, knowing her life was falling apart around her. But when the older, most handsome boy she'd ever seen had tended to her scraped knees, she knew she'd idolize him forever. She'd trusted him.

Which was a big deal, since she'd learned never to trust anyone other than her aunt Roxie. Not even her parents. Especially not her parents, who had been the worst, always making her think that this time their home life would settle down. This time it would be good. This time the new spouse would stick. But it had never happened, and she'd find herself back at Aunt Roxie's and next door to Jarrod.

But then that fateful, hateful Fourth of July she'd let her heart believe . . .

She took a deep breath and let it ease out slowly as she tried to be unaffected.

Jarrod was still as single and as devastatingly good-looking as ever, and he was still next door.

But she had changed.

She was no longer that child, or that kid. Not that young woman she'd been the last time she'd been with him —

"You sure you're okay?" he called.

"Yes," she said tersely, looking back at him. "I have a lot to do. I just panicked and raced over here, taking a chance that you would be here and could help. I appreciate everything you're doing. With the crop duster," she clarified, and then felt like a ninny.

"Anytime." He tucked his right thumb into his belt loop, looking at ease.

At ease — ha! She climbed into her truck and slammed the door. Fighting not to take a peek at him, she yanked the gear shifter into reverse, then pressed the gas pedal. The truck shot back like a bullet, and she very nearly took out a fence post before she stomped on the brake. Heat suffused her cheeks as she swallowed hard and turned the wheel, jerkily starting the truck down the drive and straight back to her place.

She was a little shocked at how helpful Jarrod had been. She would have thought that, as a rancher, he'd have been more closed-minded about the whole crop-dusting issue. But then, what did she know about ranchers? Other than the handful of times she'd spent at her aunt's place, she really hadn't given much thought to what a rancher would or wouldn't do.

And in her rush to get out of the suburbs and start her new life, she hadn't given the ranch next door a lot of thought . . . or the cowboy who lived there. In all honesty, thinking about men of any sort wasn't even on her radar. So what was with her pulse every time he looked at her?

Jarrod might be good-looking, and helpful, but Cassidy was here for no one but herself.

And she'd make this work with a smile on her face, even if it took gritting that smile out on the days she felt like crying.

There had been a lot of those days in the last few years leading up to the failure of her marriage. Days that had reminded her so much of each and every breakup she'd lived through with her parents. And each time with Jack she'd vowed to make it work. But infidelity left a gaping hole in the other partner's soul, and Cassidy was concreting that hole up and never, ever going to have to worry about living through another breakup.

She was making her own happily-ever-

after, and it was going to be solitary, independent, and joyful, just like Aunt Roxie's.

# 5

"Sing it, Glen!" Cassidy paused at the ancient radio sitting on the workbench in the corner of the barn. She turned up the volume so Glen Campbell's smooth voice radiated louder from the radio that was permanently dialed into the "oldies" country station. Cassidy had been glad the barn had electricity and that the oldies station was still going strong after all these years. She sang along with the singer whose music she knew mostly because Aunt Roxie had always listened to this station over the years. Old country wasn't Cassidy's favorite, but today she was feeling nostalgic as she worked in the barn.

She stared at the stack of tires in another corner. She'd been lugging stuff out of the barn since seven this morning. Two long hours ago. She winced at a jab in her lower back letting her know she had a long day ahead of her. But she was determined that before night came along this disaster was going to have room in it for the supplies she needed for her strawberry business.

And if she had some luck, she'd find some cool things hidden among the junk she could use in her strawberry business, maybe some things Aunt Roxie had used that could be salvaged. She'd started making two separate piles, one with the interesting stuff that she didn't know exactly what to do with, like the old mantel she knew was beautiful beneath what looked like infinite layers of paint. The other pile was the completely unusable and unexplainable items. The tower of old tires went into that category. They assuredly did not count as cool stuff. Unexplainable, yes, but not cool.

"Like a rhinestone cowboy . . . da dum dum," she sang louder. She laughed at herself as she dug out an old baby bassinet, then reached for more, singing stronger as she tugged harder on the mishmash of tangled junk piled on top of each other.

Singing along as if Aunt Roxie were right there with her, giving her strength. Roxie had spirit, and when Cassidy had come to Strawberry Hill, beat down and feeling uncertain and torn by the chaos in her life, Aunt Roxie had built her up. She needed that now.

"Mornin'. How's it going?"

Cassidy screamed and swung around, her heart in her throat. Jarrod stood there in a sunbeam looking like . . . looking *amazing.* "Holy smokes, you scared the life out of me. Would you stop doing that, please?" She scowled at him and tried to ignore the voice in her head that was asking why he had to go and age so stinkin' well.

He chuckled, which only made him better looking. "I'm sorry. But I can almost hear Glen singing at my house. And you were pretty into the song too. I thought for a minute there you were going to break into a dance."

Her mouth fell open. How embarrassing. Her cheeks burned with the knowledge that he'd been standing there long enough to see her with her guard down.

She closed her mouth and cleared her throat. "I'm cleaning out the barn." Like the man couldn't see what she was doing. "It's a wreck in here." Again, self-explanatory. "It's going to be the death of me if I'm not careful," she added cheerfully, pushing for positive with the exaggeration.

There was laughter in his eyes. "That bad, huh?"

"Worse."

He chuckled again, laughing at her, she

was quite certain.

"Let me take a look. Maybe I can help you."

"Oh, you don't have to do that."

"It's not a problem."

"No, really —"

Ignoring her protest, he stepped inside the barn. "Roxie kept everything if I'm remembering correctly. And she was always going to some auction or roadside sale —" Halting, he let out a low whistle. "Whoa. Wow."

Shaking her head, she stalked over and switched off the radio. "I guess if you insist. You are remembering right. It's awful, though there is some cool stuff in here too. But I can't figure out what the tires are for."

Cassidy walked past him and reached for a tire, intent on doing something other than standing there wondering why he'd dropped by — and if she was going to have to contend with this kind of distraction and interruption all the time . . . Of course, yesterday she'd been the one who'd dropped by on him. What an embarrassing experience that had been.

Trying not to think about how she must have looked nearly running down his fence in her haste to drive off, she grabbed the tire and yanked it to a standing position. Immediately she knew she'd made a mistake as the familiar but unwanted sound of a rattlesnake filled the air —

Jarrod saw the snake the moment Cassidy pulled the tire away. Reacting instinctively, he yanked her into his arms, spun away, and didn't stop moving until they were out of the barn. She was smashed against his chest, hyperventilating.

"Snake, *snake,*" she gasped, shaking against him, yanking first one foot and then the other off the ground while looking down. He scooped her up higher as he studied the area to make sure the snake hadn't followed them.

"I *hate* snakes," she growled, now shivering uncontrollably. "If I'd have been Eve I'd have run from that snake and never looked back."

He laughed. "No joke."

"I'm not joking. It-it almost got me." She gasped again as a new wave of fear showed on her face. "I saw it strike with its big ugly head. I think I'm going to have a heart attack thinking about it."

He could tell she wasn't going to stop shaking anytime soon. "It's okay. You're fine now," he reassured her, clasping her more securely against him. His own heart was pounding like a ticking bomb, and her being all snug and close was not helping the situation.

If he were honest, and he always tried to be, even with himself, Jarrod had to admit he wasn't exactly hating the snake at that moment. Cassidy's hair teased him as it brushed his cheek. He fought not to lean in closer. She smelled faintly of something sweet despite the film of dust on her. "Come on now, breathe," he soothed as her heart pounded erratically against his own. She turned her head, and his throat went dirt dry when his lips very nearly ended up against her soft cheek.

His hands tightened on her. "I promise, you're fine," he managed, his voice gravelly even to his own ears. He didn't move as her panic-filled eyes sought his. That panic yanked his thoughts from where they'd gone and back to her fear.

Her fear cut him to the core.

She'd looked strong and ready to take on the world yesterday when she'd barreled out of her truck, eyes on fire. But the sight of a snake had terrified her. Her trembling body told him just how much.

For safety's sake — his own — he set her on her feet and took her face in his hands. "Look at me. Come on, look at me. You're fine."

She focused on him and blinked hard. Then nodded. "Okay. So did it go a-away?"

"Probably not, but I'm going to go back in there and find it and any friends and family it might have hanging out with it."

"Thank you," she said, her face white as milk. Her gaze dropped to his lips, then yanked back to his eyes. The panic in her eyes shifted to something else, and her look set his heart hammering again. Her brow wrinkled, her eyes darkened, and she backed away from him.

"Sorry. I'm not usually such a wimp. It's just that snakes are so awful, and-and that one nearly took a bite out of me. Thank you. Thank. You."

He melted at the gratitude. He quirked a grin, fighting for a foothold to maintain some distance. "Glad I was here."

She took a deep breath, and he could tell she was fighting for calm. He wondered if she was still thinking of the snake or if, like him, her thoughts were on whatever had just passed between them.

"I think . . . I'm not sure I can get myself to go back in there. And I have to get that place cleaned out so all my supplies have a place to go. And so I can see what's good and what's bad."

"I'll get you in there. I'll go in with you."

She stomped her foot. "Ugh, I feel like a *fool.* I got all dressed for this and never once thought about a snake. How crazy is that? I didn't think about the crop dusting and I didn't think about snakes —"

"Hey, whoa. You were caught up in the excitement of doing something you were looking forward to. Of course you didn't think about a stinkin' rattlesnake. It's not as if we see one every day. As much as I'm in the pastures I see only one or two most years. They don't like us as much as we don't like them."

"But it was here. And if you hadn't been here, I'd be in there now, snake bit and not sure what to do about it. I'd probably be a screaming mass of pitiful —"

"Hey, stop," he snapped. He needed to break her out of this. "It didn't happen. I'm glad I'm here. And you have my cell number to call if you ever need me to come kill a snake or anything. So you're okay. Give yourself a break. Yesterday you were warrior woman over that crop duster." He laughed. "If you'd have glared at the snake like you were glaring at me, then he'd have coiled up and died on the spot."

Her eyes widened. "Are you serious? Did I look at you like that?"

He laughed. "Like Annie Oakley or something."

"Oh."

He grinned, glad to have distracted her. "Now, come on. Let's get rid of your snake buddy. Do you have a hoe or a shovel around here anywhere?"

She pointed toward the barn. "There, against the wall."

"Great. Now stand back and let me do this."

"Are you sure? You might get bit —"

"I've dealt with all kinds of snakes in the pasture. I've got this."

She didn't look completely convinced as she rammed a hand into her hair and paused with it on top of her head, studying him doubtfully. That bruised his pride a little, he had to admit.

Finally she nodded. "Okay then. Go on in. Just be careful."

Jarrod looked at her, her translucent skin, flaming hair, and oh-so-expressive eyes — not to mention the all-too-memorable feel of her body pressed against his, their hearts pounding in unison —

Careful. He was feeling reckless at this moment, and it had been a long, long time since he'd let his self-control down long enough to feel this way.

He yanked his gaze from hers and strode toward the tools. Right now, in the barn hunting for a snake was the safest place for him.

# 6

Cassie's heart was still pounding and she wasn't sure if it was from the snake or the startling feel of Jarrod Monahan's arms around her. Knees a bit wobbly, she watched him stride toward the tools as she fought to right the craziness swirling around inside of her.

He took the shovel into his hands, and his expression was ruggedly intent as he moved toward the barn door.

*Move, sister!*

She needed the Annie Oakley part of her to show up. Honestly, if she was going to be independent, she needed to get over this fear and go after that stinkin' snake too.

Springing forward, she jumped behind Jarrod, ramming him in the backside in her haste. "Sorry," she gasped, cringing as he stopped dead in his tracks and glared at her over his shoulder.

"What are you doing?" he demanded.

"I-I'm helping you. It's my snake, after all. And, well, I don't like the idea of that awful thing getting the better of me."

"Cassidy, it's okay. I won't think any less of you. Now, go on back out there and let me take care of this."

"No. I'm coming. I couldn't look at myself in the mirror tonight if I let you do this without at least coming with you." She scooted closer — not that she could get any closer, but she tried. "Go." She waved her hand for him to go.

His jaw tightened and she thought he would protest again. Instead, he let out a heavy breath and shrugged. "Watch yourself," he demanded. "And stay right behind me. Rattlesnake bites are not fun. And they can kill you or at least mess you up really bad. This is not a matter to toy with."

"I am not stupid. I know *that,*" she huffed. "I might be scared, but there is a reason for that."

"Right." He turned back and moved toward the tires. With the shovel, he poked around the first layers, then one by one yanked the tires out of the way. As he moved them, Cassidy forced herself to grab them and roll them out of the barn to a pile outside. It didn't take long for Jarrod to make it to the row closest to the wall. She got braver with each passing moment and moved to stand behind him.

"Stay behind me!"

She jumped back. "Fine. I'm here." She placed a hand on his hip and peered around him as he went to move the last tire. Her mouth went dry and she prepared to run.

But there was nothing there. Just a hole in the wall. No snake.

Her stomach felt queasy looking at that hole. "Do you think it will come back?"

"I'm going to close the hole, but even if it does get back in here, if you put your stuff in order, you'll be better able to see it. It'll have fewer dark spaces to hide. Tires are really easy for them to coil up in."

"Okay. So I can handle that. Thank you." It was time to take charge again. To be a woman and not a mouse. She followed him back outside.

He looked around at the piles of stuff. "This is going to take awhile."

"And there could be more snakes too."

"I hate to agree, but it's true."

She'd been trying not to focus on that niggling bit of knowledge hanging out in the back of her mind. She took a deep breath. "Well, okay. Thank you for your help. I know you have things to do, so it was great of you to stop by, but you need to go do your thing now." She swallowed hard and fought to look brave.

It was a big fat lie, though.

"My thing?" Jarrod grinned at the awful face Cassidy was making as she tried to put up what he suspected was supposed to be a brave face. Nope. Not exactly the look she was probably hoping for.

"I've got bulls to tend to and move around and heifers to move around, but my men can do that. Today I'm going to do what Pops and my mom taught me to do all my life, and that's to be a good neighbor. I'm going to fix that hole in your barn."

"Are you sure? I don't feel right —"

"I'll go if you want me to," he said.

"Oh, no. I mean, if you really want to, that would be fine. But I'm helping."

"Good. Then we better get busy." Not waiting for her to suddenly change her mind, he strode past her in search of wood.

A little while later, the hole was boarded up. Cassidy had worked right along beside him. Really close beside him. He could tell she was scared but fought hard to hide it and overcome it. She was determined, he'd give her that.

They kept on clearing out things after that, working in silence, something she seemed to need before she slowly relaxed again. The fight that had welled up inside of her seemed to ease away as she lifted and carried pile after pile of junky pieces from the old barn.

He, on the other hand, had a hard time keeping his focus on the work and not on her. Cassidy had matured into a beautiful woman. There was a uniqueness to her beauty. Big eyes and high cheeks that had once stood out prominently but were now softer since the hollows of her face had filled in nicely. Her hair was still out of control, but today she'd tamed it some by pulling it back into a bushy ponytail at the nape of her neck. Curly pieces of it sprang out from the clasp and seemed to dance about her face as she moved around. Her hair fit her though, just like it always had. It was alive with energy just like everything else about her.

What was he doing? He should change his line of thinking — now.

"Your great-aunt was a hoarder of sorts," he said, stating the obvious as he ripped his eyes off her to focus on the junk.

Cassidy paused in pulling a birdcage from a shelf. "Tell me about it."

"What do you think she did with all this stuff? Or planned to do?"

"I'm not certain. Oh, but look at that old cabinet right there."

She moved toward a wooden piece about five feet tall and four feet wide. It had large square bins in it that were full of old cans and jars. It was pretty rustic, to say the least.

"This is cool. I know it looks kinda bad." She studied it. "Really bad. But if I give it tender loving care, it will be a great storage piece — for good stuff, not just junk. I think it can be used in my fruit business." She turned to him, smiling. "I'm keeping this. I don't know what Roxie did with it other than to stuff it full of cans and jars, but I know what I'll do with it. It's going to look great when I get through with it."

He chuckled, eyeing the ugly thing skeptically. "If you say so."

"No, really, it will. You'll see."

"What about all those old cans? I've never seen so many old rusted coffee cans. And tires. I can't get over all the tires."

Cassidy smiled. "I just remembered. She grew things in them."

"Oh yeah, I remember that now."

"It's cheaper than buying pots. And Aunt Roxie was all about recycling old things. She started tomatoes in the tires. That vegetable stand of hers had a lot of variety in it. I only hope I can make a go of selling both fruit and vegetables like she did. It'll probably be next year before I have an actual crop of anything because I've missed the strawberry season this year. And I have to get the land certified organic and repairs made on the house before I can turn it into a bed-and-breakfast. Even then I may not get it opened before Christmas — there's just so much to be done."

A shadow crossed her expression. "It would be nice if I could. But I just don't see it happening."

He wondered how her finances were. She looked worried. "You know there are peach trees on this land too. I bet there are peaches on them now."

Her chin snapped up. "Peach trees?"

He smiled, glad to see the excitement in her eyes. Glad to know he might have brightened her outlook. "A small orchard at the back of the property. It's kind of neglected after all this time, but I see them when I check fences."

"Oh my goodness. I had no idea. They weren't here last time I came around."

"I think Roxie got some kind of agricultural deduction for planting them. And she sold the peaches some. Want to take a look?"

"Of course."

"Then let's go."

"This is so cool. It would mean a crop this year maybe. Okay, I'm getting ahead of myself. Why didn't she put the orchard up near the house?" Jarrod was beginning to think he was right about her needing the income.

He shrugged. "She had her reasons, I'm sure. Come on. Let's go for a walk — Wait. On second thought, you don't have on boots and the pastures need to be mowed. Let's take my truck."

Cassidy followed him to his truck and climbed inside. Ten acres wasn't big, but she didn't fancy traipsing through tall grass after the snake scare. He drove to the tree line, which was where a shallow creek cut through the land. He drove through it easily enough with his four-wheel drive and then eased over the barely visible track past the trees and bushes lining the water's edge.

And there in neat rows were about twenty peach trees.

"I can't believe this. I have peach trees," Cassidy exclaimed. "Roxie must have planted them after my last visit."

Cassidy suddenly looked pensive and sat very still in the seat. "I should have come to see her more." She lifted a hand, then dropped it. "I got so busy. I just called every once in a while. I guess I thought she'd always be here. And then I kept thinking I'd get here but I didn't. And then just like that, she was gone."

"I bet that's hard to think about. She was a happy lady, though. Independent. Talked about the trips she took a few times with your grandmother when she was alive."

"Yes, she used to tell me about my grandmother. Said she was a free spirit and that I would have liked her. She'd been married and divorced twice before she died. I just wish I'd come to visit more. Roxie was all alone."

"None of us is perfect." That was all he said. Cassidy wasn't the first to feel like she'd dropped the ball where family relationships were concerned. But he was thankful his pops had always lived nearby so he'd never have to live with that regret. He had plenty of regrets when he thought of his dad, though. And he didn't like to think of him often.

His dad had once been the man he'd looked up to more than anyone. He'd thought his pops was pretty special, too, but a kid sees his dad as first and then everyone else as second. And then he'd started to see small things that caused him to lose respect. Like the way he'd taken Pops's hard work for granted. And the way he'd let his sons do the things that he should have been doing. But he was off flying around the country in his little plane.

"I've been researching strawberries and tomatoes and all kinds of vegetables. And all this time I have a peach orchard." She sounded awed by the idea as she turned to look at him with amazement in her expressive eyes.

Jarrod's mind jerked from thoughts of his dad back to Cassidy. His pulse hummed looking at her. "Something tells me you're going be able to figure out exactly what to do with them."

She took a deep breath and stuck her head out the window. "It's wonderful. I own an orchard." She laughed, then sank back into the seat, her eyes glistening. She laughed again and swiped at the tears that started running down her cheeks.

"Hey, don't cry." Jarrod fought the urge to reach out to her.

She turned again and stared out the window. "I'm sure you really are starting to think I'm a basket case. This has been a crazy day."

Unable to stop himself, he touched her arm to offer some kind of reassurance. "No, I don't. I feel like you've been through some hard times and you're dealing with a lot right now." He pulled his hand away.

She nodded and looked him in the eye. "You could say that." They stared at each other. "Have you ever been married?"

Her question took him by surprise. "No."

"Count your blessings. I'm never doing it again. Worst mistake of my life."

Stunned, he watched her climb out of the truck and close the door behind her. Her pain and anger seemed to remain inside the cab of the truck with him, and he suddenly had the urge to find this ex of hers and do some damage to the man.

She started tromping across the tall grass, and he hurried from the truck and followed her. When he caught up with her, she was studying one of the trees, her hands on her hips and the grass touching her knees. Tree limbs lay strewn among the grass beneath the peach trees. This was going to take a lot of hauling off of limbs and mowing.

"This is a mess." She dropped her chin to her chest and her shoulders slumped. When she looked up, there were still tears at the corners of her eyes.

"Is there something I can do for you? I don't know what your ex did but —"

"No." Her eyes were bright with the unshed tears. "I'm happy. Really, this is . . . I'm just emotional. I've had a lot of changes lately. And" — she sniffed — "I'm fine. I'm here and I'm going to make this work. This is me starting fresh and free. And I just found out I own a peach orchard." She laughed. "It can't get any better than that. I live in the country. I-I have an awesome neighbor who stopped his day to help me clean out my barn and run off rattlesnakes. It's all great. More than any girl could ask for."

She smiled at him and he was dazzled. Whatever she was going through, she was doing it bravely. "You're going to be okay, Cassidy Starr."

"Yes, I am. Now I just need to hire someone to mow and clean up these limbs. Do you know who I could get to do that?"

"I can get your fields mowed. I have tractors. I'll have one of my ranch hands get this done tomorrow, as long as it will dry up those tears."

Her upper lip trembled and she bit down on it. He waited for her to regain control of her emotions.

"No, that's just too much. I can't take advantage of you anymore. I —"

"You're not taking advantage," he said. "I have the equipment and the staff. I'll have this taken care of tomorrow."

Cassidy stared at Jarrod. He meant well, she was certain of it, but he'd just taken command of her life and she'd walked right into it.

"No," she said firmly, still reeling from the emotions that had swamped her earlier. This peach orchard might very well be the answer to her hopes for some early success. Unlike the strawberries she planned, it had a head start. "You've done more than enough. I moved here to do this on my own. To stand on my own two feet for once in my life —" She halted her words, wishing she hadn't just blurted out her very personal agenda.

He frowned. "But like I said, I have a tractor —"

"I know. But I did not move here to have someone do my work for me."

"It's not a crime to accept help. You are being too sensitive."

She bristled. "Too *sensitive*?" Jack had told her that many times when he'd done something wrong, trying to turn the tables on her, trying to cover up his actions by putting the focus on her.

"Jarrod, I'm not a starry-eyed teenager

anymore." She bit the words out. "I hate being treated like one."

She was not going to bring up their past. She was letting it lie dormant just like he seemed willing to do. But feeling this unwanted attraction to him wasn't helping her. It was just one more niggling indicator that she would follow in her parents' foot-steps if she wasn't careful. Neither one of them had been responsible with life choices, and she refused to go down that road. Being single would be preferable to a life of more of what they'd put her through and what she'd been through with Jack.

"You're pretty riled up —"

"Look," she huffed. She knew thoughts of Jack, his betrayal, and his condescending attitude were driving her now, but Jarrod was looking at her like she'd lost her lug nuts and her wheels were falling off.

And maybe they were.

"You don't know me," she warned. "I'm not that naïve girl I once was, and I can tell you that I'm done being played the fool. I may be too sensitive about some things, but I can assure you there are valid reasons. If I don't want to accept help that doesn't make me sensitive or fool —"

"Hold on now. I shouldn't have said what I said. You've clearly been through a rough time. But I *never* called you foolish. I'm just here offering to help."

She felt a sudden wave of uncertainty. Was she overreacting? The very idea made her flounder again, and she was so sick of that feeling. Of not knowing if what she was thinking was right or if it was over-processed.

"Thank you for what you've done, but I can handle it from here."

His eyelids dipped, his jaw tensed, and she could only imagine what he was thinking. After the longest second, he touched the tip of his hat and took a step back.

"Then we should start back. If you need anything . . ." He paused, looking a little between angry and confused. He strode to the truck and she followed.

They were silent all the way back to the house. When Jarrod stopped the truck beside her barn, he kept his wrist cocked over the steering wheel and made no attempt at exiting.

"You have a nice day," he said, shooting her a hooded glance.

The hammer in her head had started pounding away on her thick skull. Jarrod sat ramrod straight with shoulders back as he waited for her to get out. She fought to apologize, but she was justified in her anger.

She was. She climbed out of the truck and slammed the door, then took a step back. He gave her another glance and drove away.

Dust furled up behind him as he disappeared down the lane.

Good. That would be best for both of them. And with that she stormed back inside the barn and just dared that snake to show his face.

# 7

Cassidy headed to town the next morning. She tried to enjoy the drive as she flew by the pastures dotted with grazing cattle and a large number of new babies. She loved calves. Jarrod had taught her how to bottle-feed them that first year she'd come to Aunt Roxie's. He'd been a handsome sixteen-year-old then, and he'd been kind to her when she'd been a worrisome, lonely kid. She hung out with Tru and Bo, too, but it had been Jarrod she'd tagged behind the most.

His behavior yesterday had been . . . overbearing. She didn't want or need his help. And she wasn't interested in the nagging draw of the man . . . was she? Was she a glutton for punishment?

That thought kept her from sleeping well. When she was nineteen, Jarrod had callously tossed her feelings aside after a kiss. She forced that memory of the kiss and his words deep down in the dark side of her heart, where the pain and anger caused by her parents' disinterest went. She was not here to resurrect that pain. She was here to start new.

It was purely a misfortune that the property her dreams were dependent on happened to be located right beside Jarrod's house.

She drove past the Bull Barn on the outskirts of town. The local diner and hot spot for locals and visitors alike still looked as ramshackle as ever. A little farther down the street she entered town. That same sense of welcome and relief she'd felt when she'd driven up Aunt Roxie's drive filled her.

It was just a small Texas town, with scattered businesses on the outskirts and tree-lined streets and neighborhoods. As she turned toward the main intersection, she passed the Sweet Dreams Motel, the Burke Brothers Real Estate agency, and then the square. She drove past the Cut Up and Roll Hair Salon, and then a few doors down she pulled into a slanted parking space in front of the *Wishing Springs Gazette.*

Rand Ratliff, who owned the newspaper, had been one of Aunt Roxie's friends. He was sitting in his office and saw her the minute she walked through the door.

"Cassidy, you've come home at last," he called, jumping up and walking around his desk.

He was a handsome man — thin, neat, with striking gray hair and a debonair look that had always seemed a little out of place to her in a cowboy town like Wishing Springs.

"It's so good to see you," she said as Rand gave her a hug as though he hadn't seen her in years, which was true.

"Heard you were on your way. You're not here to get the house ready to sell, are you?"

"I'm actually here for good."

He looked concerned. "Doonie and Doobie said you've had a rough divorce and that you've taken back your maiden name."

"I want a last name that means something to me." Cassidy hadn't been able to change her name fast enough after what Jack had done. And when she'd called the real estate agents and told them she was returning, she had also told them why. She figured it would be easier if everyone knew about her divorce before she arrived. It would save her explaining over and over again.

"Rightly so. I'm sorry you got hurt."

She gave a shrug. "So am I. But what was I thinking? I should have known." She gave him a small smile. "I made a mistake jumping into marriage with someone before I really knew him, and so . . ." She hated talking about her past. Her mistakes.

"Chin up, young lady. You will get through this."

"Yes, I will. As always, after a breakup, I come to Roxie's. This time it just happens to be *my* breakup."

They stared at each other, and she saw compassion in his kind blue eyes.

"Roxie always wanted you to feel at home there," he said, a smile hovering on his lips. They shared a moment of understanding, each knowing Roxie had always wanted Cassidy to feel she had a place that was steadfast. And even though she'd died suddenly, she'd already made sure in her will that everything was in order for that to be a certainty. She'd even gone so far as to put it into a protected trust so no spouse could ever touch it.

That had come in handy, as it had turned out.

"Anyway, moving on." She needed to retreat from the emotions his statement beckoned. "I'm here to reopen Roxie's strawberry farm and turn the house into a bed-and-breakfast. But you know how she loved to collect things. So to do that I need to have a garage sale. A huge sale. I need to place this in your classifieds." She waved a piece of paper at him. He scanned it and grinned.

"Garage sale, my foot. This is a bona-fide one-person flea market. You'll make a mint."

She chuckled. "I'm charging garage sale prices, not Tiffany prices."

"Don't give it away for pennies." He set it on the counter in a basket labeled "Classifieds." "I'll make sure this goes in. Right now, though, I'm on my way to lunch. Come with me."

She didn't hesitate. It was time to see everyone. "I would love to."

He walked quickly back to his office and grabbed a spiffy checkered fedora off the hat rack that sat at the door. "Ready?" he asked, offering her the crook of his arm.

Cassidy slipped her arm through his. "I've missed you, Rand," she said, and she meant it. "How's your love life? Have you married yet?"

"We'll be back," he called to someone working in another room. "I'm still a single man," he said in a grave voice once they were outside. "But I have hopes."

"What about Pebble? Roxie always said you two would get together after she'd had sufficient time to mourn."

He led her to his car and opened the door

for her. "I've had a few serious issues that have caused problems. Pebble, as you know, is a wonderful woman." He studied his polished dress shoes before meeting her with pained eyes. "Cassidy, you might as well know I'm an alcoholic. I've been sober now for six months, and I'm never going back to the bottle. But you should know this now that you're back. I just spent three of those six months in a rehab center."

Cassidy couldn't believe it. Rand, an alcoholic? It was unthinkable.

She didn't know what to say as she hurried inside the car and waited for him to come around and slide behind the wheel.

"I don't know what to say. Are you okay? How are you doing?"

"I'm as good as I can be at the moment. Got my life straightened out, was able to keep the paper operating while I was in detox, and things are going fine. Now I'm trying to mend trusts that I've destroyed."

He sounded so positive. But she sensed a deep sadness in him.

"And how is Pebble?" She was being nosey now, but hey, everyone knew everything about *her,* right? "Like I said, Roxie always thought —"

"And Roxie always did talk too much.

Pebble is as sweet and lovely as she's always been."

He drove back out of town to the Bull Barn, and just before pulling into the white rock parking lot he said quietly, "I'll always love Pebble, but I hurt her. Sometimes a person has to do what is right for them, what might be hard but right. Pebble is doing that now."

Cassidy's heart caught at the certainty of his words.

She'd done that when she'd ended her broken, dysfunctional marriage. Knowing her husband had been unfaithful for most of their marriage had left her feeling so empty and alone. But she'd hung on, stayed in the house, living in denial that she was going down the same path as her parents and refusing to acknowledge that her marriage was doomed. But when she'd finally awoken from the coma, something had clicked inside of her and she'd walked away.

Now she let the harsh memories fade as the hometown energy inside the Bull Barn embraced her. The place wasn't packed yet, but it was already buzzing with chatter from the five or six tables that were full so far.

Big Shorty lumbered their way. "Cassidy, great to see you." Big but not short, not by a long shot, he gave her a smile that filled out his whole face.

"She's moved back," Rand told him. "Going to reopen the strawberry farm."

"And the peach orchard along with a bed-and-breakfast," Cassidy added.

"For real? That's great. I used to buy strawberries from Roxie and I'd love to have fresh peaches and make the best cobblers. You get a crop this year, I'll buy from you."

Cassidy was awed. "Thank you."

"No, thank you. You got produce, come see me. This place may look rough, but I pride myself on my ingredients, and though my wife and I grow a garden ourselves, sometimes I need more."

Cassidy's mood lifted even more. Every commitment to buy from her helped. "You've got a deal."

They took a table by the window while Big Shorty went to get their drink order. She studied the different rodeo champion pictures on the walls. She realized the table across the room had pictures of Jarrod's brother Tru. She'd read he was a quarter horse champion two years running, and here he was now on what was basically the Wishing Springs wall of fame. She thought of Jarrod, wondered if he'd competed after he'd left Wishing Springs that summer. He'd been good on a horse too.

She was not going to think about Jarrod.

Through the window she saw more cars turning into the white rock. Dust flew everywhere. It seemed the floodgates had opened from town and everyone had raced to find a spot at the local favorite.

The first ones she saw coming into the parking lot were two county sheriff's SUV vehicles, and she recognized Jake Morgan, the sheriff. He was a friend of Jarrod's growing up. She didn't recognize one of his deputies and a couple of other men in starched, tan button-ups, dark jeans, and buffed boots as they climbed out of Jake's vehicle. They all had their Stetsons on too. Cassidy noticed Rand looked intently interested in the group as they entered the diner.

"Who are those men?" she asked.

He tried to appear less interested, but she'd seen the reporter in him come out.

"Probably some law enforcement officials of some sort."

Within moments Doonie and Doobie came in. The identical twins were tall and lanky and thankfully had different colored shirts on. Like Rand, they were in their late fifties, or maybe just over the sixty mark. No one could tell them apart. Thus they'd always gotten away with all kinds of pranks and schemes. They were Rand's best friends.

"Do they still pull jokes on everyone?"

Rand chuckled. "Doonie got voted in as mayor about four years ago and they share the position. They won't admit it to anyone, not even me. But we've caught on to their shenanigans."

She laughed. "That sounds like them. They didn't tell me when I called to say I was coming back."

"It works out. They do a good job, and we just let them go with it." He looked serious suddenly. "They've been good friends to me." He hesitated, looking momentarily embarrassed. "They're good as gold and they love this town and only want what's best for it."

Before she could ask about Roxie's good friends Clara Lyn and Reba, they and Pebble entered the restaurant. Cassidy glanced at Rand as he ran a hand over each side of his hair. Obviously he had seen them, too, and he looked a touch nervous as his gaze was riveted to Pebble, who seemed to be looking everywhere but at him.

Pebble had been widowed by the love of her life many years ago. Roxie had said from the moment Rand opened the newspaper that he'd come back just to be near Pebble.

Cassidy got a sudden lump in her throat. She'd known fleeting attachments that her parents thought were love but were obviously something else. At least not the kind of love she dreamed of a long time ago.

What would it feel like to know someone had loved you and waited on you for years? She couldn't believe Rand had turned to drinking. She was still stunned by his blatant declaration. But like her with the divorce, maybe it was easier to get it out there in front of everyone than have to worry about it. It wasn't as if she was a stranger to him.

The diner began filling up all at once, and within moments all eyes were on her.

"Look who's here," either Doonie or Doobie said, a wide grin lighting up his lean face. He wore a blue polo shirt. She hugged both him and his brother, who was grinning just as big.

"We weren't expecting you till tomorrow," he said. He let her go and looked at Rand. "How did you score a lunch with her?"

Rand gave a gleeful smile. "She came to see me."

She laughed as if her coming to see him was a score for his team.

"Y'all can join us," she said.

"I believe we will," the brother in the red polo shirt said. They each grabbed the extra chair at the table. Just then Clara Lyn spotted her.

"Cassidy!" Clara Lyn squealed as she hustled over and engulfed Cassidy. The hairstylist rattled and jangled from all directions.

Cassidy sneezed when her nose was buried in the shorter woman's abundantly sprayed hair. She pulled back to breathe, but Clara kept a grip on her arms as she studied her.

"Oh, just look at you. You are too thin. And you look tired. That divorce has done a number on you. You've come home where you can fatten up a little and dig in the dirt a little and —"

"Let her go," Reba scolded. "You're right about all that, but there's more of us wanting to give our girl a hug." The beaming nail tech bumped Clara out of the way with her ample hip and gave Cassidy a bear hug.

Pebble stepped up the moment Cassidy was released. She was tiny but spirited, and her hug was gentle but enthusiastic.

"It is about time for you to come home," Pebble said.

Her beautiful smile was a balm to Cassidy's soul. Working the counter at Pebble's motel when she was younger had been a wonderful experience. She'd loved Pebble and her husband, Cecil.

"And just look at you. As your aunt would say, you're as pretty as a wildflower and as good to see as daffodils at springtime."

Tears sprang to Cassidy's eyes at the quote from Roxie. Goodness, she had to get a grip on these emotions that kept sideswiping her. "That sounds just like her. It is so good to see y'all. It has been too long."

"Yes, it has." Clara Lyn harrumphed. "We didn't even know till yesterday you were coming. The twins let it slip when we were at their office."

"Hey, don't mean to break up a party, but y'all planning on ordering?" Big Shorty asked, looking like a man intent on keeping the lunch crowd rolling along at an even pace.

Everyone instantly took seats. The ladies grabbed the table next to them and everyone settled in for a visit.

Cassidy had just relaxed when Jarrod and his two brothers walked into the diner.

# 8

Jarrod went on high alert the instant he scanned the diner and saw Cassidy. She met his gaze briefly, then she smiled at his brothers. They greeted her, and at the same time gave him speculative glances that he wasn't real comfortable with.

Tru gave her a hug. "It's great to see you. I had no idea you were here."

"She's moved back," Clara Lyn supplied.

"Moved back — that's good to hear," Bo said, grinning from ear to ear and shooting another glance at him, undoubtedly noticing he was being quiet.

Jarrod knew there was no way to keep them from realizing that he had omitted telling them she was in town. There was no use denying it. She lived right beside him and they knew he'd have seen her over there. And they also knew he hadn't said anything. They'd find that odd, because though they didn't know what had happened between him and Cassidy all those years ago, they knew something had happened.

"How's the barn cleaning going today?"

"Fine. No snakes today," she said a bit stiffly, which caused a lot of eyes to shift from her to him and back to her.

"That's good. Found anyone to mow your peach orchard?"

"I'm going by the feed store after this and inquiring if anyone's advertising. I assume they still have that wall of advertisement in there, for folks to put their cards and such?"

"They do," he said, feeling his shoulders pinch at the base of his neck. He had a perfectly good tractor, and if she had let him take care of it, her place would have already been mowed. He wanted to tell her this, but it would draw attention to the strain yanked up between them.

Tru looked at him with more speculation in his eyes. "We've got a perfectly good tractor —"

"I'd rather hire it done," she said quickly. "Thank you, though. Jarrod already offered."

"Well, that was nice of him," Reba said.

"Sure was," Clara Lyn added. "Let him do it."

Jarrod wasn't going to stand there and let

everyone talk her into doing something she was clearly set against. "Cassidy's got her mind made up on the subject. I wouldn't want to butt in on that." He tipped his hat. "Nice seeing you, neighbor. Jake's waiting. Ladies, fellas, have a good lunch." He turned and strode across the diner, knowing the entire time that he'd just messed up.

He could feel the eyeballs on his back.

"We've got a meeting," he heard Tru saying. "But we'll have you over for dinner one night before I have to go back on the circuit. Maggie will want to meet you."

"Yeah, Abby too," Bo added, and Jarrod grinned. Cassidy was going to find avoiding him and trying to push him away wasn't exactly as easy as she was hoping. He loved his brothers.

"I'll have Maggie set it up . . ."

Jarrod didn't hear the rest as he greeted Jake. As sheriff, Jake had called them and set up a meeting with the Texas and Southwestern Cattle Raisers Association's Special Rangers. Jarrod hadn't even mentioned to Jake that he suspected theft yet, but there was something going on in the surrounding counties and Jake liked to be prepared. He had work to deal with right now, so he didn't need to be dwelling on thoughts of Cassidy.

■ ■ ■ ■

A few days after seeing Pebble at the Bull Barn, Rand knew it was time to do something. He'd spent ninety long days in rehab to kick the drinking habit and he'd done it for Pebble. Yes, she'd told him she wanted him to do it for himself and she'd reminded him that the Lord would help him. She'd told him he was hiding behind the alcohol and that he needed to get well for himself. Not for her.

She'd told him that she would come and support him at rehab but only as a friend. And she'd done exactly that.

But what had he done for her? Except put her in an awkward position of having to be uncomfortable around him. She didn't deserve any of this.

He'd loved her since they were in high school and he'd lost her because of his drinking then. He wasn't going to lose another opportunity. He was done with the bottle for good and he'd turned his life around. He wished with all of his might that he'd made better choices.

Walking briskly down the tree-lined street, he reached the motel just as she was coming out of one of the bungalows. His stomach tilted and he forced himself to move toward her.

She was lovely standing there with her red bucket of fresh flowers.

"Hello, Rand. What a perfect day for a walk."

He removed his hat. "It is. And it looks like you're enjoying it too. Are you putting fresh flowers in the rooms?"

"I am." She smiled, and his heart skipped several beats. "Guests love the fresh flowers and I love making them feel welcomed."

"Just a smile from you does that. But the flowers add to it too." He was being bolder than he'd been since getting out of rehab, but seeing her blush and her kind blue eyes brighten did his heart good.

He was responsible for the awkward strain that stood between them now and the strain was growing.

"You weren't at the Bull Barn for lunch yesterday or today," she said.

The fact that she noticed gave him hope. "No, no, I had . . . meetings. I . . . well, I drive over to Kerrville for my AA meetings two or three days a week, and we're having some morning sessions now too. Today I had a meeting with my sponsor." He was planning on starting a meeting here in town soon. When he was more ready.

"Oh, I see. And that's going good? You seem to be doing well."

He cleared his throat and fiddled with his fedora. "Yes. About all of that." He yanked his shoulders back, forcing his backbone to stiffen and his resolve and determination to do the same. "I came to thank you, Pebble. To thank you for coming to the rehab all that time. For standing by me as a . . . friend."

"You are my friend. That's what friends do."

"Yes. And that is one of the many things that I —" He halted before he blurted out that it was one of the things he loved about her. "That I admire about you. If you commit to something you do it. And I want to thank you for your friendship the last few months." He cleared his throat. "And I need to tell you that from here on out I want you to relax. To not fear that I'm going to be trying to take — I mean, try to have more than a friendship with you. In the grocery store the other day and even at the Bull Barn it felt like we were walking on eggshells. I don't want that. I just want you to know that I'm at a comfortable place in my life and with us." He was letting her go. It was the right thing to do . . . for her.

She studied him for a long moment. Her

pretty lips clamped together just a little more tightly than usual. "I see," she murmured a heartbeat later, her eyes growing soft.

Was it pity he saw there? He needed to know that she found a redeemable quality in him. And if she saw him overcome his addiction to alcohol, then maybe she'd respect that. If he could see that in her eyes, then there was a chance that one day he might respect himself again.

"That's all I have to say," he said. "I just wanted you to know. Our friendship means the world to me. I need to get back to the office. I have a lot of stories with the Fourth of July celebration coming up next weekend." He put on his hat and turned to go.

"Rand," she called out, and he turned back. "You're doing well. I'm so proud of you."

And there were the words. But Rand didn't feel them in his soul. He tipped his hat. "I'll be seeing you. If you need anything, you know to call me. You can count on me, I promise."

It had been a long time since he'd said those words with conviction.

Her eyes mellowed and she smiled gently. "I'm believing that, Rand."

If only he could believe that. He turned

then and forced his feet to carry him away from the love of his life.

He didn't look back.

## 9

Jarrod saddled his horse and loaded him in the trailer with the horses that belonged to his men. They were going out to start doing a head count of all the cattle.

"You not get any sleep last night?" Gil, one of his ranch hands who also happened to be one of his old school buddies, eyed him hard as he exited the trailer.

"Some. I had thieves on my mind. If we want the cattle found we need to know which ones are missing. So y'all work as fast as you can." They'd be checking tags to document exactly which animals were missing, and then the TSCRA agents would load them into the databases and the auction barns would be on alert.

He didn't mention that he'd also had a redhead on his mind. That was a personal detail his brothers were now bugging him about. They had not missed the tension between him and Cassidy. Nor had anyone else in the diner two days ago.

"It's just amazing to me that they try it. I mean, in this day and age it's crazy." Gil scratched his temple.

"And yet sometimes they still get away with it. That's not going to happen on our watch." Jarrod strode toward his truck. "All right, I'll be out there later."

Gil grinned. "Whatever you say. Got a girl to see?"

Jarrod scowled. "Anyone ever tell you to mind your own business?"

"Anybody ever tell you to chill? I was just fishing and hoping. I'm thinking you're way overdue on having a date. And I heard there was some interesting tension in the diner on Monday."

This wouldn't be the first time Gil had pushed for him to start dating. "You date enough for both of us," Jarrod muttered. "I'd hate to steal your thunder. And besides, this isn't a date." Boy, was that an understatement.

Gil laughed. "Yeah, well, at least I know how to enjoy myself. All work and no play makes a fella boring."

"Funny, I think I told Bo that same thing last year, and the next thing I know he's married."

"See there, could work for you too."

"Or you," Jarrod said. "You're as bad as Bo and Tru. Shouldn't you be settling down soon? You're not getting any younger."

"I told you before, I'm not a family man. You, on the other hand, have family man written all over you. I know you've used getting this ranch out of debt as an excuse, but from everything you've said things are starting to look better. You're not going to have that as an excuse soon."

Jarrod didn't even bother saying anything else. He knew Gil was just giving him a hard time and trying to get a good-natured rise out of him.

He drove out to the road and then up the gravel drive to Cassidy's place.

He told himself not to get involved. She'd made herself clear. But he went anyway.

He'd gone over and over all parts of their conversations in his mind, and it boiled down to those tears she'd cried when she saw the peach orchard. There were some intense emotions going on inside of her to have caused that reaction. He knew she would have tried hard not to show those tears to anyone. At least that was how she'd been as a kid.

As he drove up, she was coming out of the barn. There was a yard of "stuff" lined up like a store. It had rummage sale written all over it.

She was pushing an ancient garden tiller and wore an orange ball cap. Her hair was tamed into a braid that hung over one shoulder. She almost tripped when she saw him.

"Mornin'," he said, realizing instantly that he'd made another big mistake. He shouldn't have come. She wasn't going to appreciate that he'd told his ranch hand to drive over and mow her peach orchard today.

She brought the tiller to a halt beside a pitiful excuse of a push mower. That thing had to be thirty years old. "Do those things work?"

"I'll find out soon enough. They were in a stall by themselves, so I think Roxie still used them. If they work I won't have to buy new ones. I'll be able to keep the grass around the house mowed and cultivate my garden."

He moved to stand beside her, and it took every ounce of his willpower not to offer to help.

But he could read her thoughts. She didn't want him there. He bit back the next question, which was to see if she'd found someone to mow, and if not, did she want him to have his man do it. That wouldn't be a welcome inquiry and he knew it.

"It looks rough, but maybe you'll get some more life out of it." That was all he let himself say. "Hey, I need to go, but I came to tell you Jasper has an alternative formulation he uses around organic properties. So you can rest easy. That's what I'll have him use on all sides of your land."

"That's wonderful. Thank you for changing your plans for me. Getting certified is not an easy task, and I have a lot of things to do for the land and the B and B."

"I'm glad it worked out. What all do you have to do to get certified?"

"Well, I need to have the land tested. Even if my business is small enough to be exempted, I want to know it's okay. But I have to have the fire chief come out to okay the house for a bed-and-breakfast because that has to be official. It's a little nerve-wracking. But I can do it."

He opened his mouth to tell her not to be nervous, but she kept talking.

"And I hired someone to mow. Just so you know. So no need for you to be worrying about me not being able to handle it on my own."

The fact that she sounded a little smug about hiring someone grated on his nerves like sandpaper. What was wrong with his help anyway? But he kept that to himself.

"Well, sounds like you have it all taken care of. I better get to work." He tipped his hat, climbed inside his truck, and drove back down her drive.

When Jarrod reached the end of his drive, he dialed Bill, his ranch hand who did all the ranch's mowing and dozer work.

"Hey, boss, I'm about two miles away."

"Yeah, that's why I called. Change of plans. Mow my pasture between my house and my neighbor's, but cancel plans to mow the peach orchard. She got it taken care of."

He hung up and tossed the phone on the dash.

Then he yanked the gear shift into drive and had to fight the urge to goose the gas as he drove off. Cassidy might not have wanted any help from him, but she was going to be completely shocked when she called for the Wishing Springs fire chief.

That made him smile despite the irritation he was feeling. He'd only been trying to be neighborly, after all.

But then, the woman had a right to hire whomever she wanted to mow her orchard, so he just needed to get over it.

Cassidy sank into a chair and let out a weary sigh. Things were starting to shape up. She'd been going through the kitchen all morning and felt certain it and the rest of the house was ready for the fire chief's inspection. If she could get that out of the way, she'd be one step closer to getting the bed-and-breakfast opened. She found the fire station number and called it. And she waited. In a small town the size of Wishing Springs, it was a volunteer fire department. She heard several clicks, as if the phone number was being transferred. Or forwarded. She was about to hang up when a man answered.

"Hello, Jarrod Monahan."

Cassidy hesitated. "Um, hey, Jarrod," she said, confused. "I must have called the wrong number. I'm, um, looking for the fire chief. Sorry to bother you."

"No bother. I'm the fire chief."

"You're the Wishing Springs fire chief?" she said slowly.

His chuckle rumbled over the line. "At your service."

Cassidy's ears burned hot at the smile she heard in his voice.

"You didn't say anything when you were here two days ago." She heard the sound of cattle mooing loudly in the background.

"You weren't looking for my help that day."

Her fingers tightened on the phone. "Fine. Is there a time when you could come take a look at the house and okay it for fire safety?"

"I'm in the middle of tagging calves right now —"

"That's fine. I'm not really ready yet. I'll let you know. I was just calling to make the chief aware and make certain there wasn't going to be a problem when I called in the next few weeks."

"No problem at all."

"Good. Great. I'll let you go then."

"Have a nice day, Cassidy."

She could hear the laughter in his voice. "You do the same, Chief," she gritted out through clenched teeth, fighting not to sound as aggravated as she was feeling at his little surprise.

She had moved out onto the back porch during the call, fighting the urge to hit her head against a post. It seemed she was doomed to have to contend with her neighbor. Feeling a need for some fresh air, she stalked to the edge of the barn.

Jarrod had been on her mind a lot, and now she'd found out he was the fire chief. She'd basically acted like she had the other day, and now the joke was on her. He'd known she was going to have to call him. He was probably laughing his head off right now. She stuffed her hands on her hips and kicked a patch of long grass.

"Hi there."

Cassidy spun around to find two women about her age staring at her with wide eyes. One was holding a cute toddler. She'd thought she was alone and had missed the car sitting at the side of the house.

"Hi," she called, striding back toward them.

"We'd just driven up when you came down the steps," the one holding the little boy said. "You looked like you were in a hurry."

The gorgeous blonde standing beside her looked vaguely familiar. "We really hate to intrude, but we couldn't walk away when you truly look like you might need a friend." She came forward then, long and lanky in her jeans and boots as she held out her hand and smiled. "I'm Maggie Monahan."

A light went on in Cassidy's brain. "Maggie Hope."

"That's me. And this is Abby. I'm married to Tru and Abs is married to Bo. We thought it would be nice to come meet you since we're your nearest neighbors. Well, aside from Jarrod being right there and all."

Abby smiled. "We thought you would want to know there's more out here than stoic cowboys and cows."

"I'm about cowboyed up to my eyebrows right now." Cassidy took a deep breath, trying to tell herself she shouldn't be mad that Jarrod was the fire chief. She was overreacting to the whole thing. "I'm glad to know there are women around the corner — a Texas corner," she added quickly to get past the cowboy remark that she probably shouldn't have made.

Abby bounced the little boy on her hip. "Thought you'd like that. If you need a cup of sugar or an egg or a cup of coffee and some conversation, we are right over there as the crows fly."

"Or the coyotes yell might be more accurate," Maggie added.

"True. They were doing some singing last night while I was sitting here on the porch."

"Brave girl," Maggie said. "It took me a long time and Tru's help before I felt comfortable being outside with them carrying on in the woods."

"I've lived here on and off through the years so I got used to their sound," Cassidy said, walking closer to her visitors. She reached a hand out to the toddler, who was grinning at her.

Abby was studying her intently. "He'll have you wrapped around his finger if you give him a second."

Cassidy smiled. "I'm fine with that. He's adorable. What's his name?"

"Levi. And thanks. We think so too."

Maggie nodded. "We didn't mean to intrude. Just wanted to come welcome you and let you know we're here if you need anything."

"Would y'all like to come inside? I warn you the house is a bit of a wreck. I'm sorting through things getting ready for an epic garage sale. Or rummage sale might be a more accurate term for what I'll be having. That's what all of that over there is." She waved toward the barn. "I'm sorting through things in the barn too."

Maggie looked genuinely excited. "Oh, I love rummage sales. Can we help?"

"Me too. I love to go there every year," Abby added. "We'd love to help."

Cassidy was startled by their kindness. "I would love that," she said just as Levi lunged toward her and she caught him. The cute little boy in her arms and two new friends — the day had just taken a turn for good.

Feeling her spirits lift, she led the way toward the house.

# 10

On Tuesday Jarrod had risen before dawn, picked up Pops, and driven over to Navasota for a load of horses that had been found in a bad situation. They were nearly starved and needed a new place to call home. He'd been participating in the rescue program for horses for some time. He would never understand a person who could intentionally be cruel to people or animals. He had no tolerance for it. And though there was little he could do to change the world or cruel people, he could change the lives of these horses.

When Bo married Abby, they chose to remain in Pops's house so they could watch out for him. But he was still independent to some extent. He was an early riser, too, and when Jarrod went over to see if he wanted to go along today, he'd been excited.

Pops rode in the truck sitting straight and studying the landscape. Jarrod wondered if he was remembering the years spent hauling his cutting horses all over the country to competitions and exhibitions. It was similar to the way Tru lived now, but Pops had had more downtime than Tru. There had been fewer sponsor requirements and more time training on the ranch and for regular ranching.

"Sad shame," Pops said after they arrived at the auction barn and picked up the malnourished horses. He swept his straw Stetson from his head and ran an aging hand over his graying hair, worry filling his gaze as he studied the animals. Pops knew horses. Loved horses. And even now with his mind fading, he understood these horses had been mistreated. "Somebody needs a horsewhippin'," he said.

Jarrod grinned. "I agree completely, Pops." He placed a hand on his shoulder. "Don't worry, you and me, we'll get them healthy again. You'll help me, won't you?"

Pops nodded, then scrubbed his jaw as he studied the horses. "We'll fix 'em. Get 'em ready." He pointed at one in the background. It held back from most of them and seemed wary as it watched them. "That's a good 'un."

Jarrod studied the horse too. It wasn't real big, but it had good lines. Jarrod had little hope that it would be registered, and even if it was, he doubted he'd ever see the papers. There was only a small chance of getting them, if they could trace them from the owner's documentation. But that was a long shot. Still, Jarrod knew "That's a good 'un" used to be gold if Pops said it. And even now, Jarrod knew enough to know that he'd be taking a good look at that little pony himself as they brought it back to good health.

A few days after her "talk" with Jarrod, and still miffed at the man over his little joke, Cassidy drove her truck from the house, across the creek, and up the hill to the orchard. She'd spent a lot of time online, and she'd learned that her aunt had known exactly what she was doing when she'd planted the orchard on this acre of land. Yes, it was small, but the drainage, the sunshine, and she had no doubt the soil were all perfect for growing peaches.

Feeling purpose in her heart, Cassidy got out of the truck and, knowing more about the care and development of an orchard now, went to view her trees with a new enthusiasm. Yes, because the trees had been neglected for six years, she would more than likely have a reduced crop this year. But next year? With the correct care and the addition of her strawberry crop, Cassidy would be in business. Maybe a small business, but it had potential.

Nothing could measure what the sense of hope and accomplishment for next year could mean for her emotionally and mentally.

Based on what Cassidy had just learned, she knew Roxie had pruned the trees well in their early years. They'd need some additional pruning to get them into their best shape again, but the early years of cultivation would pay off. Cassidy walked between the well-placed trees on freshly mowed grass. Her heart raced as she took in the number of ripening fruit. If she was lucky, this crop would be at its best in July, and there looked to be two different types of trees. She'd have to research and go through Roxie's papers to find out what they were, but if everything else panned out like she was thinking, then Roxie planted trees that would mature at different times, making the harvest last longer and spreading out the season.

Roxie Starr had been one smart cookie.

Standing in the orchard, Cassidy breathed in the scent of newness. She plucked a small, hard peach from a low branch and cupped it in her hand. This was how she'd felt for the last three years of her life. For the last eight years . . . for most of her years. As if she'd had no room or time to fully ripen. She had let her life be pulled and pushed in all directions, and until the day she'd realized her life had truly and completely fallen apart, she hadn't felt any hope that she could build a new life.

And that sounded weak. Cassidy had never looked at herself as weak. Maybe uncertain.

She gently rubbed the green pod in her palm, lifted her gaze to the trees, then headed back to the truck. She grabbed the hoe and planned to spend the rest of the morning working the grass out from around the tree trunks. She wanted them to look well taken care of, and that meant that, once again, she'd have to find someone to help or she'd have to bring a ladder out here. She was so caught up in what she was about to do that she barely registered the whine at first.

The second time the soft, low whimper came, Cassidy stopped pulling on a clump of grass and looked around, searching for what was making the sound.

Near the fence on the other side, on what would be Four of Hearts Ranch land, she spotted a tail curling out from the bush. A dog?

Not at all certain she should be doing this, Cassidy moved toward the fence for a better look. The bush moved slightly and the tail flopped once, weakly. And the whimper came again, once more soft and low.

Cassidy didn't hesitate again. Instead, she bent low, grabbed the barbed wire, and climbed through. She moved cautiously to the bush, and there lying very still was a scruffy, speckled dog. Caked blood on its side told her it had been like this for a while. The poor animal looked at her with weary, listless eyes.

Her heart clutched and she crouched down. "You poor dear." Fear was gone because this pitiful dog could barely hold its eyes open, much less do her any harm. Sympathy had her reaching a gentle hand to run over the matted hair, and then without another thought she jogged back to the fence, darted between the wire, and raced to her truck. In seconds she had it backed up to the fence with the tailgate down. After moving everything in the bed out of the way, she hopped to the ground and hurried to the dog. Cassidy needed to get this pup to the vet, and quick.

Without thinking twice she eased her arms

beneath the suffering animal and lifted it from beneath the thorny bush. Thorns ripped at her skin, but she ignored the sting and rose to her feet. The dog wasn't small, but it weighed far less than it should.

Carrying it to the tailgate, she gently lay the animal down. Then hating that she might be hurting him, she lifted the top rung of barbed wire and as gently as possible pushed the dog into the truck's bed. Once it was clear of the barbed wire, she let it down and then climbed onto the tailgate and stepped over and into the bed with the dog.

After making it as comfortable as possible, she hopped to the ground, slid behind the wheel, and moved the truck forward enough so she could close the tailgate. She wanted to move the poor animal into the truck, but she didn't want to disturb him too much more. So she simply drove as carefully as possible from the pastures, then past her home and to the blacktop.

Once there she could drive a little faster. She glanced over her shoulder and saw the dog hadn't moved. She pressed the gas pedal harder and found herself praying that the dog would be all right.

Jarrod was backing the horse trailer up to

the examining pens at the vet clinic when he saw Cassidy's truck pull carefully into the gravel parking lot.

"Come on, Pops. Let's go see what Cassidy's brought in for Doc to see."

"Sure thing, buddy boy."

Jarrod smiled, enjoying Pops's teasing as they walked to Cassidy's truck. Her door opened and she sprang out.

"Jarrod, can you help me?"

At first he didn't think he'd heard her correctly. When she started waving for him to come to where she was letting down the tailgate, he jogged the rest of the way to get her.

"It's a dog and it's hurt," she said, frantic. "I found him up near the orchard."

The animal had matted hair and blood caked on several areas. It was in bad shape. He didn't waste time. "I'll carry him. If he can be saved, Doc can do it." He gathered the dog into his arms. "Poor fella looks bad."

Holding the animal carefully, he carried it toward the front door. Pops altered course and hurried after them as Cassidy jogged forward and pulled the door open.

Doc's receptionist took one look at them and the bloody dog and yelled for Doc. There was no tiptoeing around at Doc's. The grizzled, white-haired veterinarian hustled out of the back and waved them into an examination room as the two people and their pets in the waiting area watched.

"What do we have here?" Doc started examining the dog, and Cassidy retold her story while he worked. "This pup's been on its own for a while. Looks like it got into a fight with something. Maybe a wild hog."

"Can you save him?" Cassidy moved closer, her expression tight with worry.

"I'll do my best. Haven't seen you around in a long time." Doc was gathering supplies from a cabinet as he spoke.

"No, sir, but I'm back now."

" 'Bout time. I don't know why folks leave town anyway," Doc grumbled, working intently. He told Missy, his assistant, to get an IV going, and she flitted around them.

"Roxie talked about you a lot, you know." He looked at her from beneath his bushy white eyebrows. "Told me she was putting you in her will."

Cassidy looked a little surprised by that. "She told you?"

He grinned. "Don't look so surprised. Roxie told me a lot of things." He looked from Cassidy to Jarrod.

Jarrod was as startled as Cassidy had looked. What had Roxie told Doc? The aging vet quirked an eyebrow, then went back to work on the dog.

Cassidy pinned Jarrod with a look that said she was wondering exactly the same thing.

Cassidy's nerves were shot over worrying about the dog, and now she couldn't figure out what her aunt might have told the vet. From the way he'd looked from her to Jarrod, she had to wonder if she'd exposed her secret. Aunt Roxie had known she was head over heels in love with Jarrod. She'd figured it out because she was extremely observant. Cassidy had moments when she'd been unable to hide her feelings or her heartache over believing he'd never think of her as anything other than the kid with the mixed-up family. If Doc knew this, surely he wouldn't say anything.

Jarrod looked as surprised as she was, and she knew he was curious about what Doc was talking about. Thankfully the moment was interrupted by a trotting sound in the hallway. She glanced toward the door just as a potbellied pig came prancing into the room.

Cassidy stepped back. The animal shot a curious look around and then came straight for her. Cassidy backed up until she was against the wall, but the pig came right up to her, cocked its head, gave a snort, and peered up at her.

"Don't mind Clover. She's just a curious ole gal that likes to shake up newbies."

Jarrod came over and scratched the top of the pig's head, and Cassidy could have sworn the pig grinned. Pops came over and petted the pig too.

"She won't bite. She's a sweetheart, actually. Thinks she's Doc's nurse."

"And don't tell her any different," Doc barked, hunching over the dog as he worked.

Cassidy reached down and gave the pig a tentative pat between the ears. Then laughed automatically for some unknown reason. She was pretty sure it came from the fact that never in a million years would she have thought two weeks ago that she would be petting a pig today.

But life had its ups and downs and surprises. And this one was actually kind of cool.

"Roxie gave me that pig, you know."

"Really?"

"Yup. For my birthday. She thought I needed a pet and this is what she picked out." He grinned from where he was steadily working. "I love that pig. Roxie always did know what was best. She had great intuition, that aunt of yours."

Cassidy was suddenly really curious about her aunt and Doc.

"Okay, I've done what I can for now." He spoke before she could come up with a way to ask about his and Roxie's relationship. "We'll keep the dog overnight and see if he makes it. Call me tomorrow and I'll tell you where we go from there."

"Is there a chance he'll make it?" Cassidy moved past the pig and looked at the passed-out dog. Her heart ached for the lost and injured animal. "I'll pay for the bill and take him in if he makes it."

"I'll call you. You bring those rescued horses by, Jarrod?"

"They're outside."

"Good. I'll be there in a minute. Let me get these other two checkups done and I'll be out there."

Cassidy thanked Doc and gave the dog one last gentle caress. The pig trotted out into the waiting area beside her, looking up at her expectantly. "Oh, all right," she said, giving in and scratching the animal between the ears. As if satisfied, Clover spun and pranced back into the clinic area, then turned the corner out of sight as her clicking hooves faded into the back rooms.

Pops chuckled. "Pigs," he said and shook his head.

Cassidy laughed. "Exactly. They're a little odd for a pet." But then she had to admit the potbellied pig had been extremely friendly. Still, thinking about curling up on the couch to watch a movie with her pet beside her didn't call up any images of cuddling a pig. A dog lounging at her feet was perfect. She really hoped Doc saved the poor pup. She would give it a great home.

"You rescued some horses?" she asked as Jarrod opened the door of her truck for her. He smiled. Suddenly it wasn't an animal she pictured cuddling up to for a late-night movie. No, it was this man. She froze.

"Are you okay?" He was standing closer than was good for her. He smelled so good she had to remind herself not to scoot even closer.

Butterflies fluttered in the pit of her stomach. "I'm fine. Just tired and worried about the dog." She glanced toward his trailer. "You rescued them?" she asked again, totally aware that he was studying her. It wasn't helping the butterflies at all.

"Yeah, we're a rescue ranch for abused horses. Sadly, I had to pick up six this morning. We all rescued something today, isn't that right, Pops?"

"Yup." Pops looked perplexed, like he was searching for a word. "Pitiful," he added, and it was. "We should shoot 'em."

Cassidy gasped.

Jarrod chuckled and leaned close. "No, he's not talking about the horses. He's talking about the people who starved them."

Relief surged through her, but it was overcast by the fact that Jarrod's lips were nearly touching her ear. "Oh, I see." She laughed shakily. "I agree, Pops. Can I see them?"

"Sure."

She moved from the truck, glad to get some space and hoping the tingling awareness that had started in the pit of her stomach and now radiated through her would go away.

Jarrod and Pops fell into step beside her. Pops had marked all of his grandsons with his looks, but Jarrod was a carbon copy. On the other hand, it was easy to see even now that Pops, like Bo, was more of a teaser than Jarrod. Jarrod had always been more serious, and that had drawn her to him. It had been that tender and serious attitude that had made him pay attention to her when she was a hurting kid. He'd taken time to give her a smile of encouragement when she'd come around. He'd ask her how she was doing, even if he was rushing off to work with Pops or to do something older kids did.

She'd been a kid whose life seemed to always be on the verge of falling apart. Something about Jarrod's serious, steadfast manner had drawn her from the moment she'd climbed through that fence and come face-to-face with him.

The poor, bone-thin horses made her heart weak. "Oh, how awful. And you take them in?" She looked up at Jarrod and he nodded. "What will you do with them?"

"I'll put them on the place and teach them to carry a rider. We'll use them to work cattle. Make them useful. I'll give them a purpose."

"You'll break them?"

"I'll gentle them. You've watched me work a colt before."

She had. And it was a beautiful thing to see. It was a dance between a man and a horse learning to trust each other. "Yes. I remember," she said quietly. It was one of the things she'd loved about him, his way with horses. She realized suddenly that she was standing in the space between his body and the arm he had propped on the pen rail, and the proximity was too personal. She stepped away, her pulse humming.

"I think that's wonderful, what you're doing."

"You'll have to come see them. I'll be working with some new colts over the next couple of weeks. We actually got one in that's really mean, though. I've been spending a lot of time with Sundance. He doesn't trust me at all and it's been a real challenge."

She understood how the horse felt. "I'm sure you'll fix that."

Something flickered in his gaze, a gentleness that seemed to soften it. "I'm hoping to."

Cassidy's mouth went dry. She tore her eyes from Jarrod's and, hearing a soft baa, she looked around, thankful for the distraction. Spotting two small lambs in the corner stall, she went over to look at them. Jarrod followed, but at least she'd had a moment to give herself an internal kick in the pants.

Doc came out the back door of the clinic.

"They're adorable," she called, bending down to stick her hand through the railing to pet the babies.

Doc scowled. "Mother died and the owner dropped them off here. We've been having to bottle-feed them for two weeks now."

"Really." Cassidy studied the twins then Doc. "What are you going to do with them?"

"Beats me. Find them a new home if not sell them at the auction. You want them?

I'm not joking. If you want them, take them. You're opening that bed-and-breakfast and folks might like the whole farm effect you'll get by adding lambs. People like the look of sheep. Kids can pet them."

"And Doc won't have to feed them anymore." Jarrod's dark eyes crinkled around the edges with a smile.

"I'm not going to lie," Doc said gruffly. "It won't hurt my feelings not to have to worry with them."

"Fine. I'll take them." Cassidy didn't even stop to ask herself if this was a smart thing. She wanted them. And she knew how to bottle-feed calves. Lambs had to be similar. "There's a fenced pen on the back of the barn. I can fix them up in there. When can I take them?"

Jarrod had moved to stand beside her. "Cassidy, they take a lot of work."

She looked up at him, aware that their shoulders were brushing each other. "I'm not afraid of a little work. They need a home." She looked back at Doc, who had an amused expression on his grizzled face.

"Well, you're in luck. They're at the end of two weeks old, so the most taxing time is over. Instead of feeding every two to three hours, you can switch to every five hours and introduce water and a little bit of solid food. Come by tomorrow after you make sure the area you've got in mind will make a good home. Then I'll fix you up with what you need. We'll know more about the pup by then too."

"Okay, you've got a deal."

Doc grinned. It was an unusual sight because he had always been such a gruff fella, though she suspected there was a heart of gold beneath that exterior show. "Roxie always did say you had a soft heart."

Cassidy stared down at the babies and briefly wondered what she'd just set herself up for, but then she smiled. "The way I look at it, what good is a farm without a few animals? Take care of my dog, Doc."

He chuckled and looked at Jarrod. "She's bossy too. I like that in a woman."

"How about hardheaded?"

Cassidy rolled her eyes. "Bye, Pops," she said as she passed the old man. He'd moved back to the horse pens and was studying the horses.

"Come ride sometime," Pops said, startling her. "You used to like it."

The sudden clarity of his statement shocked her. "You remember that?"

He looked quizzical. "Well, sure. Jarrod was a good teacher."

Cassidy nodded, completely waylaid by

his comment. She glanced at Jarrod, who looked as shocked as she was. "Yes, he was."

To her dismay, Jarrod fell into step with her as she turned to leave.

"Pops amazes me. His mind comes and goes, and memories from the past come out of nowhere sometimes."

"I'm sure it's hard on y'all."

"It is, but we're dealing with it. We've made peace with it as best we can. We share duties taking care of him. Bo's a real life-saver because his work keeps him on the place most of the time. He's the rock that holds it all together. Abby stepped right in there with him, insisting on keeping things as they were." He stopped at the truck and looked off into the distance, then back at her.

"I think it's wonderful that y'all do that for him."

"He did so much for all of us."

"What about your parents?"

His expression tensed. "They died in a plane crash a little over four years ago."

She gasped. "I-I didn't know that. Oh my goodness. I haven't really been in contact with anyone since Roxie died and no one I've seen so far has mentioned it. I am so, so sorry." Tears burned her eyes. She remembered his mom most, a pretty lady who loved the outdoors and was always trying to keep up with her boys. She didn't really remember his dad that much, except that he seemed fun. More easygoing, like Bo.

"Thanks. It's been hard. We . . ." He seemed bothered, as if internally he was deliberating. "We've adjusted to that too," he said after a heartbeat. "You know how that feels, having lost your aunt Roxie."

"Yes." She was puzzled by his coolness. "I do. I don't think I'll ever stop missing her, but I've gotten to the point where it doesn't hurt so much. I mean, we're all going to go sometime. I know she's up there in heaven overseeing beautiful gardens." She laughed at that thought. "It's how I see her."

He chuckled, relaxing a little from the tension of a moment ago. "Yeah, life goes on and comes full circle sometimes. She'd really be glad to know you're here. Not glad to know you had to go through a bad breakup, but glad you settled at her place. She loved you a lot."

Cassidy nodded, suddenly unable to speak because of the emotion crowding her throat.

He touched her cheek, startling her so that she jumped. "Whoa," he said softly. "Just catching the tear." He rubbed the wetness between his fingers, and she could hardly breathe. But she could not look away from him. "You're going to be okay, Cass. I know you've got some heavy things on your mind and heart of yours, but you're going to be okay."

The bottom fell out of her stomach. He was too close. Too . . . close. She stepped away, slid into her truck, and slammed the door. "I-I need to go."

His eyes seemed to see every dark secret inside of her. She heaved in a breath and cranked the engine. It started, thank goodness. She hadn't taken time yet to get a new battery.

He hooked an elbow inside her window. "Cass, I didn't mean to scare you off. Sorry. I just know you've got fight in you. A divorce takes time to heal just like losing someone to death, I would think."

It was her turn to tense. "What I feel for my ex has nothing to do with mourning." The tears that had been threatening dried up. "Thanks for helping me with the dog. See you later."

He stepped back, tipped his hat, and watched her drive away. She knew he did because she looked in her rearview and he never moved. Just stood there and watched her until she could no longer see him.

# 11

Watching Cassidy back her truck out to leave, Jarrod stepped forward and had to force himself not to hold up a hand for her to stop.

Cassidy was a mixture of toughness and vulnerability that got to him. She'd obviously been hurt deeply. And he hadn't missed how her eyes had softened when she'd seen those baby lambs. Why hadn't she ever had children?

"Come on, Jarrod. Horses to tend," Pops called, drawing him back to where he and Doc stood. Jarrod smiled. How many times over the years had his pops said those words?

"You're right, Pops. See you, Doc. I'll come by tomorrow. You know where to find me if you need me." He remembered Doc's statement about Roxie telling him lots of things and the sudden slight panic he'd seen on Cassidy's face. What had that been about? Had Cassidy had a secret?

"You know," Doc called, "Cassidy could probably use a little help making sure she's taking care of these two lambs correctly."

Doc matchmaking? Jarrod couldn't believe it. First Tru and Bo and now Doc. "Yeah, and aren't you the helpful one?" He couldn't help but grumble.

Doc chuckled. "You work too hard anyway. Won't hurt you to go check on that pen." He opened his office door and went inside, his shoulders shaking, he was laughing so hard.

Jarrod rubbed the back of his neck, his thoughts full. Then he climbed into his truck and drove toward Pops's place. And whether or not she liked it, Doc was right. He needed to check out Cassidy's pen.

Cassidy wasn't real sure she'd left Plano, Texas, with all her marbles and screws in place. She had a house that was still clutter central, a barn interior that could possibly be featured on one of those trash-to-treasure TV shows, and if she didn't get busy on it she was going to have a herd of folks lined up in her drive and nothing ready to pawn off on them. And she still had a house to finish clearing out and then painting to start and decorating to dive into.

But now, on top of all she had to do, she had just adopted an injured dog and two — repeat *two* — orphaned lambs.

And she wasn't even going to think about the fact that Jarrod continued to trouble her. He'd drawn her like caramel drew chocolate, and it had been undeniable several times. It made her feel weak.

The fact was, Jack would have an affair and then he'd lie. And then when it was clear that what she'd suspected had really happened, he'd try to make her feel like it was somehow her fault. Or he'd make her think he couldn't live without her. And that was all so confusing.

The worst part was she'd given in to him and she'd stayed. She wasn't even clear why he wanted her to stay. But she believed it was a power issue. He liked knowing he had the power to make her stay, and he used all kinds of mind games to make it work. The man had been full of these. Even suicide threats.

But Jarrod didn't fit into that same mold as Jack. So why was she still holding a grudge against him?

*Because he tempts you so much to turn your back on your decision to remain single and in control of your life.*

The lightbulb went on.

Cassidy stomped the brake and came to a jarring halt in the driveway as understanding dawned.

Even if Jarrod hadn't broken her silly, young heart, he would still be a red flag to her. The best thing to do was to keep her distance from him, which was more important now than ever. When she came back here, she believed she was over him. That he was no risk for her.

Foolish.

Roxie had avoided all of these problems by simply remaining single.

Cassidy needed to get a handle on this right now. Nip it in the bud, as Roxie would say — obviously something Cassidy had a problem with if her miserable, pathetic excuse of a marriage was any indication. It had taken her years to nip that in the bud, but when she finally had, she'd done it well and good.

She walked away with virtually nothing. Jack controlled everything, and though they were separated for a year, they weren't divorced because he kept dragging his feet and wouldn't agree to any terms. She'd finally changed that by walking out after she'd come out of her coma. She had funds for now, though not what she'd been completely entitled to, which meant the funds she had would run out. If she couldn't make a go of it here she might have to sell, and that, she'd come to realize, would be heartbreaking. This was her home.

Just like Roxie had wanted it to be.

But though Roxie had put it in a trust to protect it from being part of a divorce settlement, there were provisions that she could sell if she were single. It was a complicated transaction that had shown that Roxie knew how to hire great advisors.

If only Cassidy was smart enough to know how to make her own vision for the place come to life and pay off, she'd be doing okay.

Not wanting to think about Jarrod or Jack or losing the place any longer, she went straight to the pen attached to the barn when she got home and surveyed it with fresh eyes. Oh dear.

It was in terrible shape. But she had to do something. Maybe if she started hammering a few of the loose boards back into place it would look better.

She was hammering loose nails in the wooden gate thirty minutes later when Jarrod showed up.

How, she wanted to know, could she stop thinking about him when he *refused* to go away?

■ ■ ■ ■

"Hey. I took Pops home and thought I'd come see if I could help," Jarrod called as he got out of his truck. Cassidy was inside the pitiful pen with hammer in hand, and she wasn't looking real happy to see him.

"I'm doing all right —" she said.

"Hold on. Don't send me away. I know you don't want my help. I've gotten the message. But since you don't really have a lot of time, I took a chance."

She looked conflicted as she looked from him to the pen. Her shoulders slumped as she held out the hammer to him. "I would appreciate your help." She said it with less than welcoming enthusiasm.

He took the hammer. "Smile. You rescued a dog and *two* lambs today."

She gave a soft laugh. "You're right. I did rescue them, at least the pup." She waved at the pen. "Please help me pull this disaster together. But" — she held up a pointer finger — "after that you can go back to not helping me."

He laughed. "It's a deal."

He took her place beside the gate and studied it for a moment. Then he lined the nail up and pounded it into the wood in two swift, precise smacks of the hammer before propping the hammer head on his hip.

He had realized on the way home from the vet clinic that he owed her an explanation.

"I need to say this. I know I messed up all those years ago. I kissed you and then I ran off, and obviously the kiss didn't mean that much to you. But I need to tell you . . . that I'm sorry. I kissed you that night, and then I ran like a scared rabbit and didn't explain. I —"

She sank to the rickety bench beside the gate. "I know that. I'm not sure I want to talk about this. It was just a kiss, after all."

He placed a hand on the fence post and stared into the distance. "Yeah, okay. I still needed to say I'm sorry, I didn't handle things right. Not the way I should have." He'd almost told her that the kiss had meant more to him. So much more that it had sent him running scared. But he understood from their conversations that if he told her, revealed how much he cared, it would be Cassidy who did the running this time.

Cassidy rubbed her suddenly damp palms on her jeans. This was not what she needed to hear right now. "It happened a long time ago. And I was a confused young woman. I'm still a confused woman, just not so young anymore."

He placed a nail on another loose area of the fence and slammed the hammer to it, sending it home with one blow. "You're not old. And that was what scared me most. That you were confused. Look." He knelt down to the base of the fence and rested an arm on his knee. Her heart slammed into her throat, seeing him on one knee.

"The thing is, I know you've gone through a rough time. I just think it would be best if we get this out in the open and then we can move forward and be . . . friends again. We were once, remember?"

Her insides were tumbling like rocks off a mountain. Hitting hard and rolling around all jumbled together. "It's forgotten." *Liar.* "You need to know I'm not looking for anything other than friendship. And I can do without that if I need to. I'm serious, Jarrod. I wouldn't want you to get the wrong idea or anything. My whole life has been wrapped up in bad results from what most people consider blessings. Love, romance, marriage — I'm not interested in any of that anymore. I'm interested in living a quiet, fulfilled life here, and I need you to understand that. Just in case you were entertaining other ideas, you know. That kiss was a mistake just like you said it was that night." Her tone hardened on the last sentence. She'd lived with the memory of his words all these years. That kiss had meant so much to her and he'd said it was a mistake and then he'd left for Montana the next morning. Left her feeling just like she had for most of her life — that she was the mistake . . .

He held out his hand. She stared at it, conflicting emotions warring inside of her. And then, not exactly sure what he was doing, or what she was doing, she took it. His callused palm was warm and rough as it met hers, and it sent a shiver through her.

"Friends." Sincerity darkened his eyes.

She swallowed hard, trying to ease the dryness of her throat. "Friends," she managed to say without croaking too badly. Before he could feel her hand tremble, she pulled it from his and fought down the rioting reaction she was having to his touch.

She popped up from the bench, a knot lodged in her chest as she fought to gain control of her sanity. He stood too.

"That should do it on the fence gate. Now let's check the slats on the fence."

"Sure." Cassidy hurried to the far side of the pen from him, glad for the momentary distance to gain her senses back. They both studied the fence post and then began to work on repairing it. Having gotten control of her adolescent reaction, when she found a loose board she held it while he nailed it in place. Friends. They were going to be neighbors and friends. She could handle that.

She could.

When he declared the fence lamb-safe — not pretty, but safe — he checked out the shelter in the corner and gave it a thumbs-up.

"Why don't I pick you up tomorrow and we'll go get the lambs together? I'll bring some hay and we can get the other supplies from Doc."

She needed to refuse him. To do it on her own. But they'd just made a truce of sorts and he had been so helpful. A standoff by her was going to do nothing but cause undue stress, and it was childish. "That would be helpful. What about work?"

"I run the ranch, Cassidy. I have men who take care of things if I need to be somewhere else."

"Then I'll see you about two or three. I have something to do until then." She realized she was already looking forward to his company. As friends. This was much better than being angry about their past. At one point in her life she'd blamed him for the mistake she'd made marrying Jack, but that was unfair. She had been the one who'd been a fool.

But that was all over.

He touched the brim of his hat, then walked toward his truck.

"Thanks," she called. And meant it.

"My pleasure, ma'am," he said over his shoulder, but he didn't look back.

Cassidy forced herself to turn toward the barn. She had work to do. A lot of work to do. It was already Wednesday, leaving her only two days until the sale.

She worked late into the night. Might as well since she wouldn't have been able to sleep for worrying that she'd just let down her guard and she was going to live to regret it.

# 12

By noon the next day Cassidy felt better about the sale that would start bright and early the next morning. She was surprised when Maggie and Abby showed up to work mid-morning. They'd brought a playpen along for Levi, who entertained himself by watching them move things around. They priced and moved the smaller items onto the temporary tables she made out of some old doors and plywood she found in the barn.

The playpen didn't last long, though. Levi wanted in on the action. Cassidy scooped him up out of the playpen and let him play stickers with her. She wrote a price on a sticker and he stuck it anywhere on the item he wanted to. He loved it.

They stopped to eat a quick sandwich and then got back to work.

Cassidy started checking her watch about two.

"Is something wrong?" Abby asked. "You've been checking your watch a lot."

Cassidy stuck a fifty-cent price tag on a small wind chime. She'd told them about the lambs she was supposed to go pick up, then added, "Well, I was actually expecting Jarrod. He said he would take me to pick up the lambs."

"Oh really," Maggie said, questions in her eyes. "I'm kind of liking this."

Abby came out from the barn carrying the bassinette Cassidy hadn't tossed out for some strange reason. "Hey, Maggie, look at this antique cradle. If we cleaned this up and gave it a new coat of paint, it would be darling for a new baby. What?" She halted in her tracks and looked from Cassidy to Maggie. "Okay, what did I miss? You two look like something good was being discussed."

Cassidy eyed Abby. "What did *I* miss? Is someone having a baby?"

Maggie beamed. "Abby, Jarrod is going to show up any minute to take Cassidy into town to pick up her new baby sheep. And, Cassidy, I'm expecting a baby in about two months."

"Jarrod, over here again." Abby spoke with unabashed enthusiasm. "He is certainly spending a lot of time hanging around you.

This is pretty exciting."

Cassidy was in too much shock over Maggie to care in that specific moment. "You don't look seven months pregnant. Really?"

Maggie chuckled. "No, no," she managed to say, still chuckling. "We're adopting. I work with Over the Rainbow a few miles from here. It's a home for unwed, pregnant teens. One of the teens asked us to be the parents of her baby, and after much prayer and consideration we decided to do it. We want kids so much. We're really excited."

"Wow, I'm happy for y'all." Cassidy couldn't think of anyone who would be a better mother.

"So spill," Abby said after patiently waiting for Maggie to finish talking. Before anything else could be said, though, Jarrod pulled into the driveway. Abby shot her a pleased smile. "Interesting."

Cassidy ignored her.

"So how's it going?" Jarrod asked as he strode across the yard to them. "Y'all going to make some big money?"

"You bet we are," Abby said. "This is very neighborly of you to take Cassidy to pick up her animals. Cassidy, you go on and don't worry about anything. Maggie, Levi, and I will just price away while you kids are gone."

Jarrod looked suddenly leery of his sister-in-law.

"Don't look so worried, Jarrod." Abby smiled. "I'm glad you're taking some time off from working constantly."

Cassidy was very uncomfortable now about the whole situation and beginning to worry that she'd made a mistake letting him help her bring the lambs home.

"You sure are quiet today," he said after they'd driven about halfway into town.

"Just a lot on my mind. I'll be glad to get the sale out of the way and have one more thing off my list."

When they reached the vet's, Clara Lyn was standing on the porch.

"Well, hi there, you two. What are y'all up to?" She was looking from one to the other.

Extremely self-conscious for fear everyone would start to get the wrong idea about the two of them if they were seen together too often, Cassidy over explained. "I'm getting two lambs from Doc and Jarrod is helping me get them home. You know, they need extra care to make sure they make the ride home without too much trauma." *What?*

Jarrod's lip twitched and Clara Lyn grinned.

"Sure they do. I'm quite certain Jarrod doesn't mind at all. Hey, here you go." She handed Cassidy a white flyer with red, white, and blue fireworks exploding all over it, announcing the Fourth of July celebration the following week.

"We want to make sure you're aware of this. It's going to be a great day. You're bringing your peaches?"

"Yes, I should have some ripe ones by then."

"Great. Jarrod, maybe you can go help her pick some."

"I'd be glad to." His dark-blue eyes crinkled with amusement.

Cassidy's temper rose. He was finding it funny that people were starting to do exactly what she wanted them not to do. "I'll talk to you about it later, Jarrod. I have lambs to get now." She didn't wait around for more blatant hints of matchmaking. Instead, she strode through the door and immediately heard the *tap, tap* of the pig's hooves on the tile floor in the hallway.

A Wet Floor sign stood in the middle of the empty waiting room, but she didn't think anything about it until the pig came barreling around the corner. Clover saw her, squealed gleefully, and never stopped running. One second Cassidy was standing and the next the pig was sliding across the wet floor like a bowling ball. She struck Cassidy in the ankles with such force that Cassidy's feet flew out from under her and she went airborne.

It all happened so fast that Cassidy wasn't prepared, and she came down hard on the tile floor. The fall in the yard that first night at Strawberry Hill had nothing on this.

Her hip hit first and pain shot through her.

"Cassidy!" Jarrod rushed inside and knelt beside her. "Don't move."

"Oh my goodness!" Clara Lyn exclaimed, dropping her flyers as she hustled to her side, bangles jingling as she knelt down too.

Cassidy's hip throbbed. Clover instantly stuck her snout in Cassidy's ear and licked, making not moving impossible. She jumped.

"No, ma'am," Clara Lyn admonished, throwing her arms around the pig and pulling her away. "You've already caused enough trouble, young lady."

"What's all the ruckus in here? Missy leaves and I can't get a dadgum thing done —" Cassidy saw Doc's eyes widen in dismay, seeing her sprawled on the floor. "Oh. What happened here?" He bent down to join the others.

"Clover slipped on the wet floor. I'm fine. My hip is sore, but I'm fine."

Doc, as gruff as he was, looked worried.

"Missy mopped before she took the afternoon off. I'm sorry about that. Let's look you over. Don't move just yet."

"You didn't hit your head, did you?" Jarrod sounded grave, and his gaze probed hers intensely. She became aware that he was cradling her head in the crook of his arm.

"No. I don't think so. I'm glad. I already had one concussion recently, and I wouldn't want another one." The words were out before she realized she was saying them.

"When did you have a concussion?" Doc asked, probing her hip, making her wince. "Sorry 'bout that. Sore, huh?"

She nodded. "Just a little."

"What about the concussion?" Jarrod asked.

"Oh, I hope she's okay," Clara Lyn added, worry in her voice.

Doc pulled a penlight from his pocket and shined it into her eyes. "Tell us about that."

"I-I ran out in front of a car and was hit. I was —"

"You were hit by a *car*!" Clara Lyn exclaimed.

Cassidy did not want to talk about this.

"Hush, Clara Lyn. Now, go on," Doc grunted, taking her chin in his hands and turning her head as he stared into her eyes.

"I was in a coma for a couple of days —"

"A *coma*!" Clara Lyn squealed. At least she thought it was Clara Lyn. It sounded very close to Clover's squeal.

Cassidy closed her eyes and opened them to find Jarrod staring down at her with deep concern. Perfect. She did not want anyone asking any more questions about that accident. It was embarrassing enough.

"I woke up two days later, the doctors deemed me fine, and now, other than a headache when I'm stressed, there are no aftereffects." Not any that anyone could see. Her being in Wishing Springs living at Roxie's was one aftereffect that had come out of that whole fiasco. "And I'm fine now. I'm going to have a sore hip, but I'm fine." She was tired of being coddled. She moved to rise up and Jarrod helped her to a sitting position.

"Okay, move your leg and let's see," Doc instructed. She complied. Pain shot through her, but she was able to move her leg fine.

"It's good. Now, let me get up and let's load up my babies. And how's my dog?"

"Maybe you need to stay down and let's get the ambulance out here and have that hip checked out," Jarrod said. A deep scowl etched his face.

"No. Jarrod Monahan, I am fine." Her

words were clipped. She started to get up with or without his help.

"Stubborn woman. You could be seriously hurt."

"And you could be seriously overreacting." Pain shot through her lower back and down her leg, but she did her best to hide the wince.

"See there. You're hurt." He reached to assist her, his long fingers wrapping around her arm.

"I fell down," she gritted through clenched teeth, fighting to ignore the feel of his hand on her skin. "I bruised my hip. Yes, I will be sore tomorrow. But I'm fine."

Doc and Clara Lyn stood watching them and were unnaturally silent.

"See, my hip moves." She lifted her leg, ignored the pain in her lower back, and smiled cheerily at Jarrod. "Stop being so protective. Thank you for your concern, but I am not a child."

He opened his mouth to say something, then clamped it shut. She could just imagine what he was thinking.

"Doc, my lambs?"

"Oh, come right this way." A sardonic expression twisted his features comically.

The old codger was laughing at her. She shot Clara Lyn a glance, hoping for some support, but there was worry in her eyes too.

"You're limping. Jarrod, she's limping."

He wore a thunderous expression now. "Clara Lyn, does it look like I can do anything with her?"

"Ex-*actly,*" Cassidy enunciated. "I am not *yours* to 'do anything with.' "

With that she followed Doc into the other room and down the hall.

"Goodness, she does have a temper," she heard Clara Lyn declare. "At least with you, Jarrod."

"Yeah, thanks for pointing that out, Clara Lyn."

"Oh, look at the babies." Abby cooed as she held Levi on her hip. Jarrod and Cassidy lifted the lambs from the backseat of the truck where Cassidy had ridden with them on the way home.

"Dog!" Levi exclaimed, jumping excitedly on his mother's hip and reaching out toward the lambs.

Jarrod laughed with everyone at his nephew. "No, not a dog, lamb," he said, enjoying the excitement on Levi's face. "He's going to have fun with these little fellas."

He was glad for the little distraction the

tot supplied. Maybe he had overreacted. But when he saw Cassidy hit that hard floor, he'd worried she had hit her head. They'd both cooled down some after getting the lambs loaded up. He'd backed off, given her room, and was biding his time.

"Are you limping?" Maggie asked the minute Cassidy took a few steps.

"I fell. It seems that Clover turns into a bowling ball on wet tiled floors. And I was the bowling pin."

"Are you all right?" His sisters-in-law asked the question in unison.

Cassidy shot daggers at him, daring him to speak. "I'm fine. My hip hurts and is probably going to be the color of a cluster of grapes soon, but I'm fine."

He set his lamb on the ground in the pen, then took hers out of her arms and lowered him over the fence into the soft hay. Almost instantly the two babies curled up together and went to sleep.

His phone rang and he was glad for the excuse to walk away. "Jarrod."

Madge the 9–1–1 dispatcher's nasal twang greeted him. "Chief, got a grass fire on Bert Tobias's place." She called out the address. "Number one is en route."

"Thanks." He hung up and looked at Cassidy. "No need me asking if you've got this.

I'm sure you do. I've got a grass fire to tend to."

"A fire?" Cassidy asked as he got into his truck with other questions from his sisters-in-law echoing behind him. He rattled off the info he had, cranked up the truck, and then drove away. A fire he could handle.

He was beginning to wonder if he could ever handle Cassidy Starr.

They made it through the rummage sale on Saturday. Cassidy watched people carting off their newfound treasures and she knew Aunt Roxie would be happy. Each of these people enjoyed the hunt as much as Roxie had, or if not, they truly had a need for what they bought.

Who knew, *Antiques Roadside* or whatever that TV show was called could come along one day and someone could have bought a treasure from her for a couple of dollars. She had no idea what she was selling. She was just pleasantly surprised by the end of the day that the two-day-long sale had left her with very little to get rid of. She had even made a small sum of money — not the mint that Rand had predicted, but for her it had mostly been about getting rid of stuff.

Toward the end of the day, a man had been trying to decide between a couple of knickknacks. She made him a deal he couldn't refuse by selling him everything left on the shelf for the price of one — a whole dollar. If he'd wanted to haggle with her, he probably could have asked her to pay him a dollar to take them.

She did keep one Thomas Kincaid commemorative plate of a gazebo in the middle of a flowering garden. It had been Roxie's favorite. "The Prayer Garden" was what she called it. It reminded her of Roxie's peaceful spirit. Of course, her exterior was quite spunky, but it was that inner peace of hers that Cassidy was searching for.

And quick. She needed to tone down her tendency to jump into sparing matches with Jarrod. It was getting old and she had to fix that.

Though she hadn't had to worry about it too much because she hadn't seen Jarrod all weekend. He disappeared after their last confrontation, and it was bothering her.

"I'm tuckered out," Pebble said, sinking into one of the chairs beside Cassidy.

"Me too." Cassidy leaned back in the chair and smiled at the group. Clara Lyn, Reba, Pebble, Abby, and Maggie had all shown up both days, ready to help and give her support. She had enjoyed the companionship.

"Thank you all for helping. I don't know if I'd have gotten it all done without you."

"With that limp of yours, it's a good thing we showed up." Clara Lyn gave her a shrewd look. "I bet it's giving you a bundle of pain right now."

"I'm fine. Some people just overreact."

Clara Lyn chuckled. "He certainly did."

"That's just the thing," Maggie said, leaning forward in her chair. "Jarrod is the levelheaded one. Well, all of the Monahan men are, but Jarrod has always been a bit aloof. Don't y'all agree?"

"Most certainly. He's all business since all that happened with his dad," Reba said. "We've talked about it before, Clara and I, and it's almost like he took what his dad did as a personal insult."

Cassidy was lost now. "What exactly did his dad do?"

Clara Lyn's eyes widened. "You don't know? He gambled the ranch away. He had a horrible gambling addiction no one knew about, and he owed all kinds of loan sharks and banks money too. It was awful, and if he hadn't died in that plane crash, he'd have lost the ranch before his sons even knew what was going on. Just gambled it right away. When Jarrod, Tru, and Bo started going over the books their dad always kept after the funeral, they were instantly alerted to the dire state of affairs."

"Yes," Maggie added. "They bonded together and saved the ranch for Pops. For themselves and their children too."

"It's sad," Pebble said. "Addiction is a horrible thing. I have a feeling Jarrod asks himself all the time if there was something he could have done. I know I ask myself that about Rand. And I know there wasn't anything I could do. But I just think that because Jarrod is the oldest he shoulders that responsibility more than the others. Not that he should, but he is that type."

Jarrod hadn't told her this the other day. They'd gotten close to it maybe but, wow. The debt to lose a ranch that size had to be astronomical.

"Tru and I actually discussed this," Maggie said. "But nothing he or Bo do can lift the weight from Jarrod's shoulders. That's why they are encouraging him to go out some. The man has no social life."

*He doesn't date.* Cassidy's ears perked up at that despite the fact that she was not interested in a social life herself.

"And that's why we find it so interesting that you are getting reactions out of him none of us have seen before, Cassidy." Maggie was beaming at her. "Keep up the good work. He's a great person."

"Wait. I'm not looking to date anyone."

*Especially not Jarrod.*

Clara Lyn, Reba, and Pebble all gasped.

Reba got her voice first. "Well, why not? He's a hunk and a half. Or two. And so sweet. All of them are. You've seen how they are with their pops. They are real men. And Jarrod, well, he's got those brooding good looks going on."

Cassidy did not want to sit around and talk about Jarrod's good looks. She was more than aware of them.

Thankfully she made it through the next thirty minutes before everyone left. Much of the time was spent talking about the Fourth of July celebration. She had her week set, knowing there would be a lot of peach picking going on. And sometime during that time she would start tilling up the garden plot. July was not the month to plant anything in Texas because of the lack of rainfall and the heat, but she wanted to be ready for a fall garden. And from what she'd read, cultivating the soil was a good thing.

"So what do you think?" Jarrod was looking at Jake. For the last two days Jarrod had driven the perimeter of the ranch, trying to think like a cattle rustler. His men had been checking tags herd by herd, and the results were not making him happy. They were on the road to having the debt paid off and the ranch completely in the black again, but if theft like this continued he was going to be in trouble.

He'd found a pen made of portable panels on a corner of his property that didn't belong to him.

"It's evident that they're being bold. I seriously doubt they'll be back to this pen. It might even be here as a decoy to make you stake the place out while they rob you blind somewhere else. I'll call Tom and let him know what you've found."

The TSCRA agent assigned to the area had alerted them that this was going on in surrounding counties too. They also suspected it was someone living in the area, the area being a fairly large mile radius. He knew Tom and the other agents were overworked and understaffed right now. The year before had been a record-breaking year for cattle thieves in Texas, with over ten thousand head of cattle missing. He figured it hadn't slowed down this year so far.

Jake scrubbed his jaw as he studied the tire tracks backed up to the pens. "The difference in a lot of those cattle and yours is that you keep excellent records."

"I'm estimating that I'm missing thirty head so far. With the price of heifers right

179

now, we're looking at a loss in the sixty-to seventy-thousand-dollar range." He didn't need to tell Jake how much that kind of a hit was jeopardizing the survival of the Four of Hearts Ranch.

"Yeah, we've got to stop the bleeding. Okay, I'll pull what evidence I can from the site and we'll put out an alert with all auction barns. In the meantime, you keep alert. You find anything else, let me know."

"You do the same. Jake, they're not going to get away with this on my land."

Jake squinted at him, probing. "Don't do anything stupid. The law will handle this."

"I'm not planning on hanging anyone, if that's what you're worried about. But I'm not planning on sitting back and letting this continue. You and I both know that with the way they've spread out, the law and the agents are spread thin."

"That's true. I'm just telling you to be careful."

He and Jake went way back, and Jake knew he wasn't one to take being pushed around lightly. "They're messing with my family's livelihood. Don't be concerned about me."

Jake looked skeptical, but Jarrod couldn't worry about that. This was his land, his cattle, and he'd take care of what was his.

But more important, what belonged to his family. He'd let his family down once. That wasn't happening again.

# 14

Cassidy went to church on Sunday. Everyone had invited her, and after a little bit of thought she decided to go. Through her divorce and the last couple of years when things had been so bad, she'd stopped going. It had just seemed pointless. Sitting there listening to the preacher talk about hope and that God loved her and . . . Okay, so, she knew he did. And she believed, but she'd still felt like she was out here doing everything herself. And she'd drifted away.

But maybe her heart hadn't been in a place where she was letting God speak to her, so maybe she should try to listen now.

It was a cowboy church, and Cassidy was a little unsure about that. She'd heard of them but wasn't real certain what they were. Clara Lyn explained it was simply a place that celebrated the cowboy culture, though everyone was welcome.

There were cattle trailers in the parking

lot and plain uncovered concrete floors inside. Not all of the men, but many of them, had on their cowboy hats and boots and jeans. She instantly thought of Jarrod, that he would fit here, and wondered if he attended. When she saw Tru in a group of men drinking coffee and talking, she felt fairly certain that he did.

People began greeting her and her thoughts were pulled in other directions. She settled in beside Clara Lyn for the service and found herself listening as the preacher in his Stetson talked about a calf with its legs bound. It was like people being tied down by the sins, the hurts, and mistakes of their past. And that trusting in the Lord was letting God remove the rope and set them free.

So the sermon had been a little different, but it stuck with her as she walked out onto the lawn after the service. Everyone was talking excitedly about the upcoming weekend, and now that she had the rummage sale off her mind, she could focus on that too.

She spent the rest of the day in her peach orchard. Climbing up and down a ladder picking peaches did not feel good on her hip, so she stuck to picking the lower limbs first. There were a lot of peaches, and some were not as ripe as others. But she was pleased that she would have a decent crop to sell at her booth at the celebration.

Monday morning she'd planned to go check on her dog and see if he could come home. She'd fixed him up a bed in the utility room. She had no idea if he was in any way house-trained, but he would need a place to recuperate. She was washing the lambs' bottles and getting ready to go outside and feed them when she heard a truck drive up.

She opened the door and found Jarrod walking up the sidewalk. Her pulse zipped into a free fall.

"Good morning," she said as she pushed the screen door open. "What are you doing here?" That sounded less than welcoming, she realized too late. As aggravating as it was to have him come over, she was glad to see him.

His lip hitched up into a one-sided smile that made her toes tingle. *Oh dear.*

"I'm doing a friend a favor. I brought your dog to you. I was at the clinic when Doc was about to call you to come get him, but I thought I'd save you the trip into town since I was coming this way."

"Well, thank you. I was going to go check on him as soon as I fed the babies." She walked out onto the porch. "I'm excited. I have a place ready for Duce."

"Duce?" Jarrod opened the back door of his truck.

"Yes. He's got a second chance at life, so I thought it would be appropriate. Second Chance didn't sound as good, so I went with Duce."

He chuckled. "I agree." He carefully lifted Duce out of the truck, and to her surprise the animal held up his head and studied her as Jarrod carried him past her.

"He's a good dog. He's not overly energetic because his injuries were so bad, but Doc says he gave him a sedative and you'll need to do that for a couple more days. And then I'll take the stitches out."

"You'll take them out?" She paused mid-step and so did he.

"Yes. I do that on most of my animals. Doc gets busy sometimes so there's no need to bother him."

"Oh, okay. Do you put stitches in sometimes too?"

He laughed. "Well, yes. My truck's got a first-aid kit in it that includes supplies to sew up a cow or a calf if I need to."

"I'm impressed." He looked a little embarrassed that she would be impressed.

"Most cowboys know how to do that.

Many times a cowboy on a forty-thousand-acre ranch in Montana has no backup in the winter. It's just them and the cattle when they're snowed in."

"I can only imagine." She wondered how long he'd stayed in Montana, but it was at least long enough to learn how to treat injured cattle. He looked uncomfortable, and she wondered if he might possibly be thinking about the night he told her he was going to Montana. The night he'd kissed her. He glanced at the dog and she did, too, trying not to think about that night. That kiss.

"He's got kindness in his eyes. He's easygoing. He's going to make you a good friend, I think." Jarrod started walking again.

Cassidy hurried to beat him to the door. "That's what I was thinking. But then again, he is hurt and weak. He could be a terror."

Jarrod laughed, and the uncomfortable moment was passed, though she still wondered how long the draw of Montana had kept him. "I think it'll be fine. Doc sent some antibiotics and instructions. He said the patient should be moving more tomorrow. He's still on a little heavy-duty painkiller and feeling slightly woozy, I think."

"So that explains the lazy kind of vibe

that's going on right now."

"Uh, yeah, I think that's what we're see-ing."

Jarrod flashed a devastating smile, and Cassidy forgot what she'd been about to say. "Um . . ."

"Where do you want him?" he asked over his shoulder.

She hurried to open the door and pointed into the side room. "There on the pallet."

He walked past her, brushing her arm as he did. Her pulse kicked in again and but-terflies winged their way through her, unexpected and again unwanted. This was not going to do. He walked through the door she held open and then she followed him inside.

She watched him stoop down, in jeans, and the muscles stretched taut beneath his cotton shirt as he leaned in and gently set down the dog.

"I'm so glad he's okay," she said, yanking back when Jarrod stood. He moved to let her through the doorway and brushing past him did not help calm her nerves.

Focusing on her dog, she bent down and placed her hand gently on Duce's head. "I'm so happy you've survived and are go-ing live with me now, Duce." She looked up at Jarrod. "It concerns me that he might have an owner and already have a name."

"He's not wearing a collar. So many animals get thrown away, dropped off on the road and abandoned. I have a feeling you're looking at one of them. Doc's going to let you know if anyone comes in and asks about a dog meeting Duce's description, though."

She studied Duce, his deep eyes locked on hers. "What if I get attached — no, I'm not going to think about that." She gave her dog one more affectionate rub and stood up." The dog's tail thumped softly on the linoleum and Cassidy smiled gently. She was so glad to see a little life in the dog's dark eyes. "I just need to give him my love for now, and if his owner shows up grateful that he's alive, well, then that'll be good."

Cassidy couldn't think about the repercussions of giving her love to someone or something and having it not matter in the end. When it came to her stepparents, she'd learned very quickly to harden her heart and not let any kind gesture or overture they made matter. Because the minute she let them in and started to care, they were gone and she didn't matter to them anymore. She looked at Jarrod and saw compassion in his eyes. She almost believed he'd read her thoughts.

Then again, he had always been able to know when she was vulnerable. And he'd always teased a smile from her when she was younger. She smiled now, hoping to hide some of her fears from him.

"So do you want to see the lambs?"

He smiled again. "I thought you'd never ask."

Jarrod looked at Cassidy and felt his heartbeat slam against his chest. He had an overpowering desire to pull her into his arms and hang on. Forcing himself to pull back from watching her with the pup, he berated himself for his foolishness. And he asked himself once again how he could fix it.

He'd run scared as a young cowboy. But now, all this time he'd done what he'd had to do, what he felt was his duty toward his family. Striving to make sure the ranch was what it needed to be. Trying to make up for what his father had done to Pops in nearly losing the ranch. But now looking at Cassidy, all he could think about was that life was passing him by and he wanted a life.

He wanted what his brothers had found. He wanted someone to share the ranch with. He wanted a wife to love so they could enjoy the ranch together with their children just as Pops had envisioned. And all these years, ever since he'd walked away from Cassidy, he'd never once felt anything that had scared him like that. Looking at her now, the gentleness she had with the puppy and the lambs, he —

Whoa. He halted his thoughts in their tracks. What was he doing? After she'd been through so much with her parents and their multiple divorces, after all the shipping here and there, after the brokenness that her life had been? And after she'd married this guy, this jerk, who had done the same thing to her, divorcing her?

He needed to find out what the guy did to put that pain in her beautiful green eyes. What did he do to make her closed off to the thought of romance? Jarrod hated that she was closing that door. And he was at a loss as to how to stop her from doing it.

"It's hard getting attached to something only to have it taken away." He was concerned by Cassidy's words. As he looked at her and Duce, Jarrod said a prayer right there that no one would claim her dog. At least she was opening her heart up to a pet.

"Everything will be fine."

He hoped so.

Before they reached the pen she was smiling.

"Aren't they just adorable?" She handed him a bottle. "I'll let you help me feed them."

He took the bottle. *She* was adorable. "Pretty adorable."

"I am really thrilled to have them here." She opened the gate and they entered the pen. The babies were still clumsy as they romped together in the corner. The moment they spotted Cassidy, they came dancing her way. They looked downright gleeful as they reached her.

She sank to the ground and welcomed them into her arms, letting them climb onto her lap. She cuddled them and looked up at him.

"Have you ever seen anything so perfect?"

"Nope," he said honestly. "Nothing. And the lambs are cute too." Her eyes widened and he realized he'd actually said that out loud. "I'm just telling it like I see it."

"Thank you," she said faintly, nuzzling the lambs. One of the lambs jumped up and pressed its nose into her cheek, and she bubbled with laughter. She pulled him down and gave both lambs gentle head scrubs. "Okay, my little ones, it's breakfast time. You feed Percy and I'll feed Petunia."

He crouched down, took the soft ball of wool into his arms, and nudged its mouth with the bottle. It latched on instantly. "Are you sure this is a little lamb and not a little pig?"

She laughed. "Petunia is the same way. There isn't anything wrong with their appetites."

Jarrod had to hold the lamb back when he started getting aggressive with the bottle toward the end. He kept getting distracted by Cassidy's laughter as she struggled a little with Petunia.

When the bottles were empty, he set Percy on his feet and watched him greet Petunia as Cassidy set her on her feet. They nudged each other and then curled up on the hay, content to take a nap together.

"They have the life, don't they?" Cassidy stood up.

Jarrod took her elbow and helped her when he realized she was struggling. "Is your hip giving you a lot of trouble?"

"It's hurting, but it gets better every day."

He opened the gate and they walked out into the yard. She walked beside him.

"How's it going? This plan of yours?"

"Slow." She laughed. "I have a lot to do, but I'm making up ground a little every day. I just have to remind myself that gardens don't grow overnight, nor do bed-and-breakfasts. Now that I've cleared out some space, I can start working more in the orchard and till my garden so the ground begins to get ready for my strawberries in a few months." She rolled her eyes. "And I'm about to start painting inside and will need to set up that time for you to come out and inspect it."

"I can do that anytime. I could do it now if you wanted me to."

"No, I'll let you know."

"Sounds good. You're getting closer to being in business."

"Thanks. I have to admit it all makes me a little nervous." She wrapped her arms around her waist. "I need to make this work."

"Financially?" He didn't want to pry and she might not say, but he'd wondered about the profit a small-town bed-and-breakfast could make. The peach orchard and strawberry business would be seasonal, and he could only imagine that had as many variables to it as the cattle business. She was driving an old truck and she wasn't hiring help. That all added up to make him wonder if she was struggling already, although she'd said she was looking to hire someone to mow. So what did he know? She might drive that old truck for a reason that was none of his business.

She ran the toe of her sandal in the dirt. "Yes, actually. I have funds, but, well, you know without profit funds run out." She gave a small smile and then waved it off. "It's going to be fine. I don't need this place to be a gold mine and never thought it would be. I can make it on a shoestring budget if I have to. But I need it to be a success for me."

"What do you mean?"

"I've never done anything on my own. I never went to college. I was working as a teller at a bank when I met Jack. I've never really even thought about what I wanted out of life. I plan to start an online business with jams and other specialty items once I get everything up and running too. It just takes time. But I" — she looked wistful for a moment — "I know I want the people who come here to enjoy the place too. That's a priority. It will be awhile before I have any visitors. I know that, but I guess as I get closer to knowing I'm actually going to be able to do this it makes me nervous."

He wanted her to do well. She hadn't told him how exactly her finances were or where her funds came from. Had she gotten anything in the divorce? He knew there had once been some small royalties from the same oil well that his ranch was pooled in with, but those had dwindled down to a trickle since they'd slowed production a couple of years ago. He bet it wasn't much more than enough to maybe pay the taxes . . . maybe not even that. "They'll be happy. You're building a great atmosphere." He studied her and she gave him a smile.

"Thanks. It's going to work." She sounded reassured.

"You know, I know it's not exactly the same thing, but I feel that way about the ranch. Pops did an amazing job building the Four of Hearts. He just had a talent for it. I don't know if you've heard what my dad did, but he put the ranch in jeopardy before he died."

"I heard a little about his nearly gambling it away."

"It's been a mess. Tru, Bo, and I have worked really hard to keep it safe, and it will carry on the legacy to everyone's children like Pops had always dreamed. But my part of that is the actual ranch management. Pops taught me everything I know, and now it's my shot to make it bigger and better and to make him proud." He'd never told anyone this.

She studied him thoughtfully. "You feel the pressure of that, don't you?"

"Yeah, I do. I'm dealing with some pretty

hard feelings toward my dad, but I'm up for it. He put this in my lap and fixing what he nearly destroyed drives me. Like you wanting to do something for yourself. You need to do it, for yourself."

"Yes, I do." Her expression grew earnest but her eyes hardened. "I have dealt with some pretty harsh emotions the last two years — truthfully, over the last six years. I realized early on that my marriage wasn't what it should have been. But it wasn't until the last couple of years that I knew how wrong it was. I was just treading water, trying to deny that my marriage was a sham. Jack didn't want me. You get numb after a while but . . ."

The morning breeze lifted one of her curling strands of red hair and it brushed against her cheek. She batted it away, looking tense again now that they'd crossed into this new, painful territory.

"Can I ask what happened?"

"My marriage was a joke. I —" She clamped down on her lips suddenly, halting whatever she'd been about to say. "I was a fool." Anger tensed her expression.

He leaned a hip against the door of his truck, no longer ready to leave. He wanted to pull her into his arms. He wanted to hold her and tell her that she'd obviously married an idiot. What had drawn her to the man she'd married six months after leaving here?

"I married a man who found infidelity to be exhilarating, and I think having a spouse made the game better for him. I'm not really certain. He just kept having affairs. I'd find out and he'd apologize profusely and say it would never happen again. And then . . ." She laughed harshly. "Then he'd blame me." Her eyelids dipped over suddenly embarrassed eyes. "He might have been right even toward the end because I just didn't care any longer. I was only holding on because I didn't want to be like my parents."

Jarrod's jaw tensed as he ground his back teeth together and fought down the burning boil of anger rising inside of him. He'd suspected something along these lines because her anger was so deep. Actually hearing it was like tossing gasoline to the fire.

But she didn't need his anger right now. She needed his reassurance. "You're going to be all right, Cassidy. You need to believe in yourself and stick to your plan. Work it and look for every opportunity that comes to enhance it." He paused, seeing that uncertainty in her eyes. "Your ex wasn't just a fool. He was award winning." Before he could stop himself, he brushed his fingers along her jaw, then drew back. "I have to go. Ranch work calls. But if you need anything, I'm right over there."

By the time he reached his house, he was still telling himself he had stepped across the line and she was probably going to have her guard up the next time he saw her. He may have messed up royally — again.

He'd intended to tell her about the rustlers, but the conversation had gone in a different direction. He'd have to tell her, though. Her being out here alone on the side of the ranch where the cattle seemed to be disappearing made it necessary for her to know there were thieves roaming around. She needed to keep her eyes open.

His phone dinged as a text message came through. Maggie was reminding him that everyone was having dinner with Pops the next night before she and Tru left for a clinic Tru was holding. She wanted to make sure he knew she was inviting Cassidy too.

He smiled. Perfect.

# 15

After Jarrod left, Cassidy went in and checked on Duce. He was such a sweet dog. A little out of it, but he wagged his tail when she came into the room. Crouching down, she ran her hand over his coat and the network of stitches. The hog had torn up the poor animal, which made her certain she didn't want to run into one herself. She'd seen pictures of some of their tusks and it wasn't a pretty sight.

"I tell you, Duce, that hog got you good, didn't he?" Duce wagged his tail and lifted one ear as he watched her. "And Jarrod is going to take these out. That fascinates me." She examined the stitches more closely.

She wanted to go work in the peach orchard, but she hated to leave Duce alone. She also knew she had to get the peaches in but she hadn't hired any help yet. She had better get busy. "Okay, I have to go for a couple of hours. You just lie here and chill out."

Feeling bad, she grabbed a couple of bottles of water and went outside into the morning heat. Her tools were still in the bed of the truck so there was nothing to load, and within seconds she was bumping along through the pasture.

Every time she drove to the orchard she thought of Jarrod. He'd caressed her cheek.

She'd tried to ignore it. But that was useless. So she'd tried to ignore that his touch had set her world spinning. Before she got out of the cab, her cell phone rang. It was Maggie.

"Hey," she said. "Given any good advice today?" She smiled, knowing Maggie had said yesterday that she had her weekly syndicated advice column to write today for the *Houston Tribune.* People all across the nation read her column looking for relationship advice and inspiration — just like she'd done.

"Oh, I hope so. Someone has written in a second time, and, well, I feel like it's a very important letter. I'm praying I'm giving sound advice. I'm a little worried, but that's where I have to trust my instincts. And the Lord."

"It sounds like a lot on your shoulders."

Maggie sighed. "Sometimes. But I love it,

and I always remind them that this is just me as a friend, that I'm not a professional."

"I think they know that." Cassidy understood. When she'd been struggling with her marriage and her problems, she'd almost written to Maggie's advice column herself and asked for advice. She hadn't had a friend she wanted to confide in and she really needed one. All of her friends were "their" friends, and in truth, when she thought back on it, she realized she'd been pretty isolated at times. Jack "worked" late so much that she stayed home most of the time. What was the use of talking to anyone, anyway?

"I just want to help. But anyway, why I called . . . Everyone can be here tomorrow night, so we want to invite you for dinner finally. Will that work? We leave the next morning for three days and then we'll be back for the Fourth, but it'll be hard to know everyone's schedules that weekend and I don't want to put off having you over another week. Please say you can come."

Cassidy laughed. "I'll come. I can't wait."

"Great! We are so excited. Around six. Nothing elaborate, just dinner and company."

"Sounds good. I'll bring some peaches."

"Oh yay. Do you have a lot?"

"It looks like plenty, with more on the way."

"You be careful out there by yourself." Maggie sounded worried.

"I'm fine. I better get busy. See you tomorrow." She was smiling as she pocketed her phone and pulled her tailgate open. She pulled the large wash bucket she'd found in the barn to the edge of the truck bed and left it there, then grabbed one of the smaller red buckets and strode to the first tree.

She hadn't made it out to work around the tree trunks since she found Duce on Sunday, but she was just as careful. So far she hadn't seen even a glimpse of another stinkin' snake or a wild hog. And that was fine by her. A gun is what she needed. Just in case. She knew Aunt Roxie had a shotgun that used to be hidden in her closet. Cassidy was going to get that gun and learn how to shoot it. Maybe she'd ask someone to show her. Maybe Jarrod might do that for her.

And so within seconds of beginning to pick the peaches again, her thoughts went directly back to Jarrod. She still couldn't believe she'd told him about Jack.

Why had she exposed her personal humiliation to him? Because that was what it was.

And yet he'd vehemently called Jack the fool.

She pulled a plump golden peach from the tree and absently placed it in the red bucket, then reached for another one. Jarrod hadn't thought she was the fool.

She couldn't say she agreed with him, but he'd been pretty convincing, and remembering the look on his face caused her pulse to race once more. He'd been serious. There was no way to hide that kind of sincerity.

But still. That didn't change anything.

After Jarrod left Cassidy's, he went into Kerrville to the sporting goods store. He bought a few supplies, then went straight home. He had some work to do and stake-outs to begin. He'd fill Cassidy in on the rustlers tomorrow night, and maybe if he was lucky he'd know more about them after tonight. He'd at least know he was more prepared. Going to the barn, he saddled his horse, then led him to the house where he tied him to the porch post while he went in to grab a bed roll and fill his saddlebags with supplies. He also took a couple of canteens of water, which he tossed over his shoulder as he grabbed his gun and extra ammunition.

He didn't call Tru or Bo. Tru had a major

exhibition coming up and Bo had an over-load of stirrup orders he and his staff had to meet. No, this was Jarrod's area of the business, and both his brothers had held up their end of the bargain bringing in income to pay off the loans. And up to this point Jarrod knew he'd done a good job keeping the ranch afloat. But now, with it being time to sell cattle and turn a profit, everything he'd been working for was in jeopardy. If he didn't stop the stealing, at the rate the loss was adding up they could be in trouble again with the last loans.

And though he hated to admit it, he couldn't let any of his men in on what he was doing. He had no idea if someone had fooled him. Whoever was committing these acts of thievery had a mile radius, and that meant to Jarrod that it could be anyone. Even one of his men.

The only problem with him doing it all himself was that the ranch wasn't small. And he had to figure out when and where they might strike before he could catch them.

That was going to be about as easy as finding the proverbial needle in a haystack.

Within thirty minutes from the time he'd arrived home, and with daylight burning, he settled the saddlebags behind his saddle and rammed his rifle into the sheath. After he led Tracer into the pasture and closed the gate, Jarrod mounted up. The saddle creaked as he settled into it, and he looked around the land Pops had worked so hard for.

Determination tightened his gut. "Let's ride, Tracer," he said, and with the mere touch of his knees the gelding took off at a lope.

They had a lot of ground to cover going cross country, but Tracer was up for the challenge and so was Jarrod.

Tuesday morning Cassidy was pleased to find Duce sitting in the doorway of her bedroom when she woke. "Hey there, boy. Aren't you pushing it a little?" It was good to see his readiness to get well. She climbed out of bed and was glad to see her hip was finally back to normal too.

She sat on the floor and scratched the dog between the ears, then gave him a back scratch. She found he was putty in her hands after that.

"You like this, I see." She laughed as he nudged her for more. "We are going to get on well." Thankfully he'd figured out what the doggie door was for and had been getting up and going to the bathroom outside.

He just hadn't been real excited about it. But today she watched him through the window as she made coffee. Despite the stitches, he ambled across the yard a fairly good distance out before taking care of business. This was very good news indeed.

When he was done he came as far as the porch, curled up on the rug, and there he stayed. She walked to the open doorway. "So are you telling me you're done with this inside stuff?"

He wagged his tail and raised his eyes to look at her, but didn't bother to lift his head from his crossed paws.

"Well, if you're happy, I'm happy."

Taking her coffee, she walked to the living room and studied the walls.

To her surprise, Duce padded through the kitchen into the dark room to sit down next to her. He studied the room too.

"You know what, big guy? It's time to paint." She took a couple more sips of her hot coffee, set the cup on a table, and started moving furniture into the middle of the room. This could not wait any longer. This room needed sunshine and color. The rose kitchen would be next, but today the ugly green had to go.

After she'd managed to get the couch and chairs moved, she changed into paint clothes and wrangled her morning hair into a clip before stuffing a ball cap over the top. The song "Wild Thang" played in her head as she tamed the mass, and she wondered if she should cut it. It did drive her crazy sometimes.

She drove to the superstore on the outskirts of town. Hoping not to run into anyone she knew, she tugged her ball cap low and ducked through the store to the paint area, grabbed the color she wanted, and managed to get out without seeing anyone. She was back home painting before ten o'clock.

"Betcha didn't think I could get back here so quick, did ya?" she said to Duce. He was sitting in the doorway, watching her. He was a good dog, but she could tell by the sadness and the wariness in him that he'd not been in a good home.

"You need to hold your head up, little man," she said as she rolled the pale-yellow paint over the aged ugly green that had been on the walls for forever. "You need to start being happy. Just like me. It's time to stop looking back and look forward. You and me, buddy. You and me."

Duce's chin tilted and one ear quirked as if listening to everything she said.

She was starting to feel better. The anger

she felt at Jack was still there, deep down, but she was doing okay. She didn't know how to get rid of those feelings, but she could compartmentalize them from the rest of her life. And it was going great.

Great.

"Can a cowboy come in?"

She yelped and spun around, paint roller in hand. Jarrod stood in the front doorway. "You scared me."

"Sorry. Didn't mean to. I saw the front door opened as I was riding by. Duce has just lost points in the guard dog department. He looked over his shoulder when I rode up and never barked a note."

"He's a softy." Cassidy put her paint roller in the pan, then walked over to the door. To deny that she was glad to see him would be a lie. "He's moving around more today. Obviously feeling better."

"Good." A slow smile eased up the corners of his mouth. "Maybe when he's more active he'll be a watch dog too."

"Maybe so. You rode over?" He looked tired, and he had a five o'clock shadow despite its being ten in the morning. He looked very good, though. She put the brakes on those thoughts.

"I did. I was passing by on my way back to the house this morning. I was on a

208

stakeout last night."

"Stakeout? That was not what I was expecting to hear you say. Stakeouts are for watching for illegal activity, right? Or is that what you call it when you're watching for a calf to be born or something?"

His expression turned intense. "That's why I stopped by. We have a situation that just developed on Friday. Seems we have rustlers."

Cassidy digested the information slowly. "But do they even still do that?"

"They do. A lot more than you realize. We met with the investigators last week after I'd already realized I had missing stock and suspected rustlers were the reason. They confirmed with their data that a ring they were tracking was now in this area."

"So they took some of your cattle?"

"Yes."

"I'm sorry." She wiped her hands on a rag and stuffed it in her back pocket. "Did they get a lot?"

"A trailer load."

"So let me guess, you did a stakeout to see if they'd hit that same spot again?"

"I did. But I'm not broadcasting that information, so I'd appreciate it you'd keep that to yourself."

"Sure. Why do I get the feeling you've got

more to tell?"

"No, that's basically it. I just wanted to let you know this is going on because it's probably going to get out around town soon, and I didn't want you to hear it secondhand. If you hear or see anything suspicious, let me know. What we know is this is an organized group. This isn't a bunch of kids or goofballs. They know what they're doing and they're good. But Jake and the proper agents have a bead on them, and I think it's only a matter of time until they're caught. I'm just not patient enough to leave it completely up to them. Nor do I care to lose any more livestock. I want you to be aware of the situation for your own safety."

Cassidy didn't know what to think. "I'll keep my eyes open."

"Good. I'll ride on home now. I'm ready for a shower. Did I hear you were coming to the house for dinner tonight?"

"I am. I wasn't sure if you would be there."

"Why do you think I came back from my stakeout?"

"Because you were tired and needed a shower."

"Because you are coming to dinner. What if I pick you up? There's no use us both driving when we're going the same direction."

"No, you don't need to do that."

He scowled. "So we're back to you telling me what I need to do and don't need to do."

"No, it's just that you have better things to do than cart me around."

"I think you're afraid of me. I want to pick you up. I'll come by at six." Three strides and he was off the porch, and within seconds he was almost to his horse.

"But —" *Afraid of him, my foot.*

"No buts, Cassidy. I'll be here." He never stopped to look back or anything. Just climbed onto his horse and rode away looking straight ahead.

Cassidy scowled. "Duce, the man is a bulldozer when he wants his way." As if to show his great interest, Duce curled up in the doorway, placed his chin on his crossed paws, and closed his eyes. "Oh right, so you don't want to hear what I have to say. Fine friend you are."

But as she began rolling on paint again, her mind stuck on Jarrod . . . and the knowledge that in just a few hours she'd be spending the evening with him.

She began humming as she worked.

# 16

Jarrod had placed hunting cameras controlled by motion in several areas of his ranch. One place was the tree near the makeshift pen the rustlers had made. They might not come back to that pen, but if they did he might be able to get a shot of something useful. He'd also placed cameras near herds and in some other places he remotely thought might work for a great shot. And before he picked up Cassidy he told Gil where he wanted cattle moved in the morning. The traps were set.

Now he would wait. His efforts led to no sleep last night as covering ground on horseback was time consuming, but in his mind, it was the easiest way to do what he wanted in case his place was being watched.

He'd stayed in the shadows and he hadn't used a light. If there was one thing he knew, it was this property. He'd roamed it since before he should have been allowed to roam it on his own. And then later, camping out on the property had been a favorite pastime he and his brothers shared.

His mind wasn't on rustlers now. Cassidy rode beside him in the truck and he was completely distracted.

She'd just about knocked his socks off when he picked her up. She had on a pair of white jeans and a pink blouse that reminded him of spun cotton candy. And he had a big weakness for cotton candy.

"You are beautiful." He couldn't help himself.

She stiffened at his compliment. "Thank you. I got the room finished."

"That's great. Makin' progress." He wondered why compliments bothered her. Was it just from him or all men? He turned onto the blacktop. The main headquarters of the ranch was on the opposite side of the ranch from where he lived. They traveled three miles, then turned left onto another country road. Finally the large metal entrance of the ranch came into view in the distance. Pops's home and the main complex of the massive ranch could be seen up the hill.

"What did you do on stakeout last night?"

She'd thought about him — or at least about what he'd been doing. He liked that. "I put out hunting cameras. But again, this is totally confidential. I haven't even told Bo and Tru so, again, I'd appreciate it if you'd keep this to yourself."

She looked pensive. "Sure. But surely you don't think they would —"

"No. Not at all. I haven't told them because I don't want to bother them right now. Tru leaves for the exhibition in the morning and Bo has a major order deadline to get out. This is my problem. They don't need to be bothered."

"Whatever you say."

He smiled at her agreement. They rode in silence until he reached the entrance of the ranch. He drove between the steel gate with the massive steel overhang that had the ranch name in logo form on it, a four with a heart extending from the long side of the numeral. His grandmother had come up with the design. As they drove up the lane, he saw Cassidy straighten, looking up the lane at Pops's home on the right. Past Pops's home and on the left was the red barn that held Bo's Four of Hearts Ranch Stirrups business. And then a hundred yards farther down were the stable and arena where Tru's horse training business was housed. Jarrod wasn't seeing any of it as his hands tightened on the steering wheel.

"The place looks great. I remember coming here when we were kids and your pops taught me to ride."

"Yeah," he said. "But things are a little different now. The red barn is the stirrup business. The stable is Tru's domain. And he and Maggie live in the foreman's house on past the arena."

"Abby told me she and Bo live with Pops now."

He parked the truck. "I hate that he has to have someone living with him." He stared out at the pasture beside the house.

"Yeah, I get that," she said quietly. And then she reached out and touched his hand that was still tightly clasped around the steering wheel. "He's a good man. I know how hard this must be for you."

Jarrod went completely still. Looking at her hand on his, his throat went dry at her touch and her words. He met her gaze. "Extremely. But if there is one thing Pops never did it was hide from anything. He faced his life full-on. I didn't always do that, and I regret it." If she only knew how much.

She pulled her hand away, looking as if she wished she hadn't touched him, and her fingers shook as she unbuckled her seat belt and rushed out of the truck. Her touch had simply been out of comfort, but he wanted it to be more. His resolve intensified as he followed her up the back steps.

Her red curls were dancing between her stiffened shoulder blades with each purposeful step she took away from him.

"Hey there," Maggie called, opening the door before they could knock. "We are so glad you're here." She hugged Cassidy like they'd known each other forever.

"I am glad to make it. Goodness, it's been a very long time since I was in this house."

Jarrod took off his hat and hung it on the hat rack as the two women chattered together faster than bees could swarm.

"I think I'll go join the fellas." He held Cassidy's gaze for a moment. Electricity sparked between them like lightning hitting a steel rod. Pain or uncertainty or something — distrust maybe — flashed in those eyes before she looked away. He forced his boots to move, carrying him out of the danger zone.

Cassidy was so glad not to be alone with Jarrod any longer. From the moment he'd looked at her like she was the prettiest female on earth she'd been a bit befuddled.

And then, just now, he'd had a hungry look in his eyes. As if he needed her.

As if he wanted her more than breath.

Her insides were quaking with the intensity of what she thought she saw.

Jarrod wasn't a man who showed his emotions. He would have made a great poker player. So she knew what she'd just experienced was rare.

And that shook her immensely.

But Jack had also been able to hide his emotions, she reminded herself. Even after she'd finally figured out his lying, cheating ways, she'd sometimes fall for his lies — late nights at the office, business trips working on mergers and acquisitions — and when she questioned exactly who he was merging with, he'd accused her of imagining things and being overly jealous. He said he loved her and he worked hard to provide for her and the kids they would have soon.

Kids. She closed her eyes to shut out the heartache of that. She'd finally realized that almost everything he said was either a lie or a carefully concocted word set intended on getting her to do what he wanted. Having a wife looked good to his bosses. Having one he could dupe continually and still have his icing too . . . well, that worked well for him. And in his mind he was justified. After all, she got the blessing of his presence in her life so that made everything right. What a joke.

*Narcissist.* She'd heard the term and

looked it up. It had been as if she'd been reading Jack's biography. And he wasn't alone. People like him had an MO, a mode of operating.

Okay, so even though she wasn't interested in ever having a relationship with a man again, that didn't mean all men fell into that category, and certainly not Jarrod. Nothing about him was narcissistic.

Just because he had control over his facial expressions and his emotions didn't mean he was a manipulative, lying jerk. She had to make certain she didn't let herself believe bad things about people without justification. That wasn't fair of her just because of what she'd been put through.

Even if Jarrod kissed her and broke her heart, she understood he and Jack were nothing alike.

She watched Jarrod walk toward the room where the laughter was coming from. If she remembered right, that was the den, where all of Pops's trophies from his years of cutting horse competition were. Her heart was pounding.

Why had she reached out and touched him? It sent all the wrong signals. But it had been a reaction to the pain she saw in his eyes when he talked about his grandfather. It had not been meant to send a message that she was looking for anything from him. Certainly not that temperature rising, completely unnerving look she'd just glimpsed.

"You're looking mighty troubled," Maggie said, drawing Cassidy from her thoughts.

Cassidy looked at her. "No, just confused."

A smile played at the corners of Maggie's lips. "Jarrod's a wonderful man, you know. I'm really not certain why he's never married. Like with all of these Monahan men, that baffled me. Though I am eternally grateful Tru didn't marry sooner. He says his heart was waiting on me."

"That's wonderful for the two of you. Really. But me, I'm not —"

"Not what." Abby had come into the room. "The men are all entertaining Levi so I thought I'd come see what you girls are getting into." She looked from Maggie to Cassidy. "Not what?"

"Cassidy is confused about her feelings for Jarrod, I think."

"I'm *not.*" What was Maggie saying?

Maggie grinned. "I can hope, can't I? You bring out emotion in him I haven't seen before. I saw that scorcher that passed between the two of you just now." Maggie waved a hand as if fanning herself.

*"Really,"* Abby said. "And I missed it."

"No, it wasn't like that."

Maggie cocked an eyebrow. "Careful, you are about to tell a fib."

Cassidy shifted uncomfortably. Abby and Maggie chuckled together like they were sharing a joke.

"What?" She looked from one to the other.

"Nothing," Abby said. "You should come say hi to everyone. Stop looking so tense."

"That's right." Maggie gave her a gentle nudge with her elbow. "It's okay. I didn't mean to make you uncomfortable, so relax and forget what I was saying. We're going to have a fun evening."

Cassidy wasn't so sure about that now. But she forced a weak smile and tried to hide the sudden need to run — from herself.

The men were all sitting around watching Levi build a tower with blocks on the floor in front of Pops. Immediately she felt a little better. The toddler was adorable, and he beamed up at them as they entered.

Pops did, too, as did all the fellas.

"Hi, Cassidy," Bo called, then shot her a grin as Abby walked over and sank onto the ottoman beside his chair, leaned back against his chest, and he hugged her. "We're glad you're here."

"We sure are, Cassidy." Tru got up to welcome her. "Great to see you. Take my seat there beside Pops. I'll sit over here with Maggie."

"Uh, okay. Um, it's good to be here." She wasn't exactly sure about that now either, seeing as he'd abandoned his seat for her and that meant she was now about to be sitting next to Jarrod on the couch. He was watching her reaction to her dilemma, and she was quite certain he knew she didn't want to sit beside him. But there was no other place.

Jarrod's gaze held hers as she carefully sat down on the end of the couch, which wouldn't have been bad if Jarrod hadn't been sitting in the center of the couch. Instead of sitting at the far end from his brother, he'd obviously sat in the middle so he could be closer to Levi and Pops.

She tried not to think about him, or the fact that she was now sitting closer to him than she had been in the truck on the way over here.

She shifted her thoughts to Pops and the tot. They looked like two kids on the playground. Each was infatuated with the other. Kind of like she suddenly felt about Jarrod.

*Drat.* What was she thinking?

Levi carried a block over to Pops and grinned at him. "You have," he said, as if even the toddler knew he was dealing with something precious that needed special attention.

"Hi, Pops. It's good to see you again," Cassidy said.

Pops looked up and studied her for a moment. "I met you. Before."

She could almost see his mind working to find her in his memory. "Yes, sir. The other day at the vet clinic. I'm Roxie's niece."

A light went on in his eyes. "Roxie, it's been awhile."

"Oh, no, I'm Roxie's niece. Cassidy," she added gently. He frowned and confusion slackened his expression. She felt bad for having corrected him.

"Pops and Levi build empires with those blocks." Maggie gave her an encouraging smile. Cassidy had never dealt with Alzheimer's and wasn't at all sure how to behave. She took her lead from everyone else.

"Abby, Cassidy spent a lot of summers here. Pops taught her to ride." Bo grinned.

"That's right," Tru said. "How many times did you get to come down here for a visit when you were a kid, Cassidy? I remember your aunt Roxie would get so excited when she knew you were coming for a stay."

"I think I got to come four times . . . or maybe it was five times."

"Six."

Every eye turned to Jarrod. Cassidy saw a slight darkening of his skin at the base of his neck and knew for a man like Jarrod that was about as close to a blush as he was ever going to get.

"I remember," he said, looking at her with stormy eyes. "The first time you were ten and you crawled through the fence looking like a redheaded, wild child with that curly mop of yours. You nearly scared us to death when you came bursting out of nowhere."

Everyone laughed and he even smiled slightly at the memory. She cringed at what they must have thought of her. She'd been a disaster as a child. She couldn't look away from him, even as embarrassed as she was.

"Then two summers later you showed up again and drove us crazy trailing around behind us when we were trying to work. You wouldn't go away and you followed us until we had to take you on a roundup. You spooked the cattle and caused a stampede."

It was her turn to blush. "I remember. I was twelve by then and a complete disaster. I had forgotten a little of that trail ride. On purpose, I think." She laughed and so did everyone else.

"I remember that," Bo said, jumping in. "Abby and Maggie, y'all should have seen her. She was trying so hard, but she couldn't ride very well. She got points for guts and perseverance, though."

"Yes, she did," Tru interjected. "But her horse got spooked and made a run for the woods. It scared the cattle, which broke into a stampede, and Jarrod had to go chase her down and pull her horse to a stop before poor Cassidy broke her neck."

Cassidy's huge crush on the good-looking eldest Monahan brother had been rock solid after that. Six years difference in age as adults wasn't that much, but for a teen like Jarrod it was a lifetime. Needless to say, he hadn't thought of her as anything but the little girl he felt sorry for and was kind to. Her stomach tipped remembering how that had felt for her . . . young love. It had been excruciating.

"You're welcome to come over and ride anytime," Tru said, bringing her back into the conversation that she'd let lapse.

"Thank you. That sounds fun. I just have a lot to get done right now."

"Riding's good." Pops broke in with a teasing glint in his eyes. He reminded her so much of Jarrod, though Jarrod was even more serious than she'd remembered him. And from what she could tell he didn't smile enough. She wondered about that.

Was it her? Or maybe the pressures he was under.

The evening passed quickly and it was fun. They shared lots of teasing and memories. Jarrod was noticeably quiet, but no one acted as if that was abnormal.

Conversation wasn't all about her, thankfully. Maggie and Tru talked about the new baby and how the teen mother would get to come and be a part of the baby's life if she wanted to. "That's very important to me," Maggie said. "It's not for everyone. But Jenna, one of the girls I'm very close with, is in college right now, and she goes periodically to see her baby. It's working out wonderfully. But others don't want to know the parents of their babies. They don't feel like it's fair to the baby. It's a tough call."

"But this is how we wanted to do it," Tru said, lifting Maggie's hand to his lips and kissing it.

Oddly, the sweet, loving gesture made Cassidy's heart ache.

They were gathered around the dinner table, enjoying the enchiladas and rice and beans Maggie had prepared, talking about the Fourth of July celebration.

Jarrod's gaze had met hers then, causing her heart to gallop. He'd looked away quickly and had been careful not to look at her again after that.

When the evening was over she thanked everyone and then Jarrod grabbed his hat and led the way to his truck.

He held the door for her, not saying anything as she got in, but her mouth went dry as she brushed past him. As he strode around the truck, she feared when he got into the cab he would be able to hear her heart thundering.

# 17

Jarrod cranked the engine and drove. He concentrated on the road ahead of him and not the woman beside him.

"It was a wonderful night," Cassidy said, breaking the strained silence between them. Her voice was soft in the dark truck. Jarrod thought he heard a slight tremble in the tone.

"Yes. It was." He managed to speak, but his voice cracked on the word *yes.* Dinner had been torture.

And now they had a ten-mile drive back to their places.

"Oh, um, just so you know, Jasper is going to be spraying over near your place this week. Like I said, he found some organic solution we're going to try."

"Thank you again."

"You're welcome."

Silence again.

They were nearing his house when he

noticed a glimmer of light in the distance. He slowed and studied the light. It disappeared somewhere out in the dark trees.

"Is that a light out there in the pasture?"

"You saw that too?" he asked.

"It was faint but I saw something. Do you think it's the rustlers?"

On impulse he whipped into his driveway and drove up the lane, then clicked his lights off. He quickly turned the truck around in the dark and headed back down the lane. He was glad this truck ran on gasoline and that he hadn't been driving one of his Dodge Ram diesel trucks he hauled cattle trailers with. They were loud.

"What are you doing, Jarrod?"

"I'm dropping you off and then I'm going to do some tracking." His gun was still behind the seat, unloaded but ready. He'd decided the other day to keep one with him at all times. It was a necessity on the ranch in the summer anyway, in case of snakes or coyotes endangering his livestock. Or rustlers.

"No."

"I'm going after them, Cassidy."

"I know that. I meant no, don't drop me off. I'm going with you."

"No."

Except for her porch light and his headlights, it was pitch-black out as it was a cloudy night. A full moon was a long way off and tonight he was glad. He figured rustlers might not cotton to full moons so much. Of course, if they did his cameras would really like it.

He stopped beside her back door sidewalk. "I'll call you tomorrow," he said. She crossed her arms and didn't move. "Come on, Cassidy, hop out. I'll let you know what I find."

"I'm not getting out. You're losing their trail."

He could make her silhouette out from the back porch light. "Don't be stubborn —"

"Don't tell me what to do, Jarrod Monahan. I am not letting you ride off out there alone. I am going and that is final."

The clock was ticking. "Cassidy, I'm going to come over there and pull you out of the truck if you don't get out this minute. This could be dangerous."

"You just try to pull me out. I will kick you so hard you will not be able to follow those rustlers 'cause you will be seeing stars."

He started laughing. "Are you serious? Come on, Cassidy."

"I am as serious as it gets. I am not getting out of this truck."

And he wasn't going to manhandle her either. "Fine. Stubborn woman," he grumbled. He shut off his headlights and retraced their path back down the lane. He drove down the dark, deserted road, ready to pull off onto the grass the minute he saw headlights coming. When he reached the first cattle guard, he drove over it slowly and then down the gravel path.

His jaw hurt. He'd clamped down on it so hard keeping his mouth shut. Jarrod drove off the road after a little bit, not wanting to run into whoever might be out here. He pulled away from the gravel road, hitting a rut or two in the dark.

When he hit one a little harder than expected, they were both jostled in their seats. He heard a thump.

"Ow! That was my head, cowboy."

He didn't bother to apologize. She should have stayed home.

He kept driving toward the trees. Once there he drove along the edge, searching for any sign of light. "Since you're here you might as well help me look for their light."

"I had planned on it. I'm certainly not sitting over here eating bonbons and getting a manicure."

"Fine by me," he snapped.

There was nothing out there. They had driven about as far as they could get without following a trail through the woods to the other side of the trees, and he wasn't real sure he wanted to do that. He wished he had his horse.

"I bet you wish you were on your horse," she said in the darkness, as if reading his mind.

"Yeah, I do."

"Maybe we should go mount up. This isn't that far from your house."

"That won't work. They'd be gone by then." He halted the truck and stared through the trees. He'd almost given up when he caught a glimmer of light.

"There." Cassidy spoke the instant he saw it.

"Yeah, I see it." It was pretty far off. And that was what he needed to know. Slowly he directed the truck into the trees along the rutted path they seldom used. He wished he could chance a light to see if it looked like he was running over their tracks. They could have used one of the other trails through the trees.

"Can we get to them without them knowing we're there?"

"Maybe. But if they see us, I've got protection, so don't worry."

231

"You mean your gun." He heard dread in her tone.

"Yup. These aren't people to mess around with, Cassidy. That was why I tried to leave you behind. This is a group of criminals who, we think, are doing this across several counties. Either that or we have a sudden rash of rustlers all over the place. More than likely it's a single group. But what they are doing is illegal. They know what they are looking at if they get caught. And it's not community service. That makes them dangerous."

"Oh."

"You should have done what I asked and gone home."

"I'm here, so that's wasted breath. Besides, you might need me."

Oh, he needed her all right, but not as a reckless tagalong. He'd recognized clearly there in Pops's den that he wanted her in his life for good. And he knew his brothers knew it too.

He would never hear the end of it after tonight. And now, here he was off in the pasture trying to round up rustlers instead of standing on her porch trying to figure out a way to get a kiss from her.

It was past time to try that kiss over again. And this time he meant business and he wasn't backing down.

They made it through the trees and crept across the pasture. He prayed the sliver of moon would remain behind the clouds. He made it to another string of trees and could see the lights up ahead. He put the truck in park and turned off the engine.

"Now what?" Cassidy asked.

He reached into the backseat and pulled his shotgun onto his lap.

"Open the glove compartment and hand me those shells, please."

She didn't move.

"Cassidy, come on."

"You could get hurt."

"They're stealing my cattle. They're the ones who need to be worrying."

He reached across her, opened the glove compartment himself, and snagged a box of shells. "You stay here." He pulled several from the box and stuffed them into his pockets.

"No, I'm coming with you."

He lost his patience. "No, you will stay here, in the safety of this truck. And don't come out until I get back here. You could accidently get shot. I'm serious."

He exited the truck, and as he lightly closed his door, making as little noise as possible, he heard the passenger door opening.

"Stop," he hissed. "Stay."

She stormed to stand beside him in the darkness. "Let's go."

He stared down at her. Now that his eyes were adjusting to the darkness he could tell hers were flashing. "This is ridiculous. You are so messing up."

"Payback then, buddy. Now stop yakking and let's go."

Cassidy couldn't believe how stubborn she was being. But she wasn't about to miss out on this adventure. Or was she missing out on making certain there was payback in this too? He'd not liked her bucking his authority, but she had news for him. She was not a schoolgirl anymore, wearing her heart on her sleeve.

And she didn't want him out here all by himself. His brothers wouldn't know where he was in the morning if something was to happen to him, and she just felt like two was better than one. Not that she was going to be a great help.

They were creeping through some underbrush and her insides were trembling with each step. Creepy crawlers might be out tonight. She tried to follow his exact boot steps because her sandals were not the best choice of footwear for this job.

She realized they were walking along a ravine. "Don't fall into that," Jarrod commented.

"I-I won't," she said, totally insulted. Just as her foot slipped and she went down.

She let out a small squeak, hit the ground hard, and rolled. All she could think about was the snakes. Forget the fact that she had no idea where she was going.

Jarrod spun when he heard Cassidy's squeal. Somehow she'd managed not to scream as she disappeared over the edge of the ravine. He dove after her, gripping his gun, glad it was still unloaded as he moved down the steep incline. He could hear her grunting each time she crashed through the underbrush.

"Cassidy," he whispered as loudly as he dared. "Where are you?"

"I'm over here," she groaned, and he angled toward her soft grumble.

"Where?" He used the screen of his phone for a little light. They were down in the ravine, so he figured they were safe from being seen here.

"Over here."

He saw her then, sprawled on the muddy

bank of the stream that ran at the base of the ravine.

He crouched down beside her. "Are you okay?"

"I'm fine." He helped her sit up. She was covered in mud and her hair . . .

"I'm getting dadgum tired of rolling around on the ground all the time. It's like I can't stay on my own two feet these days. It's really ticking me off."

He chuckled. He couldn't help it. "Well, look at the bright side. You're not lying on top of a cactus, so you're doing good."

She grunted and spat a leaf out of her mouth. "Yeah, but my rump hit more rocks on the way down than I care to count. I have a feeling I'm going to relive each and every one of them come morning."

He cringed. "I hate to agree, but it's true. And I hate to say it, but I tried to get you to stay home —"

"Right. Don't say it. Now help me stand up and let's go find some rustlers. One thing's for sure. I've officially got my camo gear on now."

"True." He holstered his phone, took her hand, and tugged her up. She came easily, despite having slid down the incline. His heart was still thundering with fear, and before he could stop himself he'd yanked

236

her into his arms and held her close, not giving a fiddle that she was getting his clothes muddy. It was a mistake. He knew it, but there was no stopping it.

She went still in his arms. "I'm glad you're not hurt," he said gruffly into her hair. She tilted her head and he found himself looking into her eyes. Even in the near black of the night he could see the whites and the flash of her irises.

He could feel her breaths coming in short intakes as she continued to stand still in his arms. The last time he'd held her like this there had been fireworks exploding, but tonight it was only darkness. Yet he knew if he lowered his head and kissed her there would be fireworks again.

"Jarrod," she whispered. "The butt of the gun is digging into my side."

He jerked his arms away, having forgotten that he still gripped the gun in one hand. "Sorry," he grunted this time. "We better go."

"That's exactly what I was thinking."

They moved silently up the hill, through the long grass and rough ground, and Cassidy never complained. Just as they reached the top he caught the lights of a truck in the distance, disappearing into the trees.

Cassidy spoke first. "They're going to be

off the property soon."

"You're right, we have to hurry."

By the time they jogged to his truck and he drove as fast as he dared back the way they'd come, the other truck and trailer was a good distance away. Once they made it to the road he could barely make out the trailer lights disappearing down the hardtop.

"Faster, Jarrod! We're going to lose them!"

He'd already hit the gas and she slammed back against the seat. "Buckle up," he warned. In the dim light of the dashboard he saw her fumble for the seat belt. At least she wasn't arguing about that.

Tires spinning, he drove across the pasture, careening over ruts and thick clumps of thornbushes that desperately needed spraying. He made it to the exit at last, and once he was on the road he turned on his lights and took chase. But they had long gone.

"Well, that just stinks." Cassidy glared down the empty road. She turned fiery eyes on him. "So now what? Did they have cattle in the back of that truck? Your cattle?"

The woman was hot. "I imagine so. I'll have to check it out tomorrow in the daylight. That's one of the places I had the cattle put and there are a couple of cameras in place. Maybe I'll have something on one of them."

"I want to check with you."

"Cassidy, maybe you should stay home and tend to all that you've got going on."

"I've got all summer. There's no rush. Besides, I've got a bone to pick with these dudes. I'm going to have a few bruises tomorrow and I blame them personally."

He cocked his head and studied her. In the dim light of the cab he could see that her hair had gathered a few things on its trip down the hillside. Twigs and leaves were matted up in that mass, and there was also a scrape on the nape of her neck he could see under the mud.

He reached out and touched it. "You're bleeding. Not bad, but you scraped your neck."

She waved a hand in the air. "Phew, it's nothing. I'm tougher than I look. Believe me."

He chuckled, then turned the truck around. It was time to take her home. "You're something, that's for certain. I haven't exactly got you figured out, Cass. You've changed."

"Jarrod Monahan, are you just now figuring that out? Because if you have even the slightest idea that I'm still that naïve, poor little neighbor girl you used to know, then you don't know me at all."

He turned into her drive and glanced her way. Conviction not only rang in her voice but in her eyes and the set of her jaw.

"Oh, I noticed," he drawled, pulling to a stop.

She arched an eyebrow. "I'm so over having folks feeling sorry for me. I'll see you tomorrow."

Before he could say more, she hopped from the truck and strode to her house. At the door she held up a hand in good-bye and slipped inside. He could see Duce waiting for her as she went in.

All the way home he should have been thinking about a plan to catch rustlers, but he wasn't. He was thinking about Cassidy.

And she was right. She wasn't the girl he'd once known. She was a full-grown woman, and if she thought he hadn't noticed that then *she* didn't know *him.*

# 18

"I'm selling the Sweet Dreams," Pebble announced from the beauty shop chair at the Cut Up and Roll Hair Salon on Wednesday morning. It was her weekly visit.

"Do what?" Reba gasped and dropped the bottle of hot-pink nail polish she'd been holding. It hit the floor and splattered its contents all about.

Clara Lyn's mouth fell open. "Hold on," she declared, raising a hand into the air, the horde of bangle bracelets jangling in chorus. "Just hold on. Surely I did not just hear you correctly. I could have sworn you just said you were selling the Sweet Dreams."

Reba scrambled to her knees and was mopping up the mess with a white towel she'd snatched off her pedi-chair. She paused to gape at her partner. "Clara Lyn, there is nothing wrong with your hearing and you know it. She *did* say that. Pebble, why would you want to go and do a thing like that? You're joking, right?"

Pebble had known they would react this way. Known they'd be shocked by the idea. She had been at first, and that was why she'd waited a few days, prayed about it, and contemplated it. "I'm not joking. I'm serious. I'm about to go have Doobie and Doonie list it."

Her friends looked from her to each other, then back at her.

Clara Lyn hurried to the front door, flipped the Welcome sign to Closed, and yanked down the window blind. Then she spun back. "Are you sick? Is there something you haven't told us?"

"That's right." Reba halted her scrubbing. She pushed her blunt-cut brown hair behind her ear and stood up. "You can tell us. We're here for you."

Pebble had made a mess of this. "Girls. Girls. Please, sit down. I did not mean to put you both into a tizzy. I'm fine. Really."

They just stared at her.

"Go on, sit down and I'll explain."

Clara Lyn sank into the pedi-chair and Reba sat on her manicure stool. Both gave her expectant glares.

"We're all ears," Clara said. "Let's hear this crazy idea of yours."

"I am ready for something new in my life.

I'm ready to shake things up a bit. And do you realize that my every move for over thirty years has revolved around that motel?"

"But you love your motel." Reba rubbed her temple. "I am really confused."

"Are you having an after-mid-life crisis of some sort?" Clara Lyn asked. "I've read that it can happen later in life. Especially to someone like you who has always been a Steady Eddie."

Pebble giggled. She couldn't help it. "No, Clara Lyn, I am not having a crisis. Well, maybe a touch of one. I am a Steady Eddie. I like being that way too. But, well, I looked at my life and I could live to be a hundred. Do you know that is *over* thirty more years? I buried my Cecil nearly eleven years ago. And I'm still doing the same thing I was doing thirty years ago when he and I bought the motel. I love it. But I want to do something else now." And that was the truth.

Reba stood up, placed her hands on her hips, and eyed her. "This has something to do with that scoundrel Rand Ratliff, doesn't it?"

"I knew it." Clara Lyn slapped a jingling hand to her thigh. "Have you decided to marry Rand?"

"No." This was getting out of hand. "Look,

girls. This is not about Rand. This is about me. Rand is, well, he is recovering. I promised him that I would stand by and be his friend through his rehab, and I have. But that is all we are, friends. I can make a decision about my life that doesn't revolve around anyone but me." She stood up shaken and a little rattled that their reaction had been quite so overboard.

"Well, don't get all huffy," Clara gasped. "This is clearly unlike you, Pebble."

"She's right, Pebble. Are you sure you're okay?"

"I'm fine. Great, actually. Once I sell the motel I might just go on a cruise, or maybe I'll go to Tuscany. What do you girls say? Would you like to do a little traveling with me?"

"Oh." Reba gasped this time. "Well, that does sound fun. I have always wanted to go to Tuscany. You know, rent one of them little tiny cars and drive across the picturesque landscape —"

"Reba," Clara Lyn barked. "You couldn't fit into one of them little cars. Your head would ram the ceiling."

"We could rent a convertible. And I could too fit into one. That handsome hunk Russell Crowe fit into that tiny car in that movie he made over there. If he could fit so could I. We. We could all fit."

Pebble's heart lifted on a cloud of excitement. "Oh, Reba, certainly we could all fit."

"Well, I'm not too certain I could do a cruise," Clara Lyn said. "Sharks and all. But maybe I could fly over there and squeeze into that car with y'all."

They all stared at each other and then burst into laughter.

"Pebble," Clara Lyn said when they finally stopped laughing, "I still am not convinced selling the Sweet Dreams is going to make you happy, but maybe we should have done this traveling thing a long time ago."

"Oh, I agree," Reba said. "But I have to ask, and please don't get upset, but what about Rand? The man is clearly head over heels in love with you, Pebble. And he has been working hard to prove that to you. I have to say I've been hoping we'd be planning a wedding soon."

Pebble's smile faltered. "I care for Rand. But I'm not certain where he and I stand. I just know I'm ready for a change in my life, and this is where I'm starting."

Cassidy could hardly wait for Jarrod to come for her the next afternoon to go look at the rustlers' tracks. She called him and left a message on his machine to pick her up at the peach orchard. Every moment counted if she was going to get those peaches picked. She should have waited to paint and picked peaches yesterday, but she'd gotten a wild urge to paint and had gotten off track by giving in to it.

Now she was going to get more behind by going with Jarrod to hunt rustlers, but she couldn't help herself. And to tell the truth, she was a little bored with peaches. Just her and peaches to pick and quiet days alone were beginning to seem endless.

She'd ordered some supplies for her strawberries and was about to start work on getting the ground ready. She also had the cool cabinet to refurbish, and she'd begun thinking about how she could take a section of the barn and turn it into some sort of store for her fruit. But she thought she might actually start refurbishing furniture for resale as well. That would take up some of the time she was going to have on her hands over the coming years.

Thank goodness she had Duce. He was a great companion, and she was so glad to see him feeling much better. She could pick him up now and put him in the truck to ride along with her and he loved it. He'd hang his head out the window and let his tongue hang out as he lapped at the wind, like he was doing now. She laughed, and in response he barked with a wag of his tail. "You're my guy," she said, reaching across to pat his hip.

She realized it was time to get his stitches taken out. They were puckered and ready to be removed, and she cringed looking at the crisscross of thread. She hoped Jarrod hadn't been pulling her leg, because if he couldn't do this she was taking her dog to Doc. She wasn't having Duce suffer through a clumsy attempt at playing doctor.

Then again, if Jarrod said he could do something, she had a tendency to believe him. There was no reason for him to boast about something like that anyway. Jarrod wasn't one to boast. Jack was the one who had the overblown ego.

Reaching the orchard, she unloaded Duce and he followed her to the first tree, sitting on his haunches to watch her work. She had just started picking peaches when she heard a purr of an engine, and she glanced around thinking she would find Jarrod driving up. She was startled to find the ladies of the Cut Up and Roll Hair Salon, along with Pebble, come riding up in Reba's truck.

"Whoo hoo," Clara Lyn hollered out the window. "We came to help you pick peaches."

"But what about work at the salon?"

The ladies all clamored from the truck. They had on jeans and big shirts and colorful, floppy hats.

Reba strode her way, grinning. "Don't you worry about the salon. We are working tomorrow and that's plenty. We decided a little sunshine and helping out our neighbor was a great idea. A whole group of ladies wanted to come out and help, but we weren't sure how much you still had to get done."

"Looks like a lot," Clara Lyn huffed, hands on her hips as she studied the trees. "Land's sake, there's a bunch of these rascals."

Pebble looked wide-eyed as she stared up at the trees. "They are beautiful. Roxie would be proud to know she planted such a great orchard."

That made Cassidy smile bigger. "Yes, it would. Y'all look in my truck and grab a bucket."

Clara Lyn came her way as Reba and Pebble looked into the bed of the truck.

"Reba and I are really running an emergency intervention," she whispered to Cassidy. "Pebble is having a crisis of major proportion. She is putting the motel up for sale."

"Oh really," Cassidy whispered, worry filling her. "What's wrong? I can't believe she is doing that. What will she do?"

"It's Rand Ratliff. He told her he didn't want her to ever have to worry her pretty self about him falling off the wagon and ruining her life. That he was just going to be her friend from here on out and she wasn't to keep worrying that he was going to pressure her into marrying him ever again. Of course, she didn't tell us that at first. She just told us she was selling the Sweet Dreams and going to start traveling. Which is all well and good and we went along with it because, girl, we can have us some fun trips. But when she finally admitted what Rand had told her, we knew it had triggered all this. She said it didn't matter, but we know different. That man. I could just pinch his head off sometimes."

Cassidy was shocked. "Wow."

"Exactly. You get the gist of it all. Pebble loves that man and is worried about him. And I'm getting the feeling that she's mad at him too. Shh, here they come. I just wanted to fill you in on what's going on."

"This is so beautiful up here," Pebble said. "Oh, who is this?" She bent down and rubbed Duce's ears. "Is this that poor dog you rescued?"

"Yes, ma'am. He's doing better. See his stitches? Jarrod is supposed to remove them today or tomorrow."

Everyone looked at her.

Reba pushed her hair behind her ears and smiled. "Is Jarrod coming around very much?"

"Well, some. But he's a busy man."

"But he can be neighborly." Clara Lyn swatted at a bee and the bracelets on her arm jangled like chimes. "He is all alone out here, you know. Roxie used to say he was the catch of Wishing Springs. She was really fond of him."

That got Cassidy to wondering how close Jarrod had been to her aunt. Had he helped her out a lot?

As if she heard her thoughts, Reba spoke up.

"You know he's the one who found her in the garden. He came over every day and checked on her."

Cassidy's mouth dropped open. "No one ever told me that. He never told me that."

"Well," Clara Lyn offered, "It was a busy time. He is the fire chief, you know, so he tends to things. But his looking after her seemed personal to him."

"Yes," Reba added. "Because I know for a fact that Roxie always baked goods and sent

250

him homemade jams and such. Your aunt had a heart of gold and a love of the dirt and it made for terrible fingernails. She would come in once a month for me to try to undo some of the damage she had done to her poor hands. And she would talk."

Pebble nodded. "She was a dear friend to me too. And to Rand. She would always tell me he was a good man."

All eyes riveted on Pebble. She blushed and her blue eyes shadowed. "He just didn't ever completely trust that he could live life without a little liquor in him, I don't think."

There was a pause and everyone hung on her last words. If Rand had told Pebble he was done trying to woo her into marrying him, then the dynamic of their relationship had changed.

Knowing how Rand felt about the sweet lady, she also knew he must have really made a strong commitment to this. He loved her. And if he wasn't going to try to win her heart any longer, Cassidy couldn't help but be curious about what he was thinking. She made a note to drop by and check on him. Because despite all the years she'd been away, she had a soft spot for the man.

"Well," Clara Lyn said, "you need to relax about Rand. You two can just be friends. He can keep going to his AA meetings and, praise the good Lord, he can stay on the wagon and with the Lord's help and ours not fall off."

Reba picked a peach. "Doobie told me Rand got his six-month sober pin at the last meeting. He and Doonie went with him. They are a great support for him. There for the longest time they didn't take his drinking as seriously as they should have."

"None of us did." Clara pulled two peaches from the tree. "Why, it was as if we accepted that he got drunk sometimes and that was part of who he was. I know I was guilty of it. And all along poor Pebble was fighting the battle all by herself. I feel terrible."

"I've told you to stop feeling guilty." Pebble looked at Clara Lyn and then at Cassidy. "It is true everyone wasn't as worried as they should have been. But when it all came to the surface, everyone jumped in and gave him strong support. I am very appreciative of that."

Cassidy had a heaviness in her chest. She'd had friends who had to have known she was struggling with how Jack behaved, but they never mentioned it or reached out to her. Instead, they all pretended there wasn't a big white elephant in the room —

his infidelity. She was certain many of them knew about it. For all she knew, he may have hit on some of them.

She decided to speak up.

"Sometimes it just takes one person to stand up and help others see the error of judgment." She held Pebble's gaze and felt her smile all the way to the cold core of her heart.

"I believe so. But in truth I wasn't doing my part either. I finally told him I would stand by him if he got help, but only as a friend. And now . . . now I do have to admit that I miss him."

There was a wistfulness to her voice that had all of them looking at each other and trying to figure out what to say or feel about this.

"Well then," Clara Lyn said finally, "why don't you tell him that?"

"Because he's at a vulnerable time in his life. He has made the commitment not to go back to drinking, and if I mess with that delicate balance then I could very possibly cause him to flounder. And I cannot be a part of that. Besides, I'm doing my own thing from here on out. He and I have our separate lives to contend with, and I'm going to be selling — Cassidy, I know Clara Lyn told you a few minutes ago that I'm going through a crisis and selling the motel. It's true I'm selling, but I'm not going through a crisis."

"I might not have told her," Clara Lyn harrumphed.

Pebble chuckled. "Yes, you did, and you know it. And it's okay. You're just looking out for me. But you can stop it. Okay? I'm fine."

Cassidy listened to the friends banter. She also understood that this was something Pebble would have to figure out on her own. No one else should or could shoulder that responsibility. You can't change someone else, no matter how much you want to. She couldn't change her mother and father. And she certainly couldn't change Jack, and sadly, in the end she didn't care to. She just wanted out. Out and away from the man, no matter that it made her feel like a failure. Looking back, there was no regret there. She would never want anything about that life back.

She was actually glad they'd never had children. And she'd wanted children for so long. But she was twenty-eight now and not looking for a new relationship. She would never know the joy of motherhood.

But God had seen fit to provide friends now, and if she could she'd give the Lord a hug. She realized suddenly that for the first time she'd actually thought something positive about the Lord. And it felt good.

There was a sound of twigs breaking, and she turned to see Jarrod riding toward her on his horse. And he was leading an extra horse.

"Oh my goodness gracious," Reba gasped. "My heart is about to beat out of my chest. That man can do for a horse what diamonds do for a woman. He just glitters, he looks so good up there."

"Oh, he *does*," Clara Lyn drawled.

Cassidy's pulse was careening through the roadblocks she'd set up between what she did and didn't want. She groaned, having to agree with the excitable beauty operators. He was as amazing today as he'd been the first time she'd laid eyes on him. Better, actually. And that seemed impossible.

She was in trouble.

Jarrod wasn't expecting to find Cassidy had company. Which was good, because she needed friends. Maggie and Abby loved her. And Clara Lyn and her cohorts would be good for her, too, reminding her of her aunt Roxie.

"Afternoon, ladies," he drawled, smiling as if they weren't looking at him like he'd just dropped in from Mars. Cassidy was looking at him as if he'd appeared out of nowhere, too, which got him to thinking maybe he was interrupting something. "Um, you did want me to come take you for a ride, didn't you?"

He said nothing about the rustlers.

"Yes, I did." She looked at the ladies and he could tell she wasn't sure how to handle this.

"No problem. Since you have company, I can check fences on my own and maybe you can come another time."

"Nonsense," Clara Lyn gushed. "We showed up out here totally unannounced. We had no idea we would be interrupting a date."

"Oh, it's not a date," Cassidy denied too quickly, then blushed. "I mean, Jarrod just offered to take me riding. I had dinner with the family last night and we talked about it."

She was cute when she rambled, and he found he was enjoying her digging those holes. All the ladies were looking at her like she'd lost her marbles, and he wasn't exactly sure what to make of that. But then he knew the ladies from the Cut Up and Roll loved to matchmake. And personally that was fine by him. He had plans to do some matchmaking for himself.

"Would you mind if we stay here and pick some peaches since we're already here?" Pebble asked. "You'll have more for the booth this weekend. And, well, it's such a lovely day that it's doing my heart good to be out here."

"Roxie always said picking peaches soothes the soul," Reba added.

"I'll stay here and pick peaches with y'all," Cassidy said.

"You will do no such thing."

"That's right," Clara Lyn added.

Reba waved her toward the horses. "We mean, you go for your ride. We've got this picking going good and the fresh air is doing us wonders."

"Go on now. Get up on that horse." Clara Lyn shooed her along. "I personally would toss my cookies if I tried to get up there. I'm scared of heights, but you know what you're doing."

And so Cassidy found herself sticking her foot into the stirrup, and in the next moment, like remembering how to ride a bike, she automatically swung into the saddle and secured her other boot in the other stirrup. "So, I guess we're going for a ride."

Jarrod's lip hitched and he flashed that

Monahan do-her-in smile. Her insides quaked and her knees felt weak. Thankfully she was sitting in the saddle, so as long as she didn't faint she was okay.

"Let's get going then." He tipped his hat at the ladies who were smiling like he'd just proposed.

Cassidy was proud of the fact that it felt quite normal to be in the saddle, though it had been a good eight years since she'd ridden. She was a little bouncy as she relearned to relax and go with the horse's movements. Jarrod, on the other hand? He rode like he and the horse were one. It was beautiful.

"I decided using you as a decoy ride was the perfect way to hide that I suspected anything went on out here last night."

"Oh, so my going along with you turned out to be a good thing." She felt a little vindicated about the whole thing. In a good way. And excitement bubbled inside of her at being with him . . . No, she corrected sternly. She felt good to be on an adventure. This was unexpected and welcomed.

They rode across the stream and back toward her barn. She remembered Duce and glanced back to see him sitting, uncertain what to do.

"Stay, Duce," she shouted, hoping he understood commands. To her delight he barked, then turned back to the ladies.

"He's a good dog. A very good dog," she said. "I can't imagine someone just losing him and not wanting him back." The fear that an owner might still show up nibbled inside her.

"I agree. He seems to have been taught some things. Some dogs are quick to learn on their own or are taught by other dogs. There is no telling what Duce's story is, but all I know is he's one lucky dog because you saved him. I'll take those stitches out when we get back."

"Thank you."

They passed the barn and stopped at her house. "I need to run inside real quick." She decided a bathroom break would save her from having to commune closer to nature than she cared to later on, but she didn't really want to just come out and say so.

"That's fine. I'll wait here."

"Okay. Back in a sec." She swung a leg over and hopped to the ground and hurried into the house. Once inside it didn't take long, and she found herself running her hands through her hair before she left the bathroom. She had been a mess when she got home last night. When she'd turned on the light and saw her reflection in the mirror, she'd almost died. She had picked up all kinds of things on her slide down the bumpy slope.

He was waiting patiently when she returned.

"You don't seem sore at all," he observed after she remounted and they started moving again.

"Oh, a little. But surprisingly not too bad. Now, after this ride I might be singing a different tune. Riding does tend to use muscles I forget I own."

He chuckled. "That's true. It's just part of me, so I tend to forget that sometimes."

They rode down the road and crossed the blacktop. The horse he'd brought her was sandy colored with a beautiful, flaxen blond mane. "What's her name?"

"Charity."

"I like it."

"She's a gentle horse. We rescued her from starvation a couple of years ago. She was already saddle ready, so I was totally amazed that someone would neglect a good horse like her. But with the drought we had going on, it was happening all the time."

"It's terrible. Did you get a lot of horses?"

"A good many. We don't keep them all. The state finds homes for them, but I get to pick the ones I want in return for all the feed I use and the time spent with them. She was definitely one I wanted."

Cassidy rubbed the horse's neck. He must have brushed Charity's coat, because she was silky and dust-free. "I really like her."

"You're welcome to come ride her anytime you want."

He smiled and her toes curled a little. Okay, a lot.

He stopped at the gate beside the cattle guard and dismounted in one fluid movement. He opened it and led his horse through, then waited on her. Once she was through, he closed the gate again and then settled back into the saddle. Goodness, she could watch the man move for days and never get tired of it. And as a kid she had.

She'd done it from the hay barn at a distance and then later as much as possible when she was invited to go for a ride or on roundups with them, which she had loved.

"So how does it feel?" he asked. "You look like you're enjoying finding your cowgirl side again."

She laughed. "It feels good. And it's beautiful out here. It was kind of dark last night." She saw rolling hillsides, dotted with large oaks and stands of mesquite trees, just enough to give the cattle shade if they wanted it and other wildlife a place of refuge.

"You can say that again. Is your neck okay?"

"It's fine. It was just a scrape." The buzz overhead had them both looking up. The yellow plane flew across the road over her fields.

"Don't panic. He's carrying organic weed control."

"I remember." Looking about she saw bramble-looking bushes with thorns. They dotted the land in clumps.

"That's some of the wild rose that will take over if I don't get it under control soon."

"I see that. I'm glad I didn't tangle with one of them last night."

"I am too. I'd have been picking thorns out of you and you wouldn't have been too happy with me."

She laughed and they entered the stand of mesquite trees. "Jarrod, Clara Lyn told me you were the one who found Aunt Roxie. And that you checked on her regularly. I want to thank you for that."

He slowed the horses and studied the tracks. "No need to thank me. She was my neighbor and a good friend. I was just returning the favor of her friendship. She

262

loved you very much, you know. Worried about you like you were her child."

Tears sprang to Cassidy's eyes. "Thank you for everything."

"You're welcome." He gave her a small smile. "It's okay, Cass. Tears show your love for someone. Don't be embarrassed."

She sniffed. "I'm not. I did love her so."

Jarrod dismounted and bent to look at some tracks. "This was the way the rustlers' truck came. Here are the tracks." He took out his phone, clicked to the camera, and shot some quick photos.

After a minute they rode deeper into the back pastures, with Jarrod keeping steady watch for signs. He knew exactly what he was looking for. When they came to the herd, he pulled a small leather notebook from his shirt pocket. He opened it, consulted numbers on a page, then pocketed it again.

"What is that?"

"That's my personal tally of my cattle." He nodded toward a tree not too far from her. "Smile for the camera."

She swung a startled glance toward the tree. She studied it and could see nothing. And then she spotted a small box that was almost the same color of the tree. Once she knew it was there she could see it, but at night it would never be seen. And even in the daylight someone would have to be searching for it to find it.

"Oh wow. Are you going to check it?"

"Sure am. But first let me count heads."

It didn't take him long. "We're missing twelve. Six mamas and six calves. I'll need to go over the tags to find specific numbers, but they've stolen again. That's a definite." His voice was gritty and low and she didn't miss the look in his eyes.

"How much is a heifer selling for right now?"

"Two thousand on the low side. Thirty-four hundred on the high side for premium stock like we raise. The market's up, which is one reason rustlers are so busy right now."

She did the calculations and gulped. *"That much?"*

"Now you see what we're looking at. That's not pennies we're talking about."

"I had no real idea. Goodness."

He loped his horse over to the tree, and from the saddle he reached up and opened the camera cover, then removed a small card. He dropped it into his pocket and pulled another card from his jeans pocket. He inserted that, then closed the camera again.

"We'll check this out on my computer," he said.

Cassidy felt sick to her stomach. The ranch was his responsibility. Yes, Tru and Bo had contributed to getting the ranch out of debt, but she now understood the ramifications of the cattle thieving. It just hadn't dawned on her how astronomical the loss could be.

Not to mention that she knew Jarrod would feel like he was failing his family if he couldn't keep the ranch healthy.

She wanted so much to help him.

She rode beside him on the short ride toward his place. "I can let you dismount at your place if you'd like. I can lead Charity home."

"Are you kidding? I want to see the film. I've come this far. I can't stop now."

He laughed. "Okay, sounds good to me."

Her stomach dropped looking at him. She tore her gaze away and studied a pair of birds in the distance doing a dance high in the sky. It hit her that she was riding beside the man she'd dreamed of for years. So many times when she'd been back home, trying to deal with the craziness going on around her, she'd thought of Jarrod. Of his calm steadiness. Of his amazing smile and the dream that one day he would be hers when she grew up — pure young girl's fantasy.

She glanced at him and swallowed the need to reach out and tell him everything was going to be okay, like he'd told her so many times when she'd been a hurting kid.

"Have y'all ever been robbed like this before?" she asked, fighting to find steady ground. She watched the way he moved easily and perfectly with the movement of the horse. The man rode horses like they'd been made just for him. And when he leaned forward, low over the horse's neck, and they galloped across a pasture, it was as if they were flying . . . She'd always loved to see him do that.

"Yeah, we have through the years. You know, here and there, but nothing like what this is starting to add up to. Then again, this doesn't hold a candle to the stealing my dad did."

"The gambling?"

He nodded, anger in the movement. "Stealing is all it can be called. He basically stole from Pops. His own dad. It's sickening." The anger reverberated from him, so deep she felt it almost reach out and touch her.

She was speechless. She knew that kind of anger.

"What's worse," he continued, "is that he didn't get it." He looked about the land surrounding them. "This land is the family legacy. Pops built it to leave behind, but my dad didn't understand that it's not only about the land. Pops's main legacy, the one that really counts, is his life and the way he lived it. The legacy of a life well lived. Yeah, we could have lost all of this and it would have killed us, but in the end it's Pops's memory that will live on. That's what we will pass down generation to generation. Nothing, not even his illness, can rob us of that. My dad couldn't take that away."

Cassidy's throat clogged with aching emotion and she blinked back tears.

Jarrod glanced at her and then looked closer. "What's wrong?" he asked gently.

She shook her head and looked away. She'd been robbed, too, she realized. Jarrod's hand on her arm halted the horses in the yard. "What are you thinking about?"

"My marriage. Jack robbed me of eight years of my life. I don't even like to think back to any of those years. I feel like it was wasted time."

"I can see that. But, Cass, it's time to move on."

She stared at him, and the pain deep inside, the anger she had to tamp down deep so it wouldn't flood out of her, caused her stomach to hurt and her chest to tighten. And the headache she hadn't had for days suddenly thumped hard. She rubbed her temple.

Jarrod was off his horse in an instant, and before she knew what was happening he reached up, circled her waist with his arm, and lifted her from the horse and into his arms. And he held her there. Her pulse shot to the sky and she stared into his eyes, stunned by his actions and the electrifying way she connected to the concern in his gaze as his eyes dug deep into hers.

Emotions tangled between them and she couldn't breathe.

His eyes dropped to her lips and then yanked back to her eyes. "I can't stand to see you hurt," he growled. "I can't."

She believed him, and when something inside of her ripped, she struggled to hold it together.

He dropped his forehead to hers. "Tell me what happened the day you were hit by that car." He pulled back. "And don't say it was nothing. I saw you that day at the clinic when you fell and Clara Lyn was freaking out. You didn't want to talk about it and you didn't tell the whole story."

She couldn't think in his arms, though.

"Put me down and I'll tell you."

He set her on her feet and she moved away from him. She'd wanted him to kiss her. To continue holding her. She'd wanted . . . what she didn't need. Telling him about her past was exactly what she needed to put the boundaries back in place. And that would keep her from letting down her guard.

Jarrod hadn't meant to hang on to her. He'd been angry talking about his dad as usual, but when he'd glanced at Cassidy his heart had almost ripped out at the pain he'd seen in her eyes. He'd had to dig deep. But then holding on to her he hadn't wanted to let her go. He had to know what caused all that hurt inside of her.

"I saw my ex with another woman. It wasn't the first time. It was after he'd sworn once more — I don't even remember how many times now — that he would never ever do it again. I had always believed him. Well, not exactly. I just stuck with him again and again, thinking this time he might have changed. But in reality I stuck with him because I just couldn't accept the idea of divorce. That day when I saw him with someone else, I spun and ran. I didn't look at the intersection. I just ran out in front of that car. We were separated at the time, and

I had filed for divorce, but he'd been at me, trying to get me back. It was the oddest thing. He didn't really want me but he didn't want to let me go. My fear of being like my parents kept me confused and caused me to waffle on finalizing the breakup once and for all. I think that too was part of his game."

She stuffed her hands on her hips and scowled. "I don't know exactly why he played the game, but I do know that a good, hard knock in the head was what I needed to wake me up. And that's the truth."

He could barely control the scalding hot anger as it surged through him at her words, at the look on her face. "So he tried to get you back while he was continuing to cheat on you?"

"Yes. Sick, huh? And then, after all that whining and begging he did, there I lay in that hospital in a coma. When I woke up the man was nowhere to be found. I'm sure he was with her." She laughed bitterly. "Pretty stupid of me."

"Of him. Stupid of him."

She concentrated on petting Charity, then, taking the horse's reins, she walked him to the barn. Jarrod led his horse and followed her.

"That was it for me. I'm driving that

rattletrap truck because I walked away from my eight-year marriage with almost nothing. It wasn't worth the fight."

He couldn't believe what he was hearing. "After everything he put you through?"

"I didn't want to spend any more time negotiating, which was another stupid move on my part, not one I would recommend to most women or men who are in the same boat. At least by Texas law our assets were split down the middle, but he'd rung up so much debt — winin' and dinin' women is expensive, I found out. I'm positive he'd hidden assets somewhere, but it would have required a long fight for me to find them and I just wanted out."

"Understandable." He looked at the ground.

"Where does Charity go?" she asked in an impatient tone. He understood the feeling completely. He pointed to the second stall. She opened the latch and led her horse inside.

He tied up his horse and quickly removed the saddle. His stomach knotted tight. He needed something to do, too, because he'd never wanted to punch a man's lights out so bad in all of his life. Not even in his rowdy teen years. "The whole thing is perverted," he gritted out as he dropped the saddle on the stand beside the stall.

She laughed bitterly as she released the cinch and then slid off the saddle. She hadn't forgotten what Pops taught her. "Tell me about it." She pulled the saddle into her arms and carried it out of the stall and set it on the stand. "And now I have eight years of my life that are basically missing. Eight years just better lost than remembered." She paused to look at him, her eyebrows knitted together over angry eyes. "Oh, they're there, dadgumit. I just try hard not to think about them. They make me feel dirty, and so very foolish. It's awful," she drawled. "I wish . . . I wish that I'd awakened from that coma with the entire eight years lost to me."

"I never thought of it like that. You really got a raw deal, Cass. You didn't deserve that. You really didn't. But you need to let it go. I can see it's tearing you up."

She pinned glittering eyes on him. "I can tell you the same thing about your dad."

"Point taken. But I can tell you again that your ex wins the award for the dumbest man alive for letting you go."

Her expression hardened. "He didn't *let* me go. He fought hard to keep me, on his terms. Like I said, he had numerous flings, affairs, and flirtations for years and I stayed. It's so humiliating to look back on now. He used so many mind games to keep me, like 'I can't live without you.' Yeah, right. But there I was, afraid I was like my parents. The thought of adding divorcée to my identity killed me. I was floundering between fear and the need to cut the toxic ties when I was hit by the car. I seriously can't stand this angry person living deep down inside of me."

He saw the pain and anger flashing in her eyes. "It's his loss, you know. How long has it been?"

Pushing her to talk about her ex was crazy, but Jarrod couldn't help it and he couldn't explain it either.

"No," she grimaced. "The divorce was final three months ago, but as I said, we'd been separated for a year, living in separate houses, and for longer than that emotionally. You're right, I should have divorced him a long time before I finally walked out. But I was the one to leave in the end. I truly didn't want to continue my parents' cycle, but I had tried everything."

She reached into the bucket and grabbed a brush, then slipped through the gate and began brushing down Charity. She brushed for a moment, then pointed the brush at him. "And biblically too, there was that . . ." She swung back, working briskly but carefully. "I went to counseling by *myself* trying to fix my marriage. Can you believe that? I learned quickly that one person can't save a marriage. It takes two, both wanting it to change. All he wanted me for was to manipulate and control. But to love and be faithful was too much to ask of him." Her shoulders slumped and she dropped her forehead to the horse's shoulder, her hand resting on its neck. "I was such a fool."

Jarrod forced himself to keep his cool. No matter what she said, to stay with her ex through all of that, she'd loved him. Surely she couldn't have let him treat her so callously if she hadn't. Jarrod couldn't believe even as much as she despised divorce that her fear of that outcome could have held her.

"Do you still love him?" He couldn't help asking, though the thought made him sick.

She spun toward him, her eyes and mouth twisted with disgust and horror. "*No.* Are you kidding me? My love for Jack, if I ever really had any, died long ago. A person can take only so much before love dies. I was there out of duty, obligation maybe to the vows I took before God. And to stop the cycle of divorce in my family."

She gave a bitter laugh. "I have to work hard not to hate him. Believe me, I'm not that good either. I try to live a good life, but my faith is a little ragged at the moment. I can't love unconditionally. My actions don't seem to show that because I didn't follow through with the divorce immediately, but it's the truth." She shuddered and turned back to her horse, gave a few more swipes, then just stood there. "Me being a fool wasn't about love but about staying there too long."

He moved to stand beside her and covered her hand with his, stilling the brushing. "I'm glad you're starting over. Cass, no one could hold something so awful against you. You deserve better."

She glanced at him. "All I want now is peace. I've learned my lesson finally and I'll never ever have to go through this again. I'm never taking vows again. I'll never have to weigh the merit of the vow 'for better or worse.' I'm done."

The pain and conviction in her words gripped him. "That's pretty harsh."

Her shoulders slumped. "It might be harsh, but now you know what kind of emotional junk I lived through. This, talking about it, thinking about it, brings it out of the darkness where I shoved it. It makes me feel like I'm reliving it all over again."

He scowled now. "Maybe talking about it

is good for you. And believe me, I know about deep, dark anger. I have some of that shoved into the corners too. Sometimes you have to let things go. And while we're on that topic, your parents' mistakes, remember only they know why they were not able to stay in a relationship. You had solid reasons for walking away."

This conversation had gone way out of bounds.

"Did I? I took a vow that in the end I couldn't live with."

He didn't like how hard she was being on herself. "So you're telling me the Lord would require you to stay in that sort of marriage? I don't believe that. If you want to get into a debate about it, I believe the Lord understood that when trust is broken, sometimes a relationship is irrevocably damaged. I certainly don't believe the person who was wronged in the relationship should be the one to suffer and have to live with all the junk created by the other party. I just don't believe he'd hold that against you. And verses in the Bible back that up. I think in Ephesians or Corinthians. You made a mistake, Cass. Nowhere near breaking your parents' records either." His blood pressure was in outer space.

And she was turning a deep rose, either

from anger or embarrassment. "I was to blame too. I had very poor judgment." She winced. "The apple doesn't fall far from the tree, so to speak."

"Hogwash. So you're saying because my dad happened to be a lying, gambling jerk who tossed his own dad and everything he'd worked for to the wolves to supply his selfish addiction that I should give up because I'm going to be just like him?"

"Don't be ridiculous. Of course I'm not saying that."

"Then you need to get past this." The horses nickered around them, reminding him that they were standing in the barn. Looking at her, he understood that everything that had come before in his life wasn't important in the context of the future he wanted with her. The realization caused him to feel lightheaded.

"Cassidy, from this point on, nothing behind you matters. You've taken a step to a new future, so let the past go. Let the anger go."

He stepped close and took her by the shoulders. "Cass, if you keep that mind-set, then I don't stand a chance of proving to you that I made the biggest mistake of my life nine years ago. That night I kissed you, then ran like a scared pup. I should have grabbed hold of you and never let you go."

She inhaled a sharp breath.

He tugged her a step closer to him. "If I'd done that then you wouldn't be standing here in all this pain. Cass, I want a shot at showing you that I —"

"Stop." She spoke while softly trying to yank away from him. He held her firmly, unable to let go.

"Cass, we need a shot as adults to see what we could be together." He pulled her close, cupped her face with one hand and caressed her cheek with the pad of his thumb. And then he lowered his lips to hers.

# 19

Jarrod's lips claimed Cassidy's with the firm pressure of a man who knew what he wanted. Her knees went weak. Cassidy melted against him, as if all the years between the first kiss and now had vaporized and only this was left. His hands moved to hold her close, and his mouth worked over hers with passion that drew a response from her just as passionate.

She was breathless when he lifted his head from hers, a dazed look in his eyes as he stared into hers. And then he kissed her again, and she could not pull away, though warning bells were ringing in her ears. Her arms went around him and she clung to him as joy sang through her.

"You're an incredible woman, Cass," he murmured against her lips. "I have wanted to kiss you from the moment you opened the door last night before dinner at the house."

Cassidy's hand rested on his heart and she let the world slowly stop spinning. What was she doing? She couldn't step into another emotional situation. The way her heart was thundering, and looking into Jarrod's eyes, she knew she might not be able to survive an inevitable breakup with him.

She shook her head. She'd already opened up too much with him.

Exposed the rawness of her heart, her soul.

"I can't do this. I can't." Pushing out of his arms, she stalked from the barn and into the brilliant sunlight. It burned through the fog of her muddled brain and clarity shone through once more.

Her cheeks burned from the embarrassment of flooding Jarrod with her failure of a past and then falling into his arms. She was mortified — and miffed.

With Jack, she'd been a victim of her own making. And she had vowed to never, ever do that again. She knew that with Jarrod she was far more vulnerable than she'd ever been with Jack.

"Cassidy, hold up." He caught her and took her arm, turning her. "You're just going to walk away?"

"That's what you did the last time you kissed me."

He grimaced. "That was a mistake."

"And this kiss wasn't? I just told you my whole sordid past. And that I'm not ever doing this again." She waved a hand. "I wasn't just saying that. I am not going through that ever again."

"Cass, I was young and that kiss scared the daylights out of me and I ran. But I'm not like that jerk. I would never hurt you like that."

"Don't, Jarrod. I can't do this."

Silence stretched between them as the heat of the day set in and hung around them.

He held her gaze, his jaw tense as the moments passed.

"Fine. For now. Let's go catch some rustlers." He strode past her up the steps and to the back door. He pulled the door open and held it for her, his expression grim.

Fine. She was angry too. Anger was good. It put a wedge between them. She didn't move at first. But they'd never get back to where they'd been earlier if she didn't. She followed him up the steps and moved past him into his home. His scent, leather and spicy, clung to her, and she had to yank her thoughts away from thinking about how good the cowboy smelled as she passed him.

*Angry,* she reminded herself.

Here she'd told him every awful detail of her past, something she'd never told anyone. And then she'd kissed the man like there was no tomorrow.

Absolutely nothing about the experience made her feel better. The kissing, yes. Momentarily. But not airing her dirty laundry. And he'd thought it would help. The awful memories had not only given her an awful headache; they had made her vulnerable and weakened her resolve to be strong.

She halted in the hallway so he could lead the way to wherever they were going. She would just have to let the kiss slide away and hopefully be forgotten.

She had to salvage her pride somehow.

"Do you live here alone?" She said the first thing that popped into her brain.

He didn't say anything for a moment, and she wondered if he'd let them get back on steady ground again.

At last, with a look of impatience he ran a hand through his short hair. "Yeah, Cass. I live here alone. For several years I lived in the small cabin Pops built on the property. Since I'm not one to spend a lot of time indoors — and not one who enjoys the sound of four walls saying nothing — I never needed much space. But after Mom and Dad died, this place was just sitting here. I've always liked it so I moved in." He was leading her through the den that was filled with brightly colored throws and dark furniture that had probably been his mother's decorating. She couldn't imagine Jarrod going shopping.

"I wasn't exactly sure how I'd handle it since, as you know, I wasn't in the best frame of mind about things at that point. But I've done all right. And the cattle portion of the ranch was over here so it just made sense."

"I always liked the house. Of course, your mom was always baking cookies." She smiled, relieved to be thinking about something positive. "I can still remember those chocolate ones with the powdered sugar on top."

His smile could melt hearts. "Yeah, chocolate crinkles. My favorite. I haven't thought about those in a while, but, boy, could I sure eat one now. Or ten."

They both laughed at that and their gazes locked once more. So much being said and nothing at all.

Cassidy had the sudden urge to try to bake him some cookies. Not a good idea.

He led the way into the office. It had thick

leather chairs and a large desk. He grabbed a small cane back chair from the corner and set it beside the desk chair. "Have a seat and we'll plug this in."

She did and he sat beside her. After turning on his computer, he stuck the small disk into the port and waited. There were a lot of photos, not very good, but there.

"So it looks like four of them?" she asked, trying to count the grainy forms.

"If they'd been closer it would have been better, but where they set up their makeshift corral was a little too far away." As they scrutinized the photos, he leaned in and she did too.

"Two of them look about your size, tall, built —" She hadn't meant to say that and quickly added, "The other two are shorter."

Jarrod leaned back and let out an exasperated sigh. "Too bad. I wish we could see their features. Or the number on the truck's tailgate. Something."

"I can't even tell what make the truck is."

He tapped his fingers on the desk, then leaned in, intently focused on the pictures. "Nope. Nothing. My brilliant idea has flopped."

"But maybe just for last night. There are other spots. You'll get lucky on one of those."

"Or if I'm lucky some of the heifers will show up at an auction and the TSCRA agents will catch the number on the computer database."

They were quiet for a moment.

"I guess I better get back home. I'm pretty sure the ladies have gone by now, but I still have a lot to do."

"And I need to remove Duce's stitches."

"I can load him up and have Doc do it."

He scowled. "I'll do it, Cass. I've already told Doc I would."

"Then that's fine." It was far from fine, but what else could she say?

They drove to her house. Duce was sitting on the porch waiting for them.

Jarrod brought a small tackle box into the house with him and set it on the kitchen table. He pulled out a pair of stainless steel tweezers, medical-grade scissors, and antiseptic.

"You might want to help hold him in case he decides to move around."

She sat on the floor and pulled her dog into her lap, leaving his hip and leg exposed for Jarrod. To her surprise Jarrod's hands were nimble, and he'd snipped the compilation of stitches within seconds. He picked up the sterilized tweezers and quickly but carefully tugged each one free. His head was bent over his work and Cassidy had to force herself not to touch him. When he looked up they were too close for comfort, and she quickly looked back at Duce. She held his head against her shoulder, and his dark eyes studied her with complete trust as he allowed Jarrod to work. Trust . . .

"You are a very good pooch," Cassidy said to him softly. She contented herself with rubbing the dog's ears rather than running her fingers through Jarrod's dark hair.

It was all over swiftly. Jarrod picked up his kit and was ready to leave in moments.

"Thank you," she said, wishing the atmosphere between them wasn't so strained.

"Anytime. Cass, don't close yourself off."

She stiffened. "I'm here to start a new life, Jarrod. And contrary to all that stuff I let fly earlier, I plan to enjoy my life. So . . . if you can, would you just forget I aired my dirty laundry to you and let's move forward?"

*And let's forget you kissed me. And I kissed you back.*

"Because that's what I'm going to do." She plastered on her brightest smile. And she meant it. The more she thought about it, the more she realized he was actually right. "Talking about it did help me. I realize there is absolutely nothing I can do to change the past. Nothing. What happened with Jack makes me feel awful, so I'm letting it go. From here on out, don't you dare feel bad for me."

He nodded after a second, his gaze probing deep, then his lip lifted ever so slightly and his eyes crinkled just a bit at the edges. "Okay, you've got a deal. From here on out, the past is the past. It's a new day, Cass."

Cassidy's stomach dropped. She really wasn't sure what she was seeing, but he grinned and then left. She wondered if that was a wink she saw before he drove off.

And suddenly she wasn't at all certain what had just passed between them.

"Have y'all read Maggie's column this morning?" Clara Lyn asked, hustling over to where Reba was helping Cassidy unload peaches from her truck into a wagon for the Fourth of July celebration. She waved the newspaper at them.

"I've just been loading peaches this morning," Cassidy said, curious. What had Clara Lyn all flustered?

"Is it good?" Reba asked. "I was running late getting here this morning and didn't get to look at it. You're so excited she must have had a really good letter."

"Oh, it's good all right. Listen to this. 'Dear Maggie, I made a huge mistake a long time ago and I hurt the woman I love. She's been through a lot and I feel responsible, but at this point I feel helpless to help her. She deserves all the happiness there is but right now she's hurting and I believe making the mistake of her life . . . and I don't know how to stop her. I need your advice.' "

Clara Lyn's eyes widened. "It's signed 'Torn in Texas.' Y'all might think I'm crazy —"

"As a bat," Reba teased her, grinning, and Cassidy chuckled at Clara Lyn's scowl.

"Oh hush, this is serious. Do y'all think that sounds like something Rand would write?"

"No, surely not," Reba said slowly. "But yeah. It could be."

Cassidy was startled. "You know, maybe . . ."

"I've read it and reread it and I just have this gut feeling this is Rand. Here is Maggie's advice. She always gives the best advice . . . so thoughtful. 'Dear Torn in Texas, it does sound like you must have really messed up. I'm no expert, so take it only as from my heart. Sometimes consequences last forever no matter how much you regret them. What I like about your letter is that I think you understand that and your worry is truly about how to help this person. The problem is you may not be able to. You may just have to let her move on with her life her own way, mistakes or not. If you love her still, perseverance may win her back in the end.' "

"I like it," Reba said. "Do you think he's worried that she'll sell the motel and move off somewhere? He should make a move, but he's drawn back instead."

"I think he thinks she's better off without him," Clara Lyn said.

"Yes. And maybe she is."

Cassidy did not want to agree, but as much as she loved Rand, she knew Pebble would be taking a risk loving him, always worrying if he might fall off the wagon. But she sure hated feeling that way. It actually hurt her heart for him.

She still had Rand on her mind thirty minutes later as she finished carting all the peaches to her tables.

"You sure do have a great crop," one of the twins said as the two brothers made the rounds.

"Doonie will eat all your peaches if you don't watch him," Doobie joked, letting her know who was who. They surveyed the baskets of peaches.

"I'm impressed," she told the twins. "This

is looking like it's going to be a huge success."

The mayor grinned, and she thought his chest puffed out a bit. "I came up with the Thanksgiving in July concept three years ago to add an extra twist to the Fourth of July celebration, and I have to say it's really caught on."

"Especially after Maggie's column came out," Rand added, coming to stand beside her.

He looked good, with his crisply starched oxford and his tan trousers. He had his tweed fedora perched on perfectly combed, thick gray hair, and his pale-blue eyes were alert and inquisitive. She was glad to see he looked so good. After hearing what Pebble had to say about their relationship, she was increasingly curious about the dynamics between them.

"Last year it was pretty exciting," Rand drawled. "I can't wait to see what excitement happens this year when Doonie and Doobie start frying up those fifty turkeys they have orders for."

Clara Lyn had told her people gave orders for fried turkeys and the men cooked them up. The money went to support Over the Rainbow. Cassidy thought it was great how the community came together to support such a good cause. The home gave a place for these young women to go, and then made certain the babies were given life and a home where they were loved.

Maggie and Tru had gotten in late last night, and Maggie and Abby were going to man the Four of Hearts Ranch table while the men helped with the turkey frying. The talk was that the volunteer fire department was on full alert, but since half the men cooking this year were in the department, everything should be fine. She'd heard tales about things that had happened. Turkey frying was apparently a dangerous endeavor.

"Hey, girl." Maggie straightened up a row of stirrups. "So how's the progress going?"

"Slow. After today I'll be ready to concentrate on plowing up the garden plot and attacking the terrible, horrible wallpaper in the kitchen."

Abby coughed, laughing. "I think I would have had to paint that kitchen first."

"Oh, I know what you mean, but it's going to be a job. I'm ready now."

She needed something to occupy her mind other than thinking about catching cattle rustlers and about kissing Jarrod. "How about you? Aren't you going to decorate for the baby?"

Maggie beamed. "I was planning it the

whole time we were on the road. I think I just about drove Tru crazy with all my magazines and paint swatches. But I managed to get it all decided with his input, which was wonderful. He's very good at smiling over at me as he drives that big truck and saying, 'Whatever you want, darlin', is good for me.' I love that cowboy."

They all laughed. Cassidy loved the whole vibe they put off as a couple. And Abby and Bo were the same. Instantly her thoughts went to Jarrod. One day he'd have someone like this and she was so surprised that he didn't already. He was the whole package, and it was just crazy that he was still an eligible bachelor.

But not for long, she felt like. He was lonely. She could tell that. He'd made a few statements that had caught her attention. And he would be thirty-four years old now. Thirty-four and never married. That was unbelievable to her.

It didn't matter, she reminded herself.

Rand came strolling back over with his camera in hand. "Let me get a picture of you with your peaches. I'll put it in the celebration spread along with your number and a notice about the B and B. I'll mention the strawberries, too, that you'll have them in the spring. How's that sound?"

"That's wonderful," she said, beaming.

"I haven't had that kind of response before. I kind of like it." His gaze shifted across the way to where Pebble was helping a group of pregnant young women unload candles from a box to a table.

She thought about that letter to Maggie.

"Okay, smile for the camera," Rand said, and she did, catching a glimpse of Jarrod watching her from a distance. After Rand snapped a few shots, he looked at them in the viewfinder. "I got a good one."

"Well, sure you did, Rand," Doonie crooned. "She's as pretty as a peach so there's no getting a bad one. Now" — he looked from her to Abby and Maggie — "when we close down the sales booths at two so everyone can enjoy the games, y'all get ready to participate. Right now I better go get the grease heated up or we'll be cooking turkeys at dark when the fireworks start."

He left at a fast clip and Maggie made a beeline toward the Over the Rainbow table.

"What games do they set up?" Cassidy asked Abby and Rand.

Abby smiled. "I hear there'll be a three-legged race and horseshoe tossing later this afternoon. Then everyone will pack up and come back later for the fireworks."

"That's right," Rand said. "There's going to be a dance later too."

She'd been trying hard not to think about the fireworks. She'd not been able to get Jarrod off her mind and she blamed the celebration as part of the problem. Someone called Abby's name and she moved away to visit with them, leaving Cassidy and Rand alone.

Busy thinking about that long-ago kiss she and Jarrod shared while fireworks exploded, Cassidy hardly noticed Abby had gone. Had it seemed so wonderful because her young imagination had been running wild over her first kiss? But she'd found out that it had been real, that he could still kiss her senseless.

Remembering now was torture.

"I'm not sure if I'll be here tonight. I have a lot to do." She was being honest.

"Now, that's no way to have fun," Rand said.

"Why don't you go over there and take Pebble's picture?" She was trying to get the focus off herself.

Rand shook his head, but she didn't want to take no for an answer.

"You should go. You've made such progress, and I bet she'd like you to at least say hello."

"You sure do remind me of your aunt Roxie sometimes. That woman used to goad me all the time about Pebble."

"And you loved her for it."

"I cannot deny that. She was a lovely woman. But Pebble and I . . . it's complicated and I didn't help anything with my drinking. Truthfully, she deserves a lot better than me."

Cassidy put a few more baskets of peaches on the table, not sure what to say to that because Pebble did deserve better than what he'd given her. "Then I guess I'll just say I'm sorry it's not working out for the two of you."

Rand let his camera hang free from the strap around his neck as he pulled a small notebook from his pocket. "She'll be fine, and that's all that matters to me. Consequences for my actions shouldn't affect her. Now, I need to make sure we have all the pertinent information right for the caption beneath your photo." He asked her for the Strawberry Hill address, when she estimated the B and B opening would be, and when her first crop of strawberries was going to be ready.

She gave him all the information and realized she was shooting realistically for the bed-and-breakfast to be open before Christmas. And from her research she knew if she protected them from frost and freeze, there was a good chance she could see her first strawberries by February. That was less than seven months and would take a lot of time. But hey, time was all she had. She was going to be single, so she had no one to worry about but herself. There should be no problem getting everything done in the next five months. No problem at all.

She spotted Tru and Jarrod in the distance, studying the fryers and instructing Doobie and Doonie to move them farther away from the building they were near. How would her relationship with Jarrod be by then? Would she have grown comfortable with him as her neighbor? Would she have stopped these nagging thoughts, wondering if she could be happy never to feel his kiss again?

Rand cleared his throat and she realized he'd seen her staring at Jarrod. She suddenly felt too warm.

"You and Jarrod live out there on the far side of the ranch all by yourselves. I've been wanting to ask if you've seen anything unusual out there around your property or Jarrod's."

That was an odd question, but then she remembered Rand was a newspaper man.

And she remembered the day in the diner when those men had lunch with Jarrod and his brothers. She knew Rand's reporter antenna had been up because she remembered how he had studied them all during lunch. He'd suspected something.

"Like what?" she hedged. She couldn't lie, but she also knew Jarrod didn't want to be in the papers about rustlers. At least she didn't think he did.

"Like suspicious folks snooping around along the roads checking out people's cattle."

"Have you heard something about rustlers?" She decided to turn the question on him.

"There's been a rash of it all across the county. I figure the Four of Hearts Ranch would be a prime target for something like that."

"Have they ever had cattle stolen before?"

He nodded. "Years ago. Pops caught them, rounded them up in a cattle trailer, and kept them there for a few days before he hauled them in to the sheriff." Rand grinned. "He didn't have any problems after that."

Cassidy laughed. "That's classic. I love it."

"Yeah, it makes for a great story. I better

go see if I can help them with the frying. Good luck with the peach sales. Folks should start showing up soon."

Cassidy watched him go and glanced toward Pebble. She was watching him too.

Rand seemed to have forgotten one thing in all of this, and that was that Pebble had a mind of her own. Then again, it had been years and Pebble had never said yes to a life with Rand. So maybe he did understand.

# 20

"I want to introduce you to Sandy Freemont. She is expecting our baby boy in the next two weeks."

"Oh my goodness, I am so glad to meet you." Cassidy took the girl's hand. "You've chosen a wonderful family for your baby." Cassidy was twenty-eight years old and didn't know what to say in this situation. Did she tell the girl she would have a wonderful life? That she'd made a great decision? Both comments seemed awkward.

Sandy smiled broadly. "Thank you," she said with a heavy Texas twang. "I was scared out of my boots trying to find the right family, and then I just prayed and knew Maggie and Mr. Tru were right. God's pretty cool when he points things out like that."

Cassidy was a little taken aback by the girl. "Well, I'm glad he did that for you."

Maggie was smiling too. "Sandy has a huge faith. I'm struck in awe each time I talk to her. She gave her life to the Lord not long after she got pregnant and she's not wavered."

"It must be nice to be so sure about his will for your life."

Sandy frowned. "Oh, I ain't at all sure all the time. Believe me, I've just got to keep my thoughts on him and hang on. You know, like I was a flying trapeze artist or something. Because I feel like that's how he's hung on to me. There have been so many close calls in my life, and even in the bad times I felt like there was a reason for me to keep going. And now I know it was the Lord. He was pulling me through the dark times like I was lost in a burning building or something. I couldn't see but he sure could. Anyway, I know my baby is going to be a blessing to Maggie and Mr. Tru, and I'm going to go on to graduate from high school in two years and then go to college and get a degree in something. I ain't got a real clear bead on that yet, but I'm praying hard and going to figure it all out."

Maggie was smiling joyfully as Sandy rattled on and on. Cassidy thought it was sweet, but what struck her the most was the girl's unshakable faith. Even through tough times. She wondered what it would feel like to be that sure that whatever came her way

God would work it out.

As Maggie and Sandy ambled off toward the turkey frying, Cassidy watched them go with a lump in her throat. She had felt lost in the darkness so much of her life.

"That little gal is a talker." Clara Lyn had come over the minute they'd left.

Cassidy tore her attention away from her thoughts, dazed.

Walking up right behind Clara Lyn, Reba grinned. "And I used to think Clara Lyn was a talker. I stand corrected."

"I think it's sweet." Cassidy pushed away the melancholy settling over her.

"Oh, I do too," Clara Lyn said. "A sweet talker. And speaking of sweet talkers, how's that handsome hunk of a neighbor doing?"

The crowds had tapered off, most angling toward the food booths now, but Abby returned to talk to the ladies.

"Yes, how did that horseback ride go with Jarrod?" Reba looked at her expectantly.

Abby gasped. "You went horseback riding with Jarrod and didn't tell me?"

"It was no big deal. It was nice, though. I haven't been on a horse in years."

"Well, you need to make sure to keep that riding up, okay? When Tru and Bo hear about this they are going to be ecstatic. They were starting to conspire on how to fix their

301

big brother up right before you showed up, so I think they have high hopes for the two of you."

"Y'all, it was just a ride. I'm not looking to marry again. Really, I'm not. And he knows that."

Clara Lyn crossed her arms and her bracelets jangled as she harrumphed. "When you fall off a horse you don't just lie in the dirt. You get up and get back on."

"That's right," Reba grunted. "One bad ride does not mean the rodeo is over."

Abby grinned. "That is so eloquently put. And the truth."

"But I'm fine. Reba, you're single. You never remarried after your divorce, but you seem to be happy and content like Aunt Roxie always was."

"Who says I'm content?" she drawled, giving Cassidy a blunt assessment. "Hon, I'm always on the lookout for that one special man. I believe in true love and I am holding out for it. He just hasn't ridden in on his horse, and at this point I wouldn't mind if he was riding a mule. I'm just looking for the man who will sweep me off my feet and share the rest of my life with me. A good man, and by 'sweep me off my feet' I'm talking about with sincerity and heart."

"He's going to have to be strong," Clara

Lyn said, arching her eyebrows. "Or use that mule to help him if he's going to do any sweeping you off your feet."

Reba slapped her friend on the arm. "Look who's talking. You know you gained five pounds last week when Bertha came in with that cream cheese pound cake."

Clara Lyn dropped her jaw. "It is so unfair. Our clients all know how to bake and they bake when they get depressed. Then they all want to come into the salon and tell us their woes, and out of acts of kindness and because they are on diets, they deposit those baked goods in our shop. All that gratefulness is a hard thing to resist. I tell them they are cruel and have threatened not to let them cry on my shoulder if they keep it up."

"But no," Reba said sarcastically. "They just keep on bringing them in. Speaking of which, I thought you were done giving advice." She was gawking at Clara Lyn.

Pebble had come over to say hello, and she now looked from one to the other, obviously wondering like Cassidy and Abby what the ladies were talking about. They were quite entertaining.

"Well, I tried. But you knew it was going to be impossible for me to keep my mouth shut. And speaking of advice, did y'all read

Maggie's column? It came this morning."

Pebble held up a hesitant hand. "I read it."

Clara Lyn blinked at her friend. "And what did you make of that letter from Torn in Texas Number 2? There was a Number 1 too that Reba and I found interesting."

"I read that one," Abby gasped, slapping a hand over her mouth as she looked at Pebble. Her gaze slid to Cassidy and then she cringed a little.

"Well." Pebble bristled. "I think whoever Torn in Texas is, he's making some decisions that are a little premature. I mean, about whoever this person of interest is he's decided to let go because he loves her so much, as he said. Well, I think he should reread Maggie's reply in the first letter and see that she told him he made mistakes and that he should persevere and give the person of interest time to make up her own mind."

Everyone looked stunned and was silent. Pebble's gentle face was rather flushed and Cassidy was shocked to see anger in her normally gentle eyes.

"Well, I . . ." Clara Lyn actually seemed at a loss for words. And so did Reba, who just blinked.

"You girls asked. And now you know. Yes, I believe Rand may have written to Maggie's advice column. When in fact the man should have been asking me what I think. But no. He just marched his sweet self over to my place and cut ties with me. Told me I didn't deserve to have his mess casting a shadow over me for the rest of my life. And then he left. You know about all that. But I've been thinking about it. And the more I think about it, the madder I get."

"Well, go talk to him." Cassidy couldn't help it. "Get this all out in the open."

"Yes," Clara Lyn agreed enthusiastically. "We sure will. We'll fix this."

"No, I don't want y'all talking to him. I can handle this on my own. He's done this. He's still learning. And while I appreciate the fact that he thinks he's making the right move asking our Maggie for her advice — and I think she gave him good advice — I think he should have started with me. I'm an adult and so is he. Going to rehab was a step in the right direction for him and then for our relationship. And now he's decided to do this."

Cassidy's head was spinning. Love was so confusing. She studied Pebble and could see that despite her words there was worry in her eyes. But what could Cassidy do about it? Pebble and Rand were two adults who had been dancing around this crazy relationship of theirs for years.

Jarrod was pleased that they managed to fry fifty turkeys without burning any buildings down or exploding any turkeys. He'd made a wide perimeter around the fryers to keep folks back since he wasn't certain what might happen.

The day had flown by and the turnout had been fantastic. Maggie's advice column had put the town on the map, and they were starting to prosper with a little more of the traffic that normally headed over to the more touristy Fredericksburg. Not that he was hoping the town got too much busier. And not that he was hoping it caught on as a place for women to come looking for love. Bo had been terrified that was going to happen. But thankfully Maggie's advice column and the TV interview a year ago had just grabbed people's attention. Doonie and the town council had done a good job holding different festivals to give folks a reason to visit and spend a few dollars for the economy.

He was fine with that.

But today his mind hadn't been in the game. He had rustlers hanging out in the background of his thoughts and Cassidy holed up in the forefront. And from where he was frying turkeys he had a fairly clear view of her. She stayed busy with her peaches and it looked like she was about out.

"Hey, Doobie, you ready to take over here? I've got this last one to finish frying."

"Sure I can. Though make sure the fire trucks are on call just in case." He gave a lopsided grin.

Jarrod chuckled. "Let's try to hold down on the fire. Okay?"

"I'm just teasing. I'm not planning on disaster striking anytime soon."

Rolling his sleeves down, Jarrod buttoned the cuffs and strode through the crowd. Cassidy was packing up.

"Did you have a good day?"

She looked less than happy to see him. "I sold every peach I brought. And people signed up for my newsletter and want me to contact them when everything else is ready. So it was a wonderful day."

"Great. Let me buy you a lemonade to celebrate."

"I don't think that's a good idea." She looked around and Abby gave her a thumbs-up before joining the conversation.

"I hear they're amazing. Bo is bringing me one in a few minutes. He just texted me that the frying is about done and he'll be down here to take up some slack for me and Maggie."

"Go on, Cassidy," Clara Lyn hollered from three tables down.

Cassidy stared down that way and realized everyone she knew was watching them.

She wanted to go home . . . but he looked really good. *You are so weak. Weak, weak, weak.*

Or a glutton for punishment.

Going home was the smart choice.

He leaned in, "You *chicken*?"

"Chicken?"

"Cass, I am not going to bite."

"I-I didn't think you were."

"Then . . ." He pinned her with challenge in his eyes.

"What did he say?" Cassidy could hear Clara Lyn asking.

She heard Reba chuckle. "He called her a chicken."

"Y'all, do not get the wrong idea about this," Cassidy declared to set everyone straight. They were all in her business anyway.

Abby was laughing now, doggone her. "Just go, Cassidy. Relax."

"Easy for you to say," Cassidy wanted to grumble. Jarrod jerked his jaw in the direction of the lemonade truck, and she decided she'd better go before he started clucking at her in double dare. *Chicken, my foot.*

He cupped her elbow as they walked, even knowing everyone was watching. Her heart faltered with his touch and she tried to stay miffed at him. It was the safest route for her.

"A three-legged race is underway over there. I'm thinking you and me should take on my brothers and their wives in a little while."

"No way. I'm not getting tied to you." She was perfectly serious and the cowboy laughed.

"I'm serious, Jarrod."

"I know you are." His eyes were twinkling.

Ooh, drat him. "You know what your problem is? You're living in the past. I am not interested, Jarrod Monahan." She glared up at him. "You don't listen."

He grinned down at her. "On the contrary. Yesterday you said the past was the past and I totally agreed. I'm just reminding you of what you said so you don't waste years hiding out there at Roxie's place, letting your life fly by because you're afraid to step out and take a chance on real love."

She frowned, then glanced around the crowd to see people watching them. She leaned in close and nearly hissed, "I would take a chance if I wanted to. I don't want to. I just want a nice, quiet life."

He leaned down, bringing his face close to hers. "You will be bored out of your mind, Cassidy Starr."

"Bored —" Her heart was thumping. The man was maddening. "I-I will not. I will have my strawberry farming and my peach orchard and the B and B. That will keep me busy. Bored, ha!"

He grinned again. "But that's not what you've been satisfied doing. You had more fun hunting rustlers than you did picking peaches. And riding horses. Matter of fact, I'm planning to go on a roundup tomorrow, and I have a feeling you'd love to go."

She stiffened and crossed her arms. "I went with you looking for rustlers because you were stubborn and going alone and not telling anyone. I-I was worried about you."

"So you were worried about me?" he pressed. "I like that."

"Well, you are my neighbor. And you were nice to look out for Aunt Roxie, so it was the least I could do."

He laughed. "I try to be neighborly and I enjoyed looking out for Roxie. Now, what about that roundup? I'm counting cattle and checking tags and looking for signs of rustlers. It should be an eventful day. What do you say?"

"I was going to tiller up ground tomorrow."

His eyes widened. "Oh, sounds like a lot of fun. What do you say? Come ride with me, Cass," he said, ending softly and sending a tremble through her. "And in trade, but only if you want me to, I'll help you tiller up the strawberry patch. Key word here being *help.*"

"You are not playing fair. You know I like to go on roundups."

"I do remember that."

She really did want to go. She bit her lip, contemplating her choices. "Oh, all right. I'll go." She poked him in the chest. "But no hanky-panky. You keep your lips to yourself. And we'll see about the helping with the garden. I might take you up on that offer too."

Jarrod laughed. "If you say so, beautiful. But you and I both know it's more fun when we share."

She wacked his arm. "People are watching. They already have the wrong idea."

"Says who?"

She stared at him. "What has gotten into you, Jarrod Monahan?"

He stepped close again so she had to tilt her head back to look up at him. He felt reckless at the moment. He was doing everything he could to keep his hands off her, but it was getting harder and harder to do that. "I'm going after what I want, Cass."

"Oh." She swallowed hard and her forehead dampened. "Well, it's a little too late for that."

"I'll be the judge of that, thank you very much. Did you happen to read Maggie's column the last couple of weeks?"

She gasped. "You read advice columns?"

He chuckled. "I read my sister-in-law's column. I thought she gave the guy pretty interesting answers. Did you read them?" he asked again.

"Yes, but —"

"I agree with her advice. Now, let's get that lemonade."

He took her arm and drew her to the line where many people he'd never seen before were waiting.

He'd decided to push Cassidy. He'd flip-flopped on how to handle the situation and had finally realized he needed to shake things up. She needed some adventure, and opening a bed-and-breakfast and serving strawberries to someone else's family was

not what he hoped she chose as adventur-
ous enough. She deserved to have it all.

# 21

"So now that you've got me here and you brought it up, have you had any luck with the rustlers?" Cassidy had tried not to ask the whole time they waited on their drinks, but now that they'd walked away from the crowd toward the games, she had to ask. Because aggravating as it was, he was right — she really wanted to catch the blasted rustlers.

For one thing, she loved Pops and she wanted to do her part to make sure his ranch was safe. And, well, she had been getting a little bored picking peaches and working in the house. She didn't admit it to Jarrod, though.

And despite getting a little scraped up the other night, she'd had a blast looking for the rustlers. She'd go to her grave before she'd tell him that either.

And then of course he started playing dirty. Though she never would have asked to tag along, he'd remembered how much she'd loved to help work cattle and then invited her on the ride. And that was too good to pass up.

"I haven't found out anything more."

"I've been keeping my eyes open. And just a heads-up, Rand was asking questions this morning."

"He was? That man has some keen sense of trouble. He's always watching, even when you don't realize it. He's a newsman, so I'm certain he's already heard about the various robberies across this part of the state and he's been on the lookout. What did you tell him?"

"Nothing. I distracted him with other talk. I didn't want to lie, so I took the conversation to something else as soon as I could."

Jarrod gave her that smile that tilted her world.

She laughed. "What?"

"You're a regular Nancy Drew, Cassidy Starr."

"Ha-ha. And by the way, I am not doing *that*."

She pointed to a group of kids running the three-legged race obstacle course.

Okay, she thought a few minutes later as she looked at the group gathered at the starting line of the three-legged race. Maybe she was going to do it.

"This is going to be so fun," Maggie said, assuring her.

She and Tru were tied together on one side of Cassidy and Jarrod, and Abby and Bo were tied together on the other side. Cassidy had been no competition against all of them as they insisted she join in. And Jarrod was having the time of his life at her expense. Of course, the feel of his arm warm and securely draped down her back and his hand resting on her waist had her thinking about hugs and being held in his arms and . . .

It was very distracting.

"I'm enjoying myself already," Jarrod drawled next to her ear. She stomped his instep. "Hey!"

"Hay is for cows, I think."

"And hayrides. Which they are having later on tonight."

Wary eyes met his. "No. Don't even think it."

"Suit yourself. I'll be shooting off the fireworks anyway."

Doobie held up his official starting gun, and the small crowd — including Clara Lyn, Reba, Pebble, and Rand — was hooting and hollering at them.

"Ready, set, go!" *Boom!* The blank went

off and everyone started toward the first barrel they had to go around. Jarrod was very competitive with his brothers and the other men in the race. Why, the man literally gripped her by the waist and lifted her off the ground and plowed forward.

She heard Maggie and Abby laughing and glanced over to see they were pretty much being carried too. Their legs moved together but their feet were not touching the ground.

Suddenly they were going down. Jarrod grabbed her and flipped so that he landed on his back and cushioned her fall. The next thing she knew they were tangled on the ground together.

"That was terrible." She laughed, realizing he'd taken the hit. He was hugging her close as they laughed together when a little up ahead of them Bo and Abby bit the dust too. Then Tru and Maggie followed when Maggie tried to help run and instead tripped Tru and took him down.

"Well, it seems that no Monahan is the winner today."

Jarrod grinned. "Says who?" he murmured and nuzzled her neck, dropping a kiss just below her ear.

Her hand on his chest balled into a fist, clutching the fabric of his shirt as her gaze flew to his. They were so very close, and she was suddenly overwhelmed by how much emotion he could evoke in her. And the mischievous grin that he gave her was both sexy and fun at the same time. It sent songbirds fluttering through her. She gasped and couldn't look away. "You-you made us fall on purpose."

"Maybe. Okay, I cannot tell a lie."

Her heart pounded and the songbirds dipped and soared.

Cassidy pressed a hand to his chest and pushed him away. Then she untied the string around their legs and scrambled to her feet. "Cassidy, what are you doing?"

He stood up and walked beside her as she started toward the booths.

"Hey, Cassidy, where are you going?" Abby called, causing her to stop. She turned back toward the others.

"I am going to pack up my truck."

Abby and Maggie untied themselves from Tru and Bo, and they all stood up. He was glad he had some backup after apparently pushing too hard.

But he was thirty-four years old, and a month ago he'd been feeling like he was twice his age and was as lonesome as a hound dog. And according to his brothers, about as humorless as it got. And then Cassidy had shown up and spun everything inside of him into a twister that wasn't letting up, and suddenly he was laughing like a kid and feeling more alive than he'd felt in years.

Despite everything she was saying, he knew Cassidy was enjoying it too — when she let herself.

"We'll come help," Maggie said. "We need the guys to help carry tables."

Jarrod ended up being flanked by Bo and Tru as they trailed the girls through the crowd.

"I just saw you sneak a kiss," Bo said, elbowing him. "Way to go, big brother. I like your moves."

Jarrod scowled at Bo, suddenly concerned about who else had seen what he'd done.

"She looked a little upset, though," Tru said, joining in.

Jarrod tugged on the collar of his shirt. "I might have gotten a little ahead of myself. But I honestly can't help it."

His brothers grinned.

"My advice is to pace yourself," Tru offered.

"Yeah, this isn't a sprint. It's a marathon," Bo said.

Jarrod figured that was true, but he was ready to move forward now.

He caught Clara Lyn out of the corner of his eye and she and several ladies in town were all smiles. He did a double take, and it didn't make him feel any better when her smile broadened.

A sinking feeling hit him. Rumors were going to fly if Clara Lyn saw him nuzzle Cassidy's neck.

So be it. All he could do was go with his gut.

Cassidy could not believe she'd come back for the dance.

It was all Maggie's and Abby's fault. They had nagged her and goaded her unmercifully, saying she couldn't hide out there on her farm collecting animals just because she was afraid a man might talk her into changing her mind about staying single.

"I am not afraid," she'd assured them and tried to believe it herself as she'd headed home to feed her animals. She'd been feeding her lambs and seriously thinking about getting a goat and a pig when it dawned on her that her friends might be onto something. She was collecting animals, and she was a little afraid of Jarrod, if the truth be told. But even still, she had a plan for her life and she needed to prove to him and everyone that she meant business. And there was no better time to do that than at the Fourth of July evening dance and fireworks display.

Besides, coming back for the dance and mingling with everyone was a good thing. She could live alone, but she did need interaction. So here she was.

Darkness had set in by the time she got back to town. Lights shone on the Bull Barn parking lot, where the evening festivities would take place. Big Shorty had a crew come in and in a day they'd built a deck on the side of the diner. They'd finished it off with colored lights strung overhead, giving the deck a festive look.

As she got out of her truck, she could hear the band warming up. Her stomach felt bottomless as she walked toward the gathering crowd. Cowboys milled all about, and she caught several eyes turning her way as she hunted for someone to hang out with. Coming to the party alone was one thing, but hanging out on the fringes among friendly looking but unknown people wasn't exactly appealing.

"Cassidy." She felt a sense of relief as she looked around for Abby, whose voice she recognized.

The whole family was standing near the edge of the deck, and she stumbled on a rock as her mouth went dry. Jarrod stood beside his brothers looking oh so wonderful. There was that Monahan signature look all three of the brothers had, stamped hard by their grandfather's DNA. But Jarrod . . . he just drew her. Always had.

He'd changed into black denim jeans and a pale-blue western shirt. The shirt had a light shimmer to the material that brought out the deep blue of his eyes. Even in the shady illumination of the colored lights she knew this, though she couldn't actually see them from here.

She fought down the feelings surging through her. "Hi, everyone." She didn't look at Jarrod, but she was very aware that he was looking at her. She knew because she had goose bumps running along her neck where he'd planted that kiss earlier.

"You made it." Maggie gave her a hug among everyone else's greetings. "The band is going to be fantastic. You'll have such a great time. I just feel it."

She swallowed and her eyes slanted toward Jarrod of their own accord.

He winked at her. "You ready to do a little boot-scootin'?"

"No, I'm just here to enjoy the company."

"No way," Abby said. "You are going to get out there and have some fun like the rest of us." She glanced around. "Where's Pops?"

"Over there with some of his old cowboy buddies." Tru pointed to a group of older men sitting in lawn chairs. "They're telling old stories and waiting for the hour and a half to pass before we go shoot off the fireworks."

"We always bring him out to these gatherings," Jarrod said. "We just keep a close watch on him, and so do his friends."

Everyone talked and laughed about the day, and different people dropped by to chat. Cassidy was glad she'd come, even though she was wary of Jarrod.

The band started up at that moment, and with limited dance time people poured out onto the deck. Maggie and Tru joined the first group, and she heard someone call Tru's name and yell for him to show them his moves. She glanced at Jarrod, who was now standing next to her.

"He's a really good dancer and he always gets ribbed about it."

Bo laughed. "It's only because everyone's jealous."

"Hey, you're a good dancer too." Abby took Bo's hand and they joined the two-stepping group.

"May I have this dance, Cass?" Jarrod

reached out to take her hand.

"No."

"You want to dance with me," he drawled. That slow smile edged across his face as he dragged her willpower right out of her and grabbed her hand. And then before she could say another word, he pulled her into his arms and spun her over to the deck.

Her breath evaporated as he easily lifted her up the step and set her on the deck, then held her close and moved them smoothly into the crowd. He had some moves himself.

"You are not playing fair, Jarrod." It was a weak protest.

"Cass, just forget all that other stuff right now and let yourself have a good time. Let go of all the fear and relax. Okay?"

Fear. There was that.

"Fine, but you behave."

He grinned and spun her in rhythm to the music.

How exactly was she supposed to relax when all she could think about was being in his arms?

When the song ended she started to move away, but the band went right into another song. Jarrod spun her again and led her into a waltz.

"Are you having fun yet?" he asked, close

to her ear.

His breath was warm and sent a tingle down her spine. She nodded. "I am."

Nothing had changed. She was not threatened — she wasn't. She reassured herself as her hand tightened on his shoulder. The song ended, and when his hand tightened on her waist, a little ache in her heart snuck past all her bravado. Being held in his arms felt wonderful.

"Let's go grab something to drink. That lemonade is calling my name again," Jarrod said as the third song ended. He'd done everything he could to keep her out there as long as possible. She was beginning to relax, though she was still skittish. He was hopeful that he'd eventually win her over.

"Sounds wonderful. I'm parched after all that. You are a dancing machine."

He placed his hand on her lower back and gently led her through the group.

"Hey, ladies." Cassidy greeted Clara Lyn, Pebble, and Reba, who were standing with a group of women between the dance floor and the refreshments.

"You two looked good out there," Reba said with undisguised innuendo.

"Boy, is that an understatement," Clara Lyn added, waving her hand in front of her face. "Y'all were burnin' up that dance floor."

"I really enjoyed watching y'all," Pebble said, smiling. Then a sigh slipped from her. "So romantic."

He felt Cassidy stiffen. "Thank you, ladies," he said quickly. "Now it's time for something to drink." He moved Cassidy the four steps to the drinks table, grabbed a cup, and dug some ice from the ice bucket Big Shorty had been replenishing all evening. At the moment the owner had given up his post and he and his wife were moving onto the dance floor. Jarrod was in the middle of getting ice into the second cup when Cassidy gasped and started patting his shoulder.

"Look. *Look,* he's going to ask her to dance."

"What?" Jarrod straightened and Cassidy stepped closer, her hand gripping his arm.

He looked around to see what she was so excited about. "Who? Oh." This time he gasped seeing Rand approaching Pebble, hat in hand.

Cassidy's fingers dug deeper into his arm. She planted herself closer to him and whispered, "Do you know he's been writing letters to Maggie's column asking for advice on how to get Pebble back into his life?"

That information shocked Jarrod. "No kidding?"

"Isn't it romantic? He's so in love with her that he's even willing to reach out for advice. I want them to get together so badly. I know it's complicated but —"

"Evening, ladies," Rand said, lifting his tweed hat slightly, then placing it back on his head. "Pebble, I was wondering if you would do me the honor of this dance."

Cassidy clutched Jarrod's arm, staring up at him. "Oh, Jarrod, the song is 'Remember When.' "

Alan Jackson was crooning his way into the hearts of every woman out there while the live band took a short break. "It's a great song," he said, touching her cheek.

Her eyebrows met. "For them." She stepped away from him.

Jarrod reacted. Snagging her with his arm, he held her close, glad he'd set down their cups of ice the moment she'd first grabbed him. "Hold on. Listen."

Pebble had gone completely still and so had everyone around who was watching. What would Pebble do?

She nodded at last. "I would love to." She spoke so softly they almost missed it. And then she placed her hand in Rand's.

Rand looked like he could jump tall buildings in a single leap as he led the love of his life onto the deck.

Jarrod smiled. "He's really made a commitment to change. He's always been a great guy. He just let disappointment over Pebble not admitting that she loves him and agreeing to let their relationship move forward grab hold of him. I think relying on the bottle to drown out the emotions he was feeling snuck up on him and then cost him."

"I think Aunt Roxie would be so happy to see this."

"I do too," Clara Lyn said, turning to them. She had a hand to her heart. "I'm about to bust with happiness for the progress and my legs are about to buckle with fear."

"There is fear everywhere," Jarrod said. "A person just has to decide to live with it if they want a full life."

Cassidy looked at him, then quickly went back to watching Pebble and Rand. Jarrod poured the lemonade and handed her a cup, then they moved a few steps out of the way of others who might want something to drink.

"Well," Reba drawled, "I believe in Rand. And I believe he's got this whupped because he wants Pebble and that bottle was getting in between him and the love of his life.

When a man loves a woman like that, he's not going to let anything stop him."

Jarrod looked down at Cassidy — and agreed wholeheartedly.

"They really went all out," Cassidy said when the fireworks were over. They'd been amazing. She'd watched them with some of the women, including Maggie and Abby. The fire department had been in charge of the show, and she had been relieved Jarrod was occupied. She could finally relax.

It had been an unusual evening. But even now Jarrod was safely out in the pasture cleaning up the fireworks area, so there was no temptation to kiss him. None. No creating fireworks of their own. This had been a spectacular display for a small town, and she had no desire to produce any other display for the town gossip mill.

Thankfully and wonderfully, Pebble and Rand had taken the matchmaking minds of everyone off her and Jarrod. The older couple danced several songs together, and then Rand led Pebble back to the group, bowed slightly, and went back to join his friends.

When the fireworks started Rand came and sat down beside Pebble. They hadn't said much. They just sat there in companionable silence most of the time, looking up at the sky together, commenting occasionally on a particularly spectacular burst of light. Cassidy found herself watching them more than the fireworks. Just before the show ended Rand gave Pebble's hand a gentle squeeze, then left to take a few more photos for the paper.

"They are so sweet together," Maggie whispered to Cassidy as Clara Lyn and Reba nearly tackled their friend in excitement.

"So," she heard Clara Lyn say, "how do you feel? What do you think? Aren't you going to say anything?"

"No. Not right now. I have to think."

"He's being so charming," Reba gushed. "And you know he's the most debonair male in all of Wishing Springs. And he loves you desperately."

"He's a dear, dear man. I think I'll go home now," Pebble said to her buddies, then smiled and waved good night to Cassidy, Maggie, and Abby.

"Maggie," Cassidy said, "I think it's sweet that he writes those notes to your column. And you're giving him great advice."

Maggie chuckled. "I've been hearing the rumors that it's him, but I really have no idea. I see so many similar questions and scenarios in what people send me."

"Really." Abby leaned around Cassidy to hear better.

"Yes, y'all would be surprised how similar people's problems are. It's like life repeats itself all the time. I get several letters with similar situations and pick the one I think will resonate the most with those who need my advice. Then I answer that letter in the column. So do you know how many Torn in Texas folks there could be out there?"

"Wow, I'm shocked," Cassidy said as the last fireworks display went up. "And wow, wow! That right there is amazing."

"Yes, it is. Nothing shabby about those cowboy firemen," Maggie said. "But you know, I cannot fib. Though that is usually the case, in this situation Torn's is the only letter I received like it. His letter stood out and touched me. My first response to him was really long and drawn-out, then I had to reel in my advice and shorten it. After that response I got a lot of similar letters. It was as if he set off a firestorm of men wondering if they should hold on after having messed up."

"Your job is really complicated, isn't it?" Abby said.

Maggie sighed. "Life is complicated. I really have to pray hard that I don't say something wrong that messes up someone's life. That's why sometimes I make my answer simple rather than long-winded."

"I think you do great. Your column helped me when I was going through my troubled marriage. And you're right, I just felt like someone else understood. It gave me some hope that I could get through my situation."

"I'm glad. I'm always so encouraged when someone tells me that. And now I'm so nervous thinking about becoming a mom. I'm going to be asking Abby here for advice all the time."

"Hey, you're going to be great. Don't you think so, Cassidy?"

"Oh yeah." Cassidy reached out and squeezed each of her new friends' hands. "I am so glad I moved back to Wishing Springs and met y'all. This has been a wonderful night. I'm glad y'all talked me into coming. Now, though, I'm heading out." She stood up.

"We're glad you're here too," Abby said.

Maggie chuckled. "Yes, we are. And don't think for a moment that we don't know you're sneaking off *before* you have to see our handsome, hunky brother-in-law again."

"I'm pleading the Fifth Amendment." Cassidy laughed. "See y'all later this week to help paint the baby's room."

"Painting's going to be fun," Maggie called.

Cassidy waved over her shoulder and made a beeline to the parking lot. They were absolutely right. It was better to get out now than see Jarrod again.

Tomorrow's roundup would come soon enough. By then, hopefully her head would be screwed back on correctly and she wouldn't be thinking about how wonderful tonight had been . . . especially the moments spent in Jarrod's arms.

# 22

Cassidy had successfully made it through her first Fourth since she'd been back in town. She had been smiling as she pulled into her driveway the night before. She was also exhausted, and after giving Duce a little loving on the porch where he'd begun choosing to sleep, she didn't waste much time before tramping up the stairs to her room and crawling into bed. She set her alarm just in case she decided to go on the roundup.

She woke up the next morning after a long fight with sleeplessness and squinted at the clock through blurry eyes. She wasn't sure if she should go on the roundup, but she really wanted to so she rolled over and dragged herself out of bed.

The rooster was crowing when she drove up to Jarrod's barn. Several men and Jarrod were gathered, waiting to load their horses into a trailer.

"Mornin'," Jarrod said, greeting her. "We're riding into the interior to work. I've already got your horse loaded."

The man had known she'd be here.

Within moments everyone had gotten into two double cab trucks, and the two trailers with the horses led the way past the barn and into the pastures. She found herself squished between Jarrod, who was driving, and a cowboy named Gil.

"So you live next door?" Gil asked.

"Yes, I do. And I enjoy being way out here in the country."

"I like a woman who knows her way around a horse. And appreciates the land."

She looked at the attractive guy. He had the look of a man who was at ease with anyone he was around. He was pure cowboy. "I do."

Cassidy could feel Jarrod's shoulder rubbing against hers. She tried to keep her thoughts off that and on the road in front of them. She was looking forward to helping round up cattle. She had almost forgotten how much she loved riding. She had taken to it so quickly as a kid. Of course, she'd had the incentive of being with Jarrod on roundups if she did well.

And nothing about that had changed.

They drove through the pastures, Jarrod

with one hand draped over the steering wheel and one elbow hanging out the window. There was just something peaceful about riding through this land, and she wondered how she could have stayed away so long. Peace filled her.

"It's going to be a great day," she said, and Jarrod slid his amazing eyes her way. Then he flashed that smile, and her heart clutched.

When they unloaded the horses from the trailer, Jarrod watched Cassidy practically swing into the saddle. She was so excited to be on this ride. He wasn't playing fair by inviting her along, but then at this point he didn't really care.

This wasn't just about him getting Cassidy to fall in love with him. Oh, that was the master plan, but this was also about getting Cassidy to live again. To be that young woman he'd glimpsed that last summer after she'd shaken off some of the residue of her parents' messed-up lives. If Cassidy wanted to raise strawberries for the rest of her life, he was fine with that. But he was bound and determined that she wasn't going to do it out of fear. Or because she was hiding from the world. Or from him. When she hid from love, he felt like she buried part of herself. He'd witnessed it. He might be wrong, but he'd take that chance if it meant getting to the core of what Cassidy needed.

After the celebration, he'd sat on the porch late into the night, sure he was on the right track. If he wasn't, then she wouldn't have agreed to come today.

"Okay, men, let's round 'em up and bring 'em home," he called as he loped over to Cassidy. "You ready to ride?"

Charity danced to the side and pranced with the desire to go. "Let's ride. I'm ready, and so is Charity, it appears." She laughed.

Jarrod laughed too, nudged Raider, his horse, and led the way in a lope. She followed, pulling up beside him and tossing him a smile that set his heart to pounding.

"I'm glad you came along."

"Don't pull my leg. You knew I couldn't pass it up."

He smiled. "I hoped you couldn't, anyway."

Clara Lyn stared at Pebble, who had busted through the door of the salon and looked as if she'd not slept at all. The normally calm, well-put-together motel owner looked frazzled.

"I can't help myself. I need your advice."

"No." Clara Lyn held up her hands. "I am

not giving advice these days. Especially if it has to do with you and Rand."

Reba's mouth dropped open. "Ha! You are too giving advice. You just told Lorna Crenshaw to tell that *lazy* husband of hers to get off his —"

"You know that is an entirely different situation."

"Girls," Pebble broke in, making Clara Lyn feel bad.

"Sorry," she said, giving Pebble her full attention. "What is on your mind? You look terrible, and I don't think I have ever said that to you. For goodness' sake, come over here and sit down."

Pebble sank down and looked as if she was going to jump out of her skin at any moment. "I can't sleep. I know Rand has messed up. He's an alcoholic. But he's gone through a good program, and though I know there is always the chance that he could fall off the wagon, that he could turn back to drinking, I just feel like he isn't going to. And he told me he wasn't going to ask me to have to worry about whether he's going to lose control again."

"That's the sad part about addiction," Reba said, looking at Clara Lyn with wide eyes. She didn't know what to think of their friend's behavior either. "When you love someone who has an addiction, you never truly know if they've succeeded in recovering."

"And I've been doing my research, because I nearly gave you some bad advice a few months ago." Clara Lyn hesitated. "To be quite frank, Pebble, the statistics are not that positive." Clara Lyn hated to point this out, but she was worried for her friend. "There is no way to ever truly know. It can be terribly hard on the loved ones."

"I agree, Pebble," Reba said, nodding. "I couldn't tell you what to do in this situation. I want Rand to be healed and over this mess and to never have to worry about desiring that bottle again. But only he can do that."

Pebble looked conflicted. "I know," she said. "And I'm certain Rand feels exactly the same way. And through his AA meetings and the recovery group at the church he's been attending regularly, I believe Rand has recognized what a battle he faces. That is why he pulled away. He is trying to protect me. Trying to take this worry off my shoulders."

Clara Lyn looked at Reba to see if she knew what to say. This was the toughest advice she had ever been asked to be a part of.

"But I'm an adult," Pebble said, sounding strong and irritated at the same time. "And I can make the decision on my own."

Clara Lyn scowled at her. "If that's so, then why are you here asking me and Reba? Giving us nervous breakdowns worrying about pointing you in the wrong direction?"

"Because it's a major decision and you girls are my sounding board. I know what I'm feeling, but feelings can lead you astray sometimes when good sense needs to be the guide."

"That is the truth." Clara Lyn bit her lip and tried to think objectively about this situation.

"So what do you feel?" Reba asked. That woman's romantic heart was going to get her into trouble one day. Or someone else. Clara Lyn was all for matchmaking and happily-ever-afters, and she had her eye on Jarrod and Cassidy right now. But this was Pebble.

"I love him. I always have. And I've always clung to my conservative nature and kept my distance."

Alarms were clanging in Clara Lyn's head now. "Pebble, you are a mature, adult woman who has had a good life. Your conservative nature has steered you the right way all these years, so don't go being hard on it right now."

Pebble stood up. "But that's just it. I'm ready to take some risk. Like selling the motel. I want to do some different things . . . and to believe in Rand. You've seen him. He is looking so healthy and he is stronger now. His attitude is different. He-he knows he's hurt me and he's fixing that. I believe in him."

Clara Lyn sighed. "I can't lie. Before I realized the kind of problem he had, I was always rooting for y'all to marry. We all were. And you know Roxie believed in y'all."

Reba nodded. "It's true. We all felt that way. But the risk of selling the motel and the risk of marrying Rand are not the same thing."

"You're right. But I don't believe his drinking got this bad until just last year. And then he got depressed that night at the wedding when he got drunk and told me he loved me on the microphone in front of everyone and sang that awful song."

It *had* been awful. He was not Whitney Houston or Dolly Parton, but he sang "I Will Always Love You" at the top of his lungs, slurring and weaving. "That was embarrassing for you. And for him, I imagine."

"It was. And then he just got worse and

worse." Pebble pressed her slender shoulders back. "But I believe he's overcome this. And I feel strongly that I need to tell him so."

It was a hot day in Texas. Despite the breeze, Cassidy's sweat trickled from her thick, curling hair and ran down between her shoulder blades. Her bra was soaked and so was her shirt, but she was feeling great. Even dusty and eating grit. She loved a roundup. Loved the feel of galloping across a pasture after a runaway.

"There, I'll get that one," she called when a cow bolted. Nudging Charity into a gallop, she went into pursuit. Cassidy hadn't ridden a cutting horse in a long time, but she was good in the saddle, always with a good seat and had great balance. Pops had been her teacher and he was the best. She was rusty, but doing all right today.

They'd had a busy morning and she'd loved every moment of it. Jarrod had ridden beside her most of the way. She was having a hard time not thinking about the kiss or the dancing last night — and the feel of his arms around her. He wore his chaps today, and because he hadn't shaved this morning he had a five o'clock shadow. He looked heart-flutteringly appealing.

She cut the cow off and turned her back, wheeling Charity around to change the direction of the heifer. It felt great, watching the horse respond to her direction and then feeling the freedom that came from riding strong with the beautiful animal. She loved ranch life.

"That was impressive," Jarrod said, smiling as she pulled Charity to a halt beside him.

"Thanks." She laughed, feeling breathless and happy. "I had forgotten just how fun this can be."

Jarrod chuckled, but then turned serious.

"I like it when you're smiling like this, Cass. No tears, no anger, just free enjoyment. That's what you need to be looking forward to from here on out. Not the junk of the other day."

"This is what I'm shooting for by taking my future into my control."

His gaze dropped to her lips and she felt goose bumps everywhere.

"And that means no room for a man?"

"A woman does not need a man in her life to feel fulfilled," she snapped, irritation sparking through her that he'd just ruined the moment.

His jaw tightened as he studied the cattle being herded through a gate into another pasture. "You're right," he said after a second, just as a cow broke and charged from the herd. Jarrod had his horse charging after it before anyone else even had time to react.

Cassidy watched him go, feeling every muscle in her body tense.

She did not need him to be a fulfilled, joyful woman.

Jarrod tried his hardest to stay clear of Cassidy for the rest of the roundup. He let her have her space, which she seemed to want. And he had other things to worry about. When they got the cattle herded into the other pasture and the corral that was there for loading, he and his men started a systematic ear tag check, marking off the numbers against his official numbers. Five head were missing from this group.

He had decisions to make on his strategy to stop this theft and he did not need to be thinking about Cassidy.

When they finally got back to the barn and his men had left, he found Cassidy in the stall, brushing down her horse. The sun filtered in on her through the open doors and his gut tightened. In his heart he knew she belonged here. Last night when they were dancing it had taken all his self-control not to pull her close and kiss her until she saw stars. He loved her. Always had. And nothing was ever going to change that.

He'd had to talk himself out of not going straight to her house after they'd cleaned up the fireworks. He wanted to tell her how he felt, but he talked himself off that cliff. He had to be patient.

For his life to feel complete he needed her. But did she need him?

If not, he might have to live with that.

"She's looking good," he said, leaning against the stall.

"I'm almost done," Cassidy said briskly. Her strokes were jerky as she brushed Charity's coat, and he noticed her hand shook as she finished.

Knowing he was wrong to do it, he moved to lift a strand of hair from her cheek. "It was a good day, Cass. But any day with you makes my day good." Sometimes with Cassidy he didn't even recognize himself.

She stilled. "You just don't give up, do you?"

He cupped her face in his hands and gently brushed his lips against hers. The being patient thought was out the window. "Not when I want something so much. I love you, Cassidy. You're driving me crazy and I just have to spell it out. You are all I want."

Her breath caught.

"Jarrod. Hold on, just . . . just back up." She moved away from him and stalked from the stall and down the center of the barn between the nickering horses. He followed, jogging to catch her.

"Come on, Cass, admit it. I believe you love me. You're going to throw that away?" Jarrod stopped when he reached the parking area and put his hands on his hips. This wasn't like him. He'd sworn he wasn't going to pressure her, but here he was doing it.

She spun at her truck, her fierce gaze drilling into him from across the fifteen-foot gulf separating them. It felt like the Gulf of Mexico.

"You stay away from me, Jarrod Monahan. I came back to Strawberry Hill with a plan. I came here knowing what I wanted the rest of my life to look like, and then you started . . . started messing with my mind. I can be fulfilled. I will be. If you would just leave me alone."

"You're messing with my heart, Cass. And you know I'm messing with yours too."

He moved toward her, slow and steady, recognizing the need for flight in her eyes.

He had pushed her too far, but maybe she needed some shaking up.

"You've got me to where I'm not tending to my business. I've got cattle disappearing like a bag of M&Ms and right now I don't give a big hoot. All I care about is holding you in my arms, Cassidy. And telling you that I love you. And that I want to spend the rest of my life showing you that you were done wrong and that you deserve better. And I'm the man for the job. Nothing else matters to me like you and that mission."

He stopped in front of her. She was all fire and warrior woman as he looked at her, and it made him smile. *Thank you, Lord, for putting her in my life.* The prayer of thanks filled him. Now he just had to pray the Lord would show him how to win her over.

"Jarrod, don't do this to me," she said softly, her voice wavering. "My heart can't take being toyed with. I just can't do it."

"I'm not toying with you, Cass. I'm dead serious."

Her gaze searched his and lingered on his mouth, then jerked back to his eyes and hardened.

"I'm serious, too, so stop. Just stop, Jarrod." Eyes glittering with anger, Cassidy scrambled into her truck, cranked the engine, and drove away.

"Cass, wait!" he called, but she didn't look back at him. She just kept driving.

And Jarrod suddenly felt like the biggest idiot on the planet.

# 23

A week had passed since she'd gone on the roundup with Jarrod. Cassidy had managed to get the old tiller chugging along and had really dug into churning up the ground for her garden and strawberry patch. She ordered supplies for her strawberry business and had begun to work on the rustic cabinet, sanding, repairing, and then staining it. It was looking great.

She was busy and overwhelmed, hot and sweaty, but that was what she needed. The hard work meant that she fell into bed worn out by the end of the day. And the sweat . . . well, she hoped it was sweating her desire for Jarrod out of her system.

It was not working.

She thought about him all the time.

That stunt he'd pulled at the barn had really made her mad, though. He knew how she felt and he still used her love of horses as a manipulation to sway her from her plan. Of course she fell for it, because she did love to ride.

If there was one thing she'd learned to recognize it was manipulation, and she despised it. But she'd missed it from Jarrod at first, and it bothered her that she had.

She drove into town and parked her truck in front of the feed store. When she hopped out, Duce jumped from his seat and walked beside her. The dog had started racing to the truck and jumping in whenever he realized she was going somewhere. It was easy to see from the way he knew his way around that he'd once been a regular rider.

Who had owned Duce? The question nagged at Cassidy. And she pushed the fear away that one day whoever it was would show up and claim her buddy. She had to get past worrying about that.

"Stay," she said as she entered the building, and Duce sat obediently on the front porch of the place, grinning up at her happily. Cassidy paused and rubbed between his ears like he loved her to do, and then she went inside through the large garage door opening that enabled trucks to back up to the dock and have their beds loaded full of feed.

The feed store was a dusty, musty old building with stacks of feed lining one wall and all kinds of items anyone might need to run a farm or ranch. Her nose twitched as she entered and she fought off a sneeze.

To her surprise Doc was there with Clover on a leash. She also saw Doobie and Doonie.

Arthur McEroy owned the place and had been in business for years. There was a coffee bar over in the corner with a brew so strong it would curl hair on a pig. She'd made the mistake of accepting a cup last time she came in and would never do that again.

The men all liked to gather there, and various groups came and went during the day. So she shouldn't have been surprised to see these three.

"Hi, boys. What are y'all doing today?" Clover came prancing to the end of her leash to rub against Cassidy's leg like a cat. She laughed and gave the animal a back rub. The pig grunted when she tried to stop and bumped her leg with her rump, code for "More, please." Her little curly tail wagged, and she looked up at Cassidy to give her what Cassidy still could swear was a grin. She really was a cute pig. And to think, Roxie had given it to Doc . . . that still baffled her. But then, Aunt Roxie had

had that knack of giving people what they needed.

Roxie.

Like she'd known she would need her home and the land, and she'd known she would need it protected by putting it in trust for Cassidy so it couldn't be sold off as Jack had so wanted to do when she'd first inherited it.

She looked up from petting the pig and realized no one had answered her question. They were all watching her. "Um, what's up, fellas?"

"Oh, I'm here getting Clover her supplements and feed," Doc said with a grunt, then jerked a thumb at the twins. "These two here, who knows? They just follow me around sometimes."

"Nothing else to do on a slow afternoon," one of the twins said.

The other one added, "We were just discussing the Thanksgiving in July celebration." He and his brother grinned that wide, lopsided smile.

"It was a grand celebration. So what are you up to, little lady?" Arthur asked, then took a swig of coffee.

"I need an almanac, I think. I was going through Aunt Roxie's books and she has a lot of them, so I'm pretty sure she must have planted her garden accordingly."

"Yup, she bought one every year," he said while walking slowly over to a stack of books sitting on a dusty shelf. "You can't go wrong using this. Old-timers stand by it." He spat a stream of tobacco into a spittoon and Cassidy cringed. He'd aimed at it like it was a bull's-eye on a target. "The gravitational pull of the moon is a strong factor in almost everything, especially a garden."

Doc chuckled. "Works pretty good holding the earth in orbit too."

"I hear it works pretty good on romance too," a twin said, his eyes twinkling. "Ain't that right, Doonie?"

The striped golf shirt was Doonie, she noted.

"That's what I hear. You and Jarrod looked real cozy at the dance last week. What's all this I'm hearing about you two?"

"What do you mean?" she asked. She followed their gazes, which were locked on the front window. Jarrod was getting out of his truck.

"Heard he's sweet on you," Doobie said.

"F-from who?"

The four men all grinned.

"You're turning pinker than Clover's snout," Doc observed, his normally grouchy expression one of suppressed mirth.

Could *he* have spread that rumor?

"We saw you two dancin' at the celebration." Doc chuckled.

Oh, right. Before she could say anything, Jarrod gave Duce a little love and then strode through the door. Cassidy forced away the warm feeling that gave her. She would not soften. The more she'd thought about it, the more obvious it was that he used her love of horses to try to sway her.

And he'd told her he loved her. That alone had her feeling unsteady.

When Jarrod saw her he stopped beside the horse tackle and stared. She suddenly felt like she was a glass of water and he was a cowboy coming in off a long dusty cattle drive, dying of thirst. It was ridiculous. She shook herself and stiffened her resolve.

"Cass," he drawled. "May I say you are looking lovely today?"

She narrowed her gaze and he grinned, and she heard snorts from the twins. The man was confirming the rumors to these old coots and she was going to have to try to live it down.

She ignored him and spun toward the counter. "How much do I owe you for the almanac, please?" It took extreme effort to hold her voice steady.

Arthur grinned. "The moon's on the

increase, you know."

"Sure is," one of the twins said. *Doonie,* she thought, shooting him a warning glare. When his brother chuckled, she shot him the same warning.

Arthur grinned wider. "You believe in the almanac, Jarrod?"

Jarrod laughed. "You fellas must have talked to my grandmother."

Cassidy gasped. "Do *not* egg them on. The almanac is all about *gardening* and you know it."

"Oh, that's what we're talking about," a twin said.

She knew good and well that they were talking about romance. Or was she being too sensitive?

"What are you talking about, Cassidy?" Doc patted Clover on the snout.

"Uh, nothing. I just need my almanac, please." She forced a smile at Arthur and tapped her toe on the cement floor, wanting nothing but to escape.

Arthur rattled off a price, then fiddled with the old cash register, taking his time as he counted out her change. As soon as he handed it to her, she picked up her book. "Y'all have a nice day," she said stiffly. Clover pranced beside her on the way to the door. Duce stuck his head inside and barked at the pig.

She halted. "Stay, Clover," she commanded, but the pig butted her in the knees with her hip and pranced around her like she was trying to keep Cassidy in this impossible situation.

Duce came inside wiggling all over as he came toward the pig. He barked again, which was not like him. Clover jumped and started squealing like someone was twisting her tail. She charged back to Doc.

Cassidy felt bad for scaring the poor pig. But she didn't slow down as she walked from the building.

Frustration had her hands shaking. She yanked open her truck door and let Duce jump into the seat. She followed and was pulling out of the parking space when Jarrod walked out of the feed store. She saw him tip his hat at her and watch her as she left. The man had turned her life upside down.

As Jarrod drove away from the feed store, he reflected on the last week. He was worn out and not gaining ground on the disappearing cattle. He'd been on stakeout at various parts of the ranch, but nothing happened. He'd gathered film from all of his cameras set up in different areas, and all was quiet there too.

And the problem with long nights with nothing to do but sit in his truck and watch his cattle or ride camp out on a high hill was that it gave him plenty of time to think about Cassidy.

She had been avoiding him and he'd been giving her space. Then when he finally saw her he acted like an oaf. He watched her leaving the feed store and wanted to kick himself. He was driving back through town on the way home, wondering what to do, when he spotted Rand walking toward the Sweet Dreams Motel, carrying a small bouquet of flowers. It seemed Rand was courting Pebble.

That made Jarrod smile. He hoped the older man was having better luck than he was. Pulling out his cell phone, Jarrod took his lead from Rand and called the florist.

The day after the feed store fiasco — something Cassidy had replayed in her mind and eventually in her dreams through the *entire* night — she was in the lambs' pen playing with the pair of darlings, hoping they could bring her blood pressure down. It wasn't really working, though. She was confused and baffled as she thought about the entire experience.

She did have this thought about all the

high-voltage anger and determination she was feeling toward Jarrod. Perhaps in her heart of hearts she wanted to throw caution to the wind and run carelessly, foolishly, recklessly into his arms, laughing in the face of all the heartache she'd gone through. Perhaps she just wanted to believe that life with Jarrod could be the fairy tale she'd once believed it could be . . . or at least some semblance of it!

Cassidy hugged Petunia, buried her face in the sweet lamb's soft coat, and wished just once in her life things would go easily. She just wanted a simple, uncomplicated life with a B and B, a strawberry farm, a garden, and a peach orchard. She did not want a handsome neighbor constantly reminding her of the things she'd decided she did not want in her life.

And causing silly, ridiculous scenes like what happened at the feed store.

She looked up at the sound of a car. A van with Blooms Galore and a large phone number scrawled across it was pulling up the driveway. Cassidy moved Petunia and Percy off her lap and stood. She recognized the petite woman hurrying across the yard carrying a vase of yellow roses as a member of the city council, Betty Brisco.

"Cassidy, you will probably be the envy of

half of four counties when word gets out that you received two dozen roses from Jarrod Monahan. That, and having danced the night away with him on the Fourth of July."

Cassidy walked from the lamb pen, holding her mouth clamped shut or else it would have been dragging in the dirt.

The flowers were perfect and beautiful. The lady held them out to her and in automatic response she took them.

"But I don't understand," she said, too stunned to form coherent words.

"What's not to understand? Your dreamboat neighbor is sweet on you. Enjoy! I've got to run — more deliveries to make."

With that the florist hopped into her van and drove off with a wave out the window.

Cassidy stared at the flowers, totally stunned.

Jarrod was in the corral working with a fairly rebellious colt. Despite their time together, the horse was still nervous and unpredictable. But Jarrod was about to ride him for the first time and hoped he didn't get himself into a wreck saddle breaking him. Tru was the champion trainer, the best at what he did, having taken after Pops.

But Jarrod had never been interested in

competition or showing. His goal wasn't a horse that would win a competition but a horse that was useful on the ranch. One he could sell to the other ranches to work their cattle. He loved being in the saddle, loved the feel of knowing he'd given the animal something useful to do with its life.

There were those who thought all horses should run free and wild, but Jarrod felt like God had made horses specifically with a purpose in mind, and that was to help a cowboy work his ranch. Everyone needed a purpose in life. Not all animals had the mind or the inclination to become useful, but horses? They were beauty in motion, and their minds were quick and loyal. They also seemed to truly enjoy their work. And they enjoyed competition, too, as was evident in the horses Tru trained.

"Easy, boy," Jarrod said quietly, slipping his boot into the stirrup as he took hold of the saddle horn. Then in as smooth a motion as possible, he stood up in the stirrup, one boot in and one hanging free. He'd give him a few more moments to get used to the feel of him. The colt jumped to the side a couple of strides but didn't kick or buck. Jarrod leaned into the horse but continued to stay on only the one side for now.

The colt was doing great, but Jarrod

needed him to acclimate to his weight since this was the first time anyone had ever tried to ride him. If Jarrod did his job correctly, the horse would never do all that wild bronc bucking Hollywood movies loved to depict. Instead, the colt would adjust and learn to trust him. It was all about trust.

Just like love.

The sound of a vehicle coming up the drive distracted Jarrod. He glanced over his shoulder in time to see Cassidy's old truck racing up the lane. She only knew one speed coming and going, and it was apparently pedal to the medal. His pulse jumped like the colt, which started hopping sideways at the unexpected sound.

Jarrod put his attention back on his ride and saw that the colt's ears were now laid back. Not a good sign.

"Whoa there, it's okay. Come on," Jarrod urged calmly.

Everything would have been fine if it hadn't been for the truck's sudden, loud backfire.

# 24

As she drove up, Cassidy spotted Jarrod preparing to ride the colt. By the way he was standing in one stirrup, she recognized that he was breaking it. It was magic to watch the man gentling a horse. He'd been doing it since before he graduated from high school, and there was just so much beauty in what he did. Yes, Tru and Pops had been the showmen, but Jarrod had his own talent with a horse.

Her stomach tumbled, from the knowledge that she was about to apologize for being rude at the feed store but also because she was going to tell Jarrod not to send her flowers anymore. Yes, she had been both shocked by and reluctantly pleased about them. But if people were talking before now, as soon as they learned about the flowers there would be no stopping the talk. Jarrod was literally giving them something to talk about.

When she turned her truck's engine off, it rattled and then backfired. The boom made her jump, but it was Jarrod and the horse that drew her attention. The colt went from semi-calm to rodeo bronc in a millisecond. Jarrod flew over its head and landed in the dust as the colt jumped and bucked.

Cassidy's heart slammed into her throat. She rushed from the truck, scrambled across the expanse separating them, and climbed the railing. "Jarrod!"

He was on his knees, shaking his head as if dazed. Then the hoof of the horse slammed into his shoulder, just barely missing his head.

Cassidy didn't think twice. She swung her legs over the fence and jumped.

She landed in the soft earth at a run, waving her arms and yelling. She didn't hesitate, she didn't think; she just ran with force. The horse bolted to the far side of the arena when it saw the crazy woman flying toward it like a banshee.

Cassidy jumped between the colt and Jarrod. Making a barrier, she planted her feet about the time the horse rounded on her and rose up on its two back legs to paw the air.

Cassidy's heart thundered. She didn't have a clue what to do in this situation.

"Get out of here, Cass," Jarrod said from between gritted teeth behind her.

"Are you kidding me? That horse almost killed you." She glanced over her shoulder to see his shirt was ripped open and a long gash on his shoulder was bleeding. *This is my fault.*

Jarrod tried to stagger to his feet. Lunging at her, he grabbed her around the waist like he'd done when he'd saved her from the rattlesnake, only this time he was unsteady and nearly took her down. The horse bolted toward them, angrily snorting. Cassidy didn't think. She just reacted, needing to get Jarrod out of the line of those hooves. She grabbed him around the waist to help him stand. Blood smeared on her shoulder.

They staggered to the side, and with all the strength she had she tried to keep them both upright as they moved toward the fence. The colt was pawing the ground and its nostrils were flared. Its ears were flat to its head and its dark eyes looked frighteningly wild.

"What's wrong with that horse?"

"Just scared," Jarrod said through clenched teeth as he reached for the chain that held the gate closed. "It's what people and horses do to protect themselves when they're scared of something. Keep going," he urged. She did as he said, keeping her arm firmly around his taunt waist. The man's middle was hard as rock. When they were both through the gate, he hooked the chain back into the slot, securing it. Putting it between them and the wild horse.

"It's glaring at us like it would like to kick our skulls in. And it very nearly would have kicked yours if it had been half a foot to the left."

"Like I said, he's scared. A horse's natural instinct is to run from danger and buck. That's all the protection God gave them from a cruel world. The backfire made him react by instinct. People do similar things, you know."

He was taking up for the horse that almost killed him. She tried to ignore the comment about people. "You're bleeding, bad. I think you could need stitches."

"I'm fine. I have an emergency kit and supplies at the barn. It's in the tack room. Don't blame the horse. It was my fault. I got distracted."

"My fault for my truck blowing up."

They made it inside the barn, and he pulled his arm from her shoulders as he grabbed hold of the workbench. He was swaying again, and blood ran down his arm.

Opening a drawer beside the sink, Jarrod

pulled out a rag and covered his gash. He shot her a sideways glance that had her breath catching in her throat.

Jack had that flirtatious look and he'd given it freely.

*Jarrod isn't Jack.*

Her pulse rattled through her like a train on shaky tracks. It blasted through her as if it were on a collision course with disaster.

She wanted to turn away and run. Wanted to get out of there now, as soon as she could. But she was responsible for the hemorrhaging gash in his shoulder. She grabbed an old chair sitting against the wall and carried it to him. "Sit and let me look at this."

He sat down without fighting.

She swallowed hard and reached for the rag, replacing his hand with hers to apply pressure to the wound.

"I'm thinking stitches. Two at least. Maybe more."

"Douse it with alcohol, dry it, then put those butterflies on it. I'll be fine."

"Are you joking? It will heal badly."

He chuckled. "So you think a scar on my shoulder is something I need to worry about?"

"Well, I guess that isn't something a man thinks that much about."

"It's part of the job. Now, if the colt had missed and kicked me in the face we might be talking about something different."

"Which very nearly happened." She wanted to lose her cream cheese bagel thinking how close that horse hoof had come to his temple. And all because of her cantankerous truck. "My need of a tune-up could have harmed you greatly."

He chuckled again. "That would have been something to put on my tombstone."

Her mouth fell open. "That is not something to joke about."

"Hey, lighten up, Cassidy. I've worked on a ranch all my life. Don't you think I have been involved in a few cattle and horse wrecks in my day? This is a liability of the work I do and you know it. Still, believe me, it's not listed on the most dangerous job list."

She grabbed the alcohol, then the gauze from the open first-aid kit and doused it with the clear liquid. "I need to get to that to wrap it," she said, and then realized as he began unbuttoning his shirt that he would need to either take it off or rip off the sleeve. Before she could say more, the shirt was dropped over his knee and he sat in front of her shirtless.

Holy smokin' pine cones! Cowboyin' kept

a body in shape.

Jarrod Monahan was lean, hard, and tanned. Her breath caught again, and she had to focus on carefully blotting the gash.

Not that he probably cared whether he was a perfect male specimen, at least she hoped not. Jack, on the other hand, loved being gorgeous.

Why did she keep comparing the two?

She kept her gaze on his gash and got it cleaned. But she felt him studying her while she worked.

"Did you need something?" he asked after a moment. Her gaze flew to his as a boulder lodged in her windpipe and she coughed.

"Excuse me?" she wheezed, her hands shaking so badly she dropped the gauze.

He acted as though her reaction were normal. "You came here for something. What were you needing?"

"Oh, I . . ." She reached for another piece of gauze and felt like bopping herself on the forehead. "I came to tell you that . . . um, to tell you not to send me flowers."

"Good. You got them. I'm glad."

"Yes, but I don't want them."

"Were they pretty?"

"Well, yes. Beautiful. But I —"

"Good. I'm apologizing for all that teasing that happened at your expense in the feed store yesterday."

That took her by surprise. "Oh."

"And trying to woo you at the same time."

"No, Jarrod, I do not want to be wooed. I do not want to give the town something more to talk about. We already did that."

He chuckled. "I don't mind them talking. And I can't promise you I'm not going to be giving them more to talk about."

"What? Why?"

He chuckled, and it sent those blasted tingles rioting through her. She finished securing the gauze over his wound but couldn't move away from him.

"Because I'm about to start some good, old-fashioned courting of the lady I plan to marry."

Deep, amazing eyes as fathomless as the ocean held hers. Cassidy melted on the inside. "No. No, no, no. N. O."

He grimaced. "Can't change what I feel, Cass."

"But I don't feel it. Or want it."

He stood, wobbled slightly, and reached for her. He pulled her against him. "I think you do. I ran like a terrified cowboy still wet behind the ears once. Do you know I got snowed in, in Montana? That I came back to Texas as soon as I could get off that line shack in the middle of that monster ranch?

Back to you? But when I got here your aunt Roxie told me you'd married. And she told me I was an idiot. And as always she was right."

He'd come back for her.

The idea shocked her. He'd changed his mind and come back for her.

"Cassidy, I love you. I can't give up without proving to you that I'm not that stupid young kid who walked away anymore. I'm the man who will love you, and stand by you, and care for you." He kissed her.

When his lips touched hers, a jolt of delirious shock coursed through Cassidy and she responded instantly. Her arms entwined his neck of their own accord. Joy filled her as he responded by pulling her tightly to him and claiming her lips more firmly. His kiss was rough, almost desperate, as if he'd been holding back for years. Emotions collided inside Cassidy as she reveled in his touch and the beat of his heart, the feel of this man in her arms. She knew now she'd always loved him.

The lure of him held her. She kissed him in return with the same desperation, born from all those lost dreams.

Sanity intruded and brutal reality slammed into her. She pulled back.

"No," she said weakly. What was she doing? "I-I can't." She tore herself out of his arms and backed away. Needing the space between them. Needing the gulf to keep her from throwing herself back into his arms.

"Too much has happened," she said firmly. "You might not be that scared cowboy anymore, but I'm not that naïve girl anymore either." She turned and fled, her heart thundering louder with every step she took away from him.

Jarrod didn't watch her walk away this time. It was the same thing over and over again. He might as well get it into his thick skull and let her have what she wanted, which was clearly not him. But she'd kissed him, responded . . .

He rammed a hand into his hair, frustration tearing him up. His shoulder throbbed, but he barely noticed over the chasm that had just reopened in his heart. As Cassidy's truck rumbled down his drive, he stalked toward the house for another shirt, forcing his mind to go back to work. To do what he did best and take care of this ranch. He needed to turn the colt back out into the pasture to cool off, then check in with Gil on how the fence building on the southwest corner of the ranch was progressing. He hadn't been going out with them to work because he had colts to gentle up before delivering them in a couple of weeks.

He had stakeout tonight too. Maybe this time he'd get lucky. The one good thing about the stakeout was that it gave him time to cool down and think up his next move with Cassidy. He needed to think clearly, but no matter where he tried to take his mind, it kept going right back to that kiss. And there was no thinking clearly then.

"We've got another one," Clara Lyn said, busting through the salon door two weeks after the Fourth of July. This year it seemed all kinds of trauma had erupted after the fireworks had long faded from the sky. Why, Pebble was still in a dither about what to do with her love life, and then there was Cassidy and Jarrod. Oh, how she'd had high hopes that those two would fall madly in love.

And they very well could be, but at the moment they were practically walking on opposite sides of the street if they got anywhere near each other. Ever since Betty Brisco had delivered those flowers from Jarrod to Cassidy there seemed to be a line drawn firmly in the sand between them.

Roxie would be rolling over in her grave if she could see the mess these two romances were in. But Torn in Texas was still alive and kicking and writing in to Maggie's column. Clara Lyn was proud of Rand for not giving up. The man was out to prove something, and she for one was starting to root for him again. Despite how aggravated she'd been.

Reba was tying on her apron, getting prepared for her first customer in thirty minutes. She was beaming like a floodlight.

"You read the morning paper, I see." She was grinning from ear to ear. "He's not giving up, is he?"

"Doesn't sound like it." Clara Lyn glanced at the paper she had folded open to the headline "Gotta Have Hope." She was just about to read it out loud when Bertha threw the door open and came hustling inside. The stout nurse was early for her weekly roll-up, but she was carrying a paper in her hand too. She held it up and waved it in the air.

"You gals read the paper this morning? We have ourselves a regular reality TV show on paper goin' on right here in Wishing Springs."

"We wondered how many others realized Torn in Texas was one of our own," Clara Lyn said.

"Oh yeah, I realized it last week. I had my

niggling suspicions before that, but after careful observation I realized this here was happening in real time in front of us."

Clara nodded and went back to the article. "Dear Maggie, I've messed up. I've rushed the love of my life because I'm so intent on making things right from the past and moving on with our lives. But now, after attempting to make my intentions known, I've upset her and may have frightened her off completely. I'm thinking it might be best for me to give up for her sake, but my heart is fighting me every step of the way. Your advice would be greatly appreciated once more. Do you have any tips that would help me either fix this or walk away like a man who wants only the best for the amazing woman who has endured so much? Always grateful, Torn in Texas."

Clara Lyn slapped the newspaper down beside the cash register. "I have to tell you, that man is really changing my attitude."

"Mine too," Reba said. "I think he's changed."

"Changed," Bertha huffed. "What about that man needs to change? He is about the most perfect man I've ever encountered."

Clara Lyn gaped at Bertha. "You think Rand is perfect?"

"I am shocked," Reba said, gasping. "I

wasn't even aware you and Rand got along all that much."

Bertha was glaring at them. She stuffed her hands on her hips. "Do you two have a fever?"

"Well, no. Do you?" Clara Lyn shot back.

"No. Torn in Texas isn't Rand Ratliff. It's that hunk of burnin' love Jarrod Monahan. And you both know the man is finer than refined sugar. I could sop that man up like molasses with a butter biscuit."

*"Jarrod,"* Clara Lyn said in unison with Reba. Shock slapped her like a mad woman.

"Well, yes. It's obvious. That man has had a thing for that girl since he kissed the daylights out of her on the Fourth of July back when she just graduated from high school. He ran off to Montana and got himself snowed in while Cassidy ran off and married some bum she barely knew. Roxie didn't explain all this to y'all?"

"Nooo." Clara Lyn could not believe it. Roxie had never mentioned anything about a kiss or Jarrod having been crazy about Cassidy all these years. She was a little insulted, to be honest.

"How do you know all this?" Reba asked. "And I am not convinced you are right."

"I saw the kiss, that's why. I was walkin' toward my car all those years ago and happened to glance toward the lake pier and saw them. Young love. Then the young heartbreaker ran off the next day to Montana and broke that girl's heart."

Reba's mouth fell open. "And we didn't know?"

Bertha looked all smug. "I didn't see any reason to tell that young girl's heartache to the world."

"Well, I am insulted." Clara Lyn could not believe the nurse's comments. "I-I do not gossip. I tell the facts that we know."

"Exactly," Bertha grunted. "So now you see why I didn't tell you the facts as I knew them. You might have told them."

"Hold it, you two. This is ridiculous. It's not Jarrod, anyway. Why would he be writing to Maggie when she lives right there on the Four of Hearts Ranch? All he'd have to do is ask her."

"Maybe he's too embarrassed to ask," Bertha said, sitting down in the chair connected to the shampoo bowl. "A man's got his pride when he's gone and messed up."

Clara Lyn stared at Reba, who looked about as confused as she was. Could they all have assumed something that wasn't really true? Could Torn in Texas be Jarrod instead of Rand?

"Clara Lyn," Reba said, tapping her toe

as the wheels turned behind her eyes. "Maybe you should ask him."

Clara Lyn looked from Bertha to Reba. Maybe she should.

## 25

Cassidy could not get herself motivated. Five days had passed since she'd confronted Jarrod and she had no willpower. She was half-heartedly ripping wallpaper off the kitchen wall when her phone rang. She grabbed it up, needing interaction of some kind, even if it was a political fundraiser or even a telemarketer. Luckily it was Abby.

"Oh, Abby, so good to hear from you. I need some good ole female interaction."

Abby chuckled. "Well, then you'll be glad of this call. Sandy is in labor so we are all on our way to the hospital in Kerrville. I know it's late, but come join us."

"I am so excited. Let me change real quick. I'm a mess. I have been ripping out wallpaper. Be there in a jiffy."

This was what she needed to take her mind off the dilemma of Jarrod. She needed to be around others. Even if he'd be there soon to see his new nephew, there would be enough distraction to help her not obsess. She needed something positive, something that was not focused on her. A new baby was fabulous. She loved babies.

Hurrying to change, she finger combed her hair into a headband, then pulled on a mint green T-shirt, black jeans, and on a whim a pair of three-inch wedge, strappy sandals. It had been awhile since she'd worn even a small heel and . . . well, why not?

She gave Duce a neck scrub on the way down the steps. "Take care of the place," she said, then tossed her purse into the seat of her truck and slid behind the wheel. Driving down her driveway, she glanced toward Jarrod's house. No lights shone in the dusk so he'd probably been gone for a while. Kerrville was the opposite direction from Wishing Springs, so she turned left. She would have to travel this quiet road for a while until it connected with another county road that would take her to the highway. She'd gone about three or four miles when she spotted a faint light in the pasture. She slowed, watching the light. Her heart was racing as she pulled to a stop next to a stand of trees and cut her lights. Was she seeing the rustlers?

Unable to contain her excitement, she wished now she'd worn her boots. What had she been thinking putting on these dadburn heels, anyway? She grabbed her phone and turned it on, then realized she'd done it again. She'd let her battery run low rather than plug it in while she'd been working in the house. She was going to have to break this bad habit.

Excitement still bubbled in her as she dialed Jarrod's number. "Come on, pick up."

Relief surged through her when she heard his voice. "Cass —"

"Jarrod," she blurted before he could say more. "I see the rustlers. They're in the pasture about three or four miles past my house. At least I think it's them. I see a dim light in the distance and it's moving like before. Like they're herding the cattle."

"Where are you?" Tension filled his voice.

"I'm parked in the trees on the side of the road with my lights off. But I'm going to try to follow them."

"Do not under any circumstances do that."

"But they might get away and it might be another month before we see them again."

"I'm on my way. I'm halfway to Kerrville but have just done a U-turn. I'm calling Jake, so you turn that truck on and get out of there. You get to the hospital and leave the rustlers to me."

"I am not leaving. They could be done before you or Jake get here," she said, repeating her concern.

And then her phone went dead.

Jarrod drove while he pressed redial. There was nothing. He pressed again. The line was dead. He hit Jake's number.

"What's up?" Jake asked. Jarrod heard some kind of noise in the background.

"I'm on my way to four miles past my house. I'm coming in from halfway to Kerrville and Cassidy's out there thinking she's going to track rustlers. And her phone is dead or something. She's not picking up."

"Jarrod, I've got a major wreck out here on the curve near Presley Creek. And both my deputies are on calls too. Keep me posted, and I'll be there as soon as I can. Don't let anything happen to her, buddy."

Jarrod's stomach clenched. "Got it." He hung up and dialed the number of the TSCRA field agent in charge, Agent Kirkpatrick. Jarrod filled him in and then hung up. He had to fight wanting to turn on his emergency lights and siren as he flew down the road. Agent Kirkpatrick had told him the rustlers were looking at some major time when they were caught and that made them very dangerous. The fact that no one had gotten near them yet meant they had no idea how they'd react to an encounter. And that meant Cass could be in over her head.

Cassidy was standing beside her truck and tried to redial, but her phone was definitely dead. She dropped it into her pocket and crawled through the fence. Jarrod would find her truck and know which direction she'd gone. She tore the headband from her hair, hung it on the fence where she'd crossed into the pasture, and tried to make tracks into the hard dirt. And then she hurried across the dark pasture toward the trees. Tonight the moonlight was her friend, giving her enough light to see her way at least some.

These heels were going to be the death of her, though.

She was breathing hard when she made it to the small line of mesquite trees. No gulley tonight, just a thick line of trees and then another pasture. The lights had disappeared, going deeper into the ranch property, she hoped, because it gave Jarrod more time to get here.

Looking around, she eased through the trees, tripped on a root, and went down. *"Umph,"* she grunted, but she didn't waste time to any pain as she scrambled up. Then, glancing across the open pasture, she could make out the faint lights again.

She stayed crouched down, which made crossing the distance more tiring. But she wanted to resemble some sort of animal if anyone were to happen to see her silhouette out here. Standing tall and straight was not a good idea. Even she knew that.

She was breathing hard again when she made it to a small corral in the valley of pasture. She saw something she hadn't been able to see in the darkness until she got closer. Did Jarrod have a camera out here? Oh man, she hoped so.

Fear should have been making her run fast back across that pasture, but this was Jarrod's livelihood they were messing with. This was Pops's ranch, the vision for a family he loved and great-grandchildren he'd yet to meet when he'd begun building this place into the amazing ranch it was. And by gosh, she wasn't going to just get in her truck and drive away when Sandy was in the hospital at that very moment having Pops's second great-grandchild. Bo had a child, now Tru was having one, and . . . well, there was a fierce drive in her heart that said Jarrod deserved a child to play on this ranch Pops had built too. And that he and his brothers were fighting to save.

"Well, well, *well,* little darlin', what do we have here?"

Cassidy froze. She had been creeping behind the old rough wood corral when the thick, slow drawl came out of nowhere. Her heart jumped into her throat and cut off her windpipe. She almost spun around, then realized there was a real possibility he had a gun and might shoot her.

"Let's put those pretty hands where I can see them, little lady."

She managed to drag in a breath and lifted her hands slowly above her head. Oh man, she was in trouble. Her stomach felt about as sick as the time she'd eaten bad seafood. If it got any worse she was probably going to turn green and barf all over this pitiful excuse for a cowboy.

"Now, turn around real slow and let old Roy get a good look at you."

Okay, so it just got super creepy. She turned around to find a Clint Eastwood wannabe with a raspy voice. The half-chewed cigar dangling from his lips wasn't lit, and as he met her gaze he took it with two fingers and drew it out of his mouth. He was holding a pistol and Cassidy tried not to focus on it. It was making her knees knock and her ankles were suddenly weak.

*Don't look down, don't look down, don't look down,* she told herself, trying not to become hysterical. She had to focus.

Jarrod would find her. He would. This wasn't the end. This wannabe wasn't going to hurt her. He was bluffing. All she had to do was stay cool. She was starting to sweat, and despite being outside she was feeling a little claustrophobic. She was in fact going to lose it. Or faint.

*Fainting isn't going to help anything.* The voice in her head growled and then kicked her between the eyes.

"You aren't going to get away with this, y-you know. The cavalry is coming. Just so you know."

He laughed loudly and ended it with the snort of a pig. *Ew.*

"The cavalry, huh?" He laughed and waved the pistol at her. "Move it. Let's tell your jokes to my buddies."

Jarrod scanned the road and pastures. His heart was pounding and his sweaty palms gripped the steering wheel. Then his headlights found her truck. He immediately saw she wasn't in it.

He was parked and jogging to the old Ford in a flash. He yanked open the door and scanned the vehicle for any signs of struggle or if she'd left him a note or anything.

Nothing.

He spun and scanned the area. He spotted a headband draped neatly on the fence. He picked it up and his throat clenched. "Cass. What are you doing?"

He bent down and studied the scuffed area she'd made so he'd know where she'd gone . . . or at least where she'd entered the pasture.

"Think, Monahan. Think." What was out here? Where had she gone . . . or no, where would the rustlers have been going?

He ran for his truck, yanked up his rifle, and reached in his glove compartment for his revolver. But he needed to decide what to do. If they were at the old corral in the valley and then came back this way to leave, and if he was on foot and stuck out there, there was no way he could stop them. But with his truck there was more likelihood he'd be seen.

He called Jake and told him what he knew. Agent Kirkpatrick was already en route.

"I'm free here now, and I've already called in backup. So soon we'll have roadblocks in place. Silence your phone, Jarrod, and dim the screen so you can text me or I can text you if need be."

386

"I will. I'm going in, Jake. Cassidy needs me."

"I'd tell you to wait on me but I know that'd be a waste of breath. You just keep your head down and stay out of sight, Jarrod. And keep the texts rolling."

"You got it. And hey, don't call my brothers on this. They're welcoming my nephew into the world right now and that's exactly what they need to be doing. Long as you've got my back, we're covered."

"I've always had your back," Jake said. Jarrod knew he was referring to their football and then rodeo days.

Jarrod hung up and did as Jake had suggested, turning his phone's sound off and the screen light to dim. He pocketed the phone, turned off his truck lights, and drove slowly down the road and across the cattle guard. He'd decided he had to get his truck a little closer and then he'd go in on foot. He made it to the mesquite trees. How far behind her was he?

Jarrod had never felt so helpless, but he refused to focus on that. He had to find Cassidy. He drove his truck into the thin strand of mesquite, then after grabbing his guns he got out and said a prayer, one of a hundred he'd already said as he'd been speeding this way. He watched the sky and could see a cloud edging toward the slight moon. He forced himself to wait. After a few seconds the clouds blocked out the moon and the night turned darker. He ran.

Covering ground as quickly and quietly as he could, he made it to the next stand of trees before the clouds moved on and revealed the moonlight again.

He dodged through thin trees, and there he could look down the slight hill to the old pens. He'd considered putting a camera here but he'd never gotten around to it, his thought being it was too deep into the interior for them to even know about it.

That's when he knew the thief was either someone working for him or had worked for him before.

And exactly why he hadn't alerted his men to what he had been doing.

He saw the trucks down in the valley — two of them. Dozens of cattle were being rounded up. This was one of the sections he hadn't asked Gil to move, which was more evidence that this was an inside job. He might not be an agent, but he knew someone close to his ranch knew where this corral was and knew this herd hadn't been moved.

They might have even known his brother and sister-in-law were having a baby tonight and that Jarrod would be preoccupied with that.

But right now he didn't care. He'd give them every heifer and steer he owned in trade for Cassidy.

Cassidy knew even more than before that she was in trouble. She recognized one of the cowboys as one of Jarrod's men. She didn't know his name, but he'd been on the roundup the day she'd gone out with everyone. There was no way she was getting out of this alive. She'd seen every one of their faces.

"What are we going to do with her?" Roy asked the three other rustlers. He looked to be the oldest, around fortyish. The others looked like they were in their thirties. And there was no way any of them wanted to go to prison.

"She's seen our faces," the one who worked with Jarrod said, panic in his tone.

Another guy scowled, and his beady eyes darted up and down Cassidy with disdain. "She'll have to have an accident. Get trampled in the trailer or something."

Cassidy glanced at the trailer full of cattle and her mouth went dry.

She wasn't ready to meet Jesus yet. If he called her home she'd go, but on his time, not these lowlifes'.

Her life flashed before her and she realized she wanted to be the one to give Pops another great-grandchild — one with Jarrod.

The thought made her smile. And made her want to cry at the same time.

She was not ready to leave this world, not when she had to tell Jarrod Monahan that she loved him and always had.

But what could she do?

Stall. Hang on. Jarrod was on the way, and if he got there in time he would know what to do.

"I'm curious what y'all are doing with these cattle?" she said. "They're not finding any traces and y'all have taken a lot of them."

The one who worked for Jarrod looked nervous and remained silent. He probably knew if something happened to her Jarrod would find them all, and it wouldn't be pretty.

Or maybe he had a conscience. After all, they'd spent that day working together.

She had to keep talking. They weren't going to spend a lot of time hanging around the pasture now that the herd had been trailered.

Beady Eyes sneered again. "Let's just say we have friends in high places."

That was interesting and reminded Cassidy that she had a friend in the highest place. She silently said a prayer asking God to watch over her. To give her strength and show her what to do.

"Like on a mountain?" she asked, acting ditzy.

"You ask too many questions," Beady snarled. "I bet ole Jarrod thinks you're a real hoot."

"Matter of fact, I think she's wonderful." Jarrod stepped out from behind the trailer and Cassidy wanted to run and tackle him. He had a rifle pointed at the two men on the left of her and a revolver pointed at Beady Eyes. There was no softness in Jarrod as he leveled his gaze on them. He looked like Matthew Quigley from her favorite western.

She felt it rather than saw it as Roy, the Clint Eastwood wannabe-but-never-gonna-be, leveled his gun on her. Great.

Then she heard the sirens.

Through the trees she saw flashing lights brighter and more plentiful than the Fourth of July fireworks. Chaos erupted when Beady Eyes grabbed her and yanked her against him. In the blink of an eye she'd become a human shield.

Not today.

Cassidy didn't hesitate. She stomped on his foot hard with the wedge of her heel, rammed him hard in the gut with her elbow at the same instant, then twisted around and brought her knee up hard. She was in a world of her own during this move and she stepped back to watch him crumble. The boom of a gun sounded over the wail of the sirens and she saw Jarrod go down.

"No!" she cried. She dove for him, but she was grabbed around the waist and hauled up against ole Roy.

"You kick me and I'll finish your boyfriend off," he growled in her ear.

"Put your weapons down. You're surrounded." The voice came from some kind of loudspeaker as spotlights suddenly illuminated them.

Roy froze but held his grip on Cassidy. Her knees went weak.

Cassidy saw Jarrod roll over, revolver in hand. He was alive. *Thank you, Lord.*

"You better listen to my friend the sheriff," he growled as law enforcement vehicles burst into the pasture around them. They charged and slung grass and dirt everywhere as they skidded to a halt. Doors flew open and officers exited the cabs, weapons drawn and aimed right at them from behind their open doors.

"Let her go, and you'll get out of this alive," Jake called, his gun steady.

Cassidy's gaze swung back to Jarrod, who hadn't wavered in his aim.

"Let her go, man," the cowboy she'd worked cattle with warned, finally deciding to speak up. "I didn't sign on for a hostage situation."

"No way. We're not a part of him," the fourth rustler said.

Cassidy's heart was thundering so hard she could barely hear. The moments ticked by, and then Roy held his gun into the air and let her go.

Though her knees were buckling, she made it to Jarrod. She knelt beside him and grabbed his face in her hands.

"Don't you dare die on me, Jarrod Monahan." And then she kissed him like there was no tomorrow.

Jarrod let the EMT finish wrapping his shoulder, then thanked her and moved out of the way as they shut down and then drove away. He'd refused an ambulance to the hospital. There was no need. He had everything he needed right here.

He was glad the bullet had hit the same shoulder the horse had attacked so he still had one good arm. The bullet had only grazed him so his injury wasn't much more than a flesh wound. When he'd gone down, he'd stayed where he was hoping for the opportunity to help Cassidy. Jake and his officers had given him that chance.

Now he just wanted everyone to leave so he could be alone with Cassidy.

Jake came to stand beside him and held out his hand. Jarrod grabbed it in a hard shake. "You did good," Jarrod said to Jake. "You had my back and then some. This old place hasn't seen excitement like this since we were kids helping Pops round up those longhorns he used to keep in this pasture."

Jake laughed. "Now those were some ornery critters."

"Yeah, tell me about it. But it was worth it. After I told you about the longhorn pen, you were probably the only person other than my brothers and Pops who would have known where to come."

"It worked out," Jake said, then glanced over his shoulder toward Cassidy, who was sitting in the squad car making a statement to his deputy. "Those fellas" — he nodded toward the rustlers being loaded in the back of a sheriff's SUV — "are going to jail, and I have a feeling once the investigation is done they'll face charges in several jurisdictions. That fella working for you has several names and has worked ranches all over Texas that are missing cattle."

Jake nodded toward Cassidy. "She's the one who did great. She didn't panic. You two will probably have a lot of questions from the TSCRA agents to answer, but that can wait till tomorrow. Y'all need to get to the hospital, you've got a new nephew to meet."

Jarrod grinned. "Give us a ride to my truck. My phone's about to blow up with text messages and phone calls from Bo and Tru."

A few minutes later he and Cassidy told Jake good-bye and then stood beside Jarrod's truck in the shadow of the mesquite trees. He didn't waste any time taking her into his arms. "Cassidy, tell me again you're okay," he said, looking down into her eyes that were glowing in the dim light from the open truck door.

"I'm wonderful. I've let go of a huge weight I've been carrying. Jarrod, I have to tell you. I love you. All I could think about when I realized those rustlers were going to more than likely kill me was that I hadn't told you I love you. And that I want to spend the rest of my life with you. If you still want the same thing."

He smiled. "What kind of question is that?

I want you more than words could describe. But what about wanting to live life on your own and not trusting men ever again?"

"It was just fear, Jarrod. And I realized I don't want to be afraid. And you were right. I love ranching so much. I still love the idea of a small farm and a B and B, but I don't want it to take the place of where you and our family should be."

She took a deep breath.

"You were so right about that, and I was just so afraid and fighting it all the way. Roxie was content the way she lived her life, but I could never feel content with that life because I'm supposed to be with you. I realized I don't want to live with bitterness from any part of my life. I'm letting it go, and that includes letting go of what both Jack and my parents did. I want a fresh start with us free from all that."

She was right. "And I want that too. I'm letting go of the anger against my dad. Life is too short, Cass." He went down on one knee and took her hand in his. "Cassidy Starr, I came back from Montana to ask you this question eight years ago, but then it was one winter snow too late. Will you marry me, Cass?"

"Yes! Right this minute if you can find me a preacher. I don't want to wait another instant."

He rose, took her into his good arm, and kissed her. When his lips touched hers, electricity sparked from every nerve ending, crying out for more.

"And, Jarrod," she said softly, "the other thing I thought about out there was what our great-grandchild for Pops will look like."

He laughed. Threw his head back and laughed so hard his shoulders shook.

"I hope she has big green eyes and wild red curls like her momma."

"And I hope he has deep blue eyes and dark hair like his daddy."

Jarrod's heart swelled with pure love. "Then I suggest we get this marriage going because I see we're going to have to fix this draw with a tiebreaker."

Cassidy took his face into her hands and looked deeply into his eyes. "I have always loved a tiebreaker. Kiss me and then let's go tell everyone."

"And I've always wanted a honey-do list. And this sounds like something I can do."

And then he kissed her and nothing ever felt so right.

# EPILOGUE

It was a gorgeous day for a wedding. The wind was a little high and there were storm clouds on the horizon, but even that couldn't put a damper on the way Cassidy felt.

They had decided on a small, uncomplicated ceremony. Neither of Cassidy's parents was able to make the date she'd chosen, but she had come to terms with that. She could be happy despite their absence. They might never change, but she could change her heart and her outlook even though she couldn't control theirs.

Nothing could change the joy she felt today. She could not contain the smile on her face as she stood among the peach trees Roxie had planted and exchanged vows with Jarrod, surrounded by his family, her new family, and friends.

Her heart full, Cassidy took it all in. She was home and she felt Aunt Roxie smiling.

Maggie held her infant son, Will, a sweet

little angel who already had Tru wrapped around his little finger. Abby held — or tried to hold — Levi's hand as he moved from her to Pops to Bo and back again, smiling and full of joy.

A small, close-knit group filled the chairs with Pops. Pebble and Rand were there together, with Pebble sporting a new wedding ring of her own. Stunning everyone, the two had eloped and they had been smiling ever since. Clara Lyn and Reba were present, too, along with Doobie and Doonie and Doc and others.

But as Cassidy turned to look into the eyes of the man she'd loved for so very long, her eyes were only for him.

It had been a shock to learn Jarrod had been concerned enough about her to write Maggie for advice. But it had also touched her deeply, and it made today even more special.

When at last Jarrod took her into his arms and kissed her, she knew joy like she'd never felt in all her life.

"There will always, always be love," he promised, looking deeply into her eyes. And he kissed her once more. "And there will always be kisses."

"Oh yes. There will be kisses." She chuckled and pulled his lips to hers.

# DISCUSSION QUESTIONS

1. When we meet Cassidy, she is bordering on depression along with grief over not having been able to hold her marriage together. Why? Have you or someone you know ever experienced this?
2. What is Jarrod feeling when we meet him?
3. Both Cassidy and Jarrod have a lot going on in their lives. But they also have an unfinished history together. Despite their history, neither of them have plans to explore what happened between them years ago. Do you believe that Cassidy's present troubles began with their history? Why?
4. Jarrod has family business as his priority. He tells his brothers that he has no time to date, that if God wants him to date he will have to bring someone to Jarrod's front door. Do you believe that's what God did when Cassidy drove up the drive to confront Jarrod about stopping the

plane? Has God ever done something like this in your life or someone you know?

5. When Duce came into Cassidy's life, why was Cassidy afraid to open her heart to the injured dog who needed her so much?

6. Jarrod's compassionate heart and care for her from the first time she'd met him had always drawn Cassidy to him. Why?

7. Jarrod doesn't want to push Cassidy too hard, but he's been given a second chance to make things right between them and he has no intention of letting his opportunity go to waste. Did he handle his second chance right?

8. Cassidy had to make a choice in order for her their romance to turn into a happy ending. She had to decide that she didn't want to let the bitter disappointments of her past steal the joy and opportunity of the future. She had to let go of the past. Do you need to let go of something in your past?

# ACKNOWLEDGMENTS

I want to take this time to thank my editor Becky Philpott for her work on this story and the wonderful insights and editorial development of this story. I'd like to say a big thank-you to the entire team at Harper-Collins Christian who helped see this book through the publication process! You are wonderful. And also to my agent, Natasha Kern — thank you for all you do!

I want to thank my friends Lisa Webb and Libby Cannon for their endless help with my questions about the cattle industry and rodeo.

And always, much love to my husband and my family who give me endless joy and inspiration and are the delights and blessings of my life!

I'm so very grateful and thankful to God for his love and the blessings he's given me.

And last, but certainly not the least, I thank you, my readers, for choosing to buy and read my books. I'm forever grateful for your support because without you the many characters and their stories I have to tell would go unknown and unloved. They and I thank you!

# ABOUT THE AUTHOR

**Debra Clopton** is a multi-award winning novelist first published in 2005 and has written more than 22 novels. Along with writing, Debra helps her husband teach the youth at their local Cowboy Church. Debra is the author of the acclaimed Mule Hollow Matchmaker Series, and her goal is to shine a light toward God while she entertains readers with her words.

*Visit her website at www.debraclopton.com*
*Twitter: @debraclopton*
*Facebook: debra.clopton.5*

The employees of Thorndike Press hope you have enjoyed this Large Print book. All our Thorndike, Wheeler, and Kennebec Large Print titles are designed for easy reading, and all our books are made to last. Other Thorndike Press Large Print books are available at your library, through selected bookstores, or directly from us.

For information about titles, please call:
  (800) 223-1244

or visit our Web site at:
  http://gale.cengage.com/thorndike

To share your comments, please write:
  Publisher
  Thorndike Press
  10 Water St., Suite 310
  Waterville, ME 04901